LOST BOYS 2.0

TALES OF B.O.O.
BOOK 2

STORM GRANT

WIT & GRIT
COMPANY

COPYRIGHT

Cover Design by Willsin Rowe, willsinrowe@ymail.com
Interior Design by Woven Red Author Services, www.WovenRed.com

ACKNOWLEDGMENTS

This book would not have been possible without the teachings and guidance of so many people. Most recently, all my writing endeavors are made possible, if not painless, thanks to my awesome brainstorming group, QuinceApple.

Special thanks to Irene Jorgensen for an excellent developmental edit and to Bonnie Staring for a terrific round of copy editing and the clever title that so suits the story. This time 'round, proofing was courtesy of Joan Leacott.

DRAMATIS PERSONAE

Borderless Observers Org. (BOO)

Formerly The Royal Society for the Investigation of Natural and Unnatural Phenomena. An internationally sanctioned paranormal policing agency tasked with foiling supernatural crimes and bringing magical beings to justice. Headquartered on the tropical island of Azunya.

PLAYER	ROLE
Thaddeus Wright	Community Center Manager—combination coach and counsellor for at-risk youth
Peter Batique (formerly Pan)	BOO Agent
Jacqueline Batique	Director, BOO
Tom Ferrell and Adrian Thornapple	BOO Agents (See *SHIFT HAPPENS*)
Jaden Raines (15), Hector Gonzales (14), and Stanley Greenberg (12)	The Lost Boys
Brother Guy Boniface	Thad's Boss
Franklin Boniface	Guy's Dad
Detective Hank Reasoner	Cop on the Case
Jack Stabler	Hired Henchman
Allison Wildgoose (11)	Victim
Emily Reasoner (11)	Detective Reasoner's daughter
Also mentioned:	Thaddeus's mother (deceased) and grandparents

CONTENTS

PROLOGUE

PAN-O-RAMA

Neverland, ten years previously

PETER HAD NEVER KNOWN FEAR.

Or at least he'd never been known to admit it.

But the sudden arrival and thunderous roar of the strange, whirling metal dragon sent a cold, shaky dread spiraling through his belly. He tried to draw his sword, but the hilt slipped through his sweaty fingers.

The dragon soared closer, a deafening, bulbous thing more like a bug than a serpent. Its spinning wings set the treetops thrashing. As it passed over the beach—Peter's beach!—it set sand and driftwood swirling, its private typhoon following along as the crocodile had once followed Captain Hook.

No dragon would threaten Peter's dominance. Neverland was his! He leapt in the air and flew toward it. "C'mon, Tinks!" he called in the silent language of the fairies, his unspoken words unaffected by the dragon's great wind.

A glance behind showed his fairy companions unable to navigate the maelstrom. He watched them shimmer off to hide in a favorite crevice time had worn in Marooners' Rock.

Who needs fairies, anyway? He'd faced worse on his own before and triumphed. Peter wheeled toward his foe, intending to meet the fearsome brute head on, to look it in its one great eye and challenge it to the battle to end all battles. As he drew near, it flew over a wide inlet, lashing him with a new torrent of wind, water, sand and debris, stinging his eyes and depositing a small fish in his hair. He tossed the flopping fish and shot high in the sky, well above the dragon's tempest.

The noonday sun glinted off its metallic hide, blinding him as much as the stinging sand had.

Instead of looking right at it, Peter navigated around the thing by watching its short, dark shadow on the sandy beach below. Where Peter's shadow should have criss-crossed it, there was nothing.

Finally, it came to rest in a clearing—the same clearing where he'd built his little house. The beast's blade-shaped wings slowed to a mere whisper. Peter flew closer, unsure now if it were a living beast or a strange kind of conveyance, like the horse-drawn carriages that clip-clopped outside the Darling's house.

Only this one could fly.

Well, so can I, thought Peter. *I'll do battle on the air or on the ground.*

For now, though, he hovered well out of reach.

Once the wings ceased turning, a tall woman alighted from inside the dragon's belly.

Curious and angry, Peter descended, landing solidly a few yards away. Inside he trembled, knees like the water that sluiced through Kidd's Creek, but he knew himself to be a brave lad so he stood his ground.

The woman stepped toward him, light shimmering from skin as dark as the mahogany treasure chest Captain Hook and his band of pirates had left behind. Three stripes darker still adorned each cheek, like a cat's whiskers. He'd seen similar scars among the African pirates, but had no idea they could be so pretty.

"Hello, Peter Pan. My name is Jacqueline Batique and I have come to take you home."

Home. The one word that held both weight and power with Peter.

And pain.

"I have no—" He coughed, spitting rudely into the unruly grasses. "This is my home."

The woman waited, watching him closely. He shifted from foot to foot. A small rock dug into his right heel.

"This *is* my home!" he repeated, stomping his foot. "Ow! Now I've hurt my foot. And it's all your fault!" His voice cracked, rusty from disuse. Conversing with the last remaining fairies was mostly in the mind.

The island had once been populated, but the pirates had slain Tiger Lily and her people, then slain each other or fled. The Lost Boys had betrayed him and left with Wendy. Wendy...

"Where's Wendy?"

Another woman stepped forward. "I'm Wendy Darling," she said. He didn't know what to make of her tone.

Or her strange, flat accent.

"You're... You've changed!" he said, pointing at her, demanding an explanation.

She wore her hair close-cropped on one side of her head and floppy long on the other, streaked with red and gold. Peter tilted his head to one side, wondering whether he liked it or not. She wore metal rings through her nose and one eyebrow. Peter raised a hand to his own eyebrows, but no rings had magically appeared. It had been a long time since he'd seen his own reflection and sometimes he forgot.

He lowered his hand, staring at it. He was nowhere near as dark as the rich warm brown of the first woman's skin, and only a shade or two darker than the pasty white intruder before him. "You're not Wendy!" he cried, practically dancing with anger, ignoring his sore foot.

"I *am* Wendy Darling, Peter. Just not the one you knew. My grandmother passed away last year. She told me all about you.

About her adventures here in Neverland and how you've been alone for many, many years."

"How many years?" Peter stepped closer. If he could see her eyes, he could tell if she lied, but she wore glasses made of little, round mirrors. All he could see was his own small reflection. "I'm not small! Take those off!"

She did as he ordered, which made him smile. He liked it when people obeyed him.

"Nearly one hundred years. My grandmother came to you when she was a child. Now it's a new century. A new millennium."

Peter screwed up his face, trying on the word. "Mill— Millanamum?"

The mahogany woman, Jacqueline she'd said, stepped up. "Millennium. It means a change in the popular calendar every one thousand years."

"I'm a thousand years old? Hey, I'm a thousand years old today! It's my birthday. My millen— My millo— My millionth birthday!" He leapt into the air and danced above them until a snicker from the newest Wendy brought him angrily back. "You mustn't laugh at me! I forbid it."

"Sorry, sorry." She held her hands up, palms outward. Was she trying to push him away? If so, her magic was weak.

Peter watched her try to force her lips down, but a grin escaped her anyway.

Furious, he flew at her, snatching at her hair, making her cry out.

"See? That's what happens to Wendies who laugh at me."

"Enough!" Jacqueline ordered. "Come stand before me, child. I have much to say to you."

Sulkily, but without question, Peter swooped earthward and landed in front of Jacqueline Batique. Her magic was strong, but he didn't have to like it. Despite his sore foot, he kicked at the rocky soil, refusing to look at her. He crossed his arms over his chest again, but a small, disapproving cough made him stand straight and meet her gaze.

"You have to be nice to me. It's my millionth birthday today."

A small, tight smile flitted across her face. "That may well be so. We are alike in that, you and I. And I have every intention of being nice to you. In fact, I have come to take you away to live with me."

"You'll be my mother?" Peter leapt up and dove toward Jacqueline, arms spread to embrace her.

She held out a single hand, freezing him in his flight.

He hovered, like her airship had, watching her. Even though not a single emotion crossed her features, Peter knew she was considering his question. He bit his lip and held his breath.

Home.

Mother.

He'd tried to forget these things, forget the very words. His stomach clenched so hard he was forced to land before he crashed into the dirt.

Finally, Jacqueline nodded once. "Yes, Peter. I will be your mother. I will take you to my home and raise you as my own."

Peter gasped, skin burning like the sun, his insides shaking with icy fear. Was this a trick? For once, he hid his excitement, schooling his features into his best "I don't care a whit" expression.

"All right. I'll go with you." Spoken casually, as if he were doing her the favor. "But I get to do what I like. And tell everyone what to do. That's the way it works here on my island."

"No, Peter. You will come and live on *my* island, and you will be a good boy and do what you are told."

"Why should I?" Peter crossed his arms over his chest yet again. "I like it here. What will you give me?"

"I shall give you the home that you need. And in a few years, we will be in need of your special talents." Her generous lips curved into a warm bow, like the lips of the mother he'd always wanted but could not recall ever having. It hurt his head and his heart to try to remember her, so he'd stopped.

But now he had a new mother, or at least the offer of one. With his heart's desire standing before him, he hesitated. He'd been alone so very long.

Jacqueline gestured to Wendy, who now came up beside her carrying a small wooden box. "We have something of yours. Do you remember this?"

Peter jumped forward. "A birthday present. It's a birthday present for *meee!*" He peered in the box. A small grayish-brown thing—not quite smoke, not quite solid—moved sluggishly in the bottom of the box.

"My shadow! My shadow!" He reached for it, but Wendy snapped the lid shut, catching his fingers.

"Ow! Ow! You've hurt me. I don't like this Wendy. I'm not coming with you."

"As you wish, young Peter." Jacqueline turned back toward the metal beast. "Stay here on your own with no one for company save a few dying fairies." She half-turned back toward him, the sun behind her outlining her face in shining profile. "Or come with me and have enough adventures to last a lifetime. Are you not tired of living alone? Are you not tired of being a child?"

As she spoke these words, Peter knew them to be true. He wanted a home and a family and a mother. More than anything.

He leapt in the air and darted into the belly of the beast. He counted four chairs and, selecting one in the front, he plunked himself down. A big, curved window arced out and over him. It was like sitting inside a huge eyeball. A fascinating grouping of dials and switches spanned the solid half beneath the glass. The latest Wendy clambered into the seat beside him, slapping his hand away from the pretty dials.

"Hands in your lap, please, Peter," his new mother said. "Wendy, could you show him how a seat belt functions?"

"What's this for?" he demanded, flinching as the less-pleasant Wendy leaned across him to fasten a strange, complicated belt across his lap and chest. "Hey, I'm lashed to this chair. Why? If I want to leave, I'll just fly away!" He stomped a bare foot on the floor, making only the tiniest, unsatisfying thud.

"If you try and fly out of here," Wendy told him, snapping switches and checking dials, "the blades will cut you to pieces." She gestured toward the roof.

Peter knew instantly what she meant.

"*Lots* of pieces," she added, showing him a mouthful of even, white teeth.

Peter thought the snide grin made her look like a bug, especially with her mirrored glasses.

She plopped some sort of hard-looking hat on her head and adjusted a black stick in front of her mouth. "So stay put."

The anger at being forbidden anything dissipated when Jacqueline laughed and handed him a hard cap to put on.

Then Wendy made the air-carriage roar anew.

"I'm going home," Peter announced unheard over the noise, sure he'd decided this all by himself. "It's time for me to grow up."

CHAPTER 1

MISSING PERSONS RETORT

Barriesville, USA, present day

GEARS GROANED AND ROLLERS SQUAWKED as the second-hand printer spit the last of the *Missing Child* posters into the output tray. Job done, it shuddered and gave up the ghost. Thaddeus Wright grabbed the pile and thumped one end of the stack against his desk until they were all nicely lined up.

"Um, Coach Wright?"

Startled, Thad dropped the posters. They fanned out across his desk. Dozens of pictures of Jaden Raines looked up at him accusingly.

And one real Jaden stood before him, wearing the same accusing, angry-sad look as he did in the shot his foster mom had provided for the poster.

"Jaden!" Thad said, half rising. He wanted to hug the kid, so glad to find him alive and looking unharmed, but the voice of his old community relations professor rose in his mind: "Never touch the children in any way, even to comfort them. It's a lawsuit in the making. Especially since you're... *you know.*"

Thad rounded his desk and stepped toward Jaden. At least he could come closer. No reason to keep the big clunky desk between them. Realizing he now loomed over the teen, he perched on the edge of his donated desk, a genuine smile blooming on his face. "Where have you been? We've all been worried sick. Your foster mom especially." He knew that wasn't completely true. She missed the check Jaden's presence brought her and was offended by the investigating detective's ongoing questions. She'd made that much clear.

"I'm so glad you've come back. If you don't like it at your current foster home, we can apply to move you somewhere else. Brother Guy can speak to your liaison. Please don't run away again." Thad spread his arms wide, pleading with the young man to listen.

"I know, Coach. I know. She's not so bad. I've lived in worse places. I tried to go to her, tell her I was okay, but she didn't listen. She doesn't even remember me a minute after we talked."

"What do you mean she doesn't remember you?" No way she'd forget Jaden. He was such a likeable young man. And the community center's star basketball player.

A flash of pain flitted through Jaden's eyes before he shrugged. "Maybe she doesn't want me there anymore."

Thad paused, toying with the gold hoop in his ear, stalling, considering his answer. He so wanted to get this right. These kids needed counseling more than coaching, but he struggled to find the right words. If only he could solve all Jaden's problems with a friendly game of one-on-one.

He strove to make eye contact. Jaden met his gaze defiantly, crossing his arms. "I know what you're going to say, man."

Thad nodded. Probably, it all sounded trite to Jaden. But Thad had to try anyway. "It's normal for you to feel—"

"Marginalized. Yeah, I know. You've said that the last six times I've come here." He made a dismissive gesture, like he was shoving Thad's words away.

"No, wait. It's true. People do care about you. I—" He paused, thinking *to hell with potential lawsuits. This kid needs me.* "*I* care about you. In fact, I was just going to put up these posters around the neighborhood."

"No, wait! Don't look away. You have to keep your eyes on me."

It was a strange thing to say, but then Jaden was obviously going through something. "Don't sweat it, Jaden. I'm not going anywhere." Thad twisted around and quickly swept up the posters into a rough stack, edges crumpling in his haste to prove to the young man that people cared. He took a second to smooth them out into a neat pile, and then wondered why he was wasting time smoothing out the posters instead of hustling to hang them up. Maybe because he felt so bad about the lost boys. He hoped the detective was wrong. That Jaden and the other missing boys had just taken off.

Better go hang these posters. When he turned around, he almost jumped out of his skin. There was Jaden himself, standing right in front of him.

"Jaden! Great to see you, man. Where've you been? We've been so worried." He wanted to hug the kid, but he knew that was a lawsuit in the making. "We've missed you," he finished, knowing it sounded weak.

Jaden's face grew red and angry, his eyes filled with tears and his shoulders thrust back. "Never mind," he said in a rage-filled voice. "I give up! You're just like my foster mother and all the others. If you look away for even a second, you forget me." He dashed from the small office, disappearing from view within three steps.

Outside, thunder boomed, a single deafening crack sounded directly overhead.

Thaddeus dropped the posters again and leapt up, ready to charge after Jaden. "No, wait. I..."

He stopped. What had he been about to do? He caught sight of the posters all over the floor. When had he dropped them? He shook his head. He'd been working too many hours. He picked up a poster. Poor Jaden.

He studied the photo. Jaden looked so much like Thad himself, with the mocha skin and the light grey eyes. They could be brothers, except Thad's mom had died when he was four. There'd be no siblings for him.

He hoped the teen was safe somewhere and that nothing truly awful had happened to him. He must be so afraid. So alone.

Thad couldn't shake that feeling that he was forgetting something.

CHAPTER 2

ALL WORK AND NO GAY

"YOU OWE ME! You owe me everything, you ungrateful snot!"

Thad leapt from his desk at the sound of yelling from down the hall. He dropped the stack of posters on his desk and strode toward the noise, then stopped.

What if there was real trouble? This wasn't the best of neighborhoods. He dashed back to his office and grabbed a baseball bat from behind the door. Better safe than sorry. He raced toward the shouts, clutching the Louisville slugger.

"You can and you will!"

The shouting came from the only other office on this hallway. He rushed to his boss's door and halted just back from the doorframe, baseball bat held high. He hesitated, unwilling to interrupt yet fearful that something bad was going down.

Hush, hush. His mother's voice echoed through his brain. *Hush and wait. Hush and wait.* He could barely remember her, but these words barked through his mind like direct orders.

The yelling stopped, thank God. Instead, he heard the voice of his boss, Guy Boniface, soft and placating, "I hear what you're saying. I'm sure if we just sit down and talk about it, we can figure out a solution to your problem. Death is something we all have to face, after all."

Thad peeked around the corner, catching his boss's eye. He could only see the angry visitor's back, but it was enough to tell that the man was old and wealthy. He carried a silver-topped cane but didn't lean on it at all. He had a matching head of silver hair and an expensive coat.

"You just wait 'til it's you facing the end, you miserable brat. Let's see how calm you are then!" The man's voice cracked mid-sentence, but he still managed to shout loud enough to set Thad's teeth on edge.

Thad wanted to rush in and help his boss, the kind and pious man who'd trusted Thad with this coaching and counseling job. How dare this stranger give Brother Guy a hard time? His grip on the bat tightened. But his mother's voice overrode any violent intent. *Hush and wait. Hush and wait.*

Her words once again turned out to be good advice. The man stopped yelling, stopped threatening. Instead, he stood there, stiffly, quietly, if not calmly, listening to Guy's words. Guy was good with people, good at inspiring and good at comforting. Now Thad observed that Guy was good at calming people, too.

Thad shivered, fingers loosening on the bat. *My first impulse should never be violence. Nothing good ever came of that. It's always better to wait. To hush and wait.* He let gravity drag the bat down until it clunked on the tiles.

"Who's there?" The silver-haired man turned toward the doorway where Thad peeked in. "Who're you?"

"Uh, I work here," Thad replied, inching a little farther forward. He got a good look at the visitor's face now. He had craggy features with permanent frown lines. One eyelid drooped a little. Maybe he'd had a stroke. He must be a parishioner coming to his spiritual leader for guidance in his time of need. It had happened before in the short time Thad had worked for the Church.

Maybe the man was one of the major donors who had made possible the conversion of the abandoned train station into a Church and community center. The bat felt heavy in Thad's hand, even though most of its weight now rested on the floor.

What if I'd hit him? I could have killed him. Killed again.

His shoulders slumped as he turned to leave.

"Come in. Come in, Brother Thaddeus. My... visitor was just leaving."

The man glowered at Thad. He turned back toward Guy again, pointing a long, bony finger at the pastor like something out of *A Christmas Carol.* "You haven't seen the last of me. I've spent a lifetime getting what I want. And you know how much you owe me." He turned and paced to the door, stopping at the doorway. Thad backed up.

The man had plenty of room to exit, but he seemed to want it all. His eyes flicked down to the logo on Thad's shirt pocket—the word *Pride* spelled out in rainbow lettering over his heart. Turning sideways as if to leave the maximum gap between himself and Thad, he edged from the room, brandishing the cane just as Thad had done with the baseball bat moments before.

"Fag!" he spat as he passed.

The word hit Thad like a punch to the gut. He stepped back, squeezing the baseball bat as his fingers clenched around the rock-hard wood. He watched the wealthy parishioner stride off down the hallway, cane thudding on the tiles but bearing no weight. It was obviously for effect rather than for support. Thad bit his tongue to keep from yelling back, reminding himself he was a grown-up now.

Inside, he trembled like the frightened little boy he'd once been, when failing to hush and wait had ruined everything.

The baseball bat burned against his palms and he noticed he'd raised it again without even thinking. He slowly lowered it, his arms aching with the effort not to use it, not to lash out and do damage to the doorframe or the recently erected sheetrock walls.

No, Thad told himself. *Discretion is always the better part of valor.* A glance at Guy assured him his boss was fine.

"Hey, Brother Thaddeus. You okay?"

Thad tried to nod but wasn't sure if he really had. Dragging the bat behind him, he made his way back to his office, where he sprawled into his squeaky old chair. The bat clattered to the floor. He let it lie where it fell.

Guy—or Brother Guy, as his boss insisted he be called—appeared in Thad's doorway a moment later. "That was— Are you okay?"

"Yeah. No, it's just..." Thad took a shuddering breath, ordering himself to grow a pair. Between his mother's voice in his head and his grandparent's misguided teachings about how a real man should act, he was practically paralyzed during a confrontation.

"Hey, look." Guy stepped into the office, coming round the desk to stand near Thad, but not too close. He'd probably had the same "no touching" training that Thad's old community relations professor had taught. Or maybe he, like the silver-haired man, didn't like fags.

That wasn't fair. Brother Guy had hired him, after all. In fact, counseling at-risk youth—including GBLT kids—was part of his job description. And who better for the job than Thad, who could really have used some counseling in his own youth?

"Sorry," he told Guy. "I didn't mean to make this about me."

Guy returned to the front of the desk, settling himself in one of Thad's mismatched guest chairs. He leaned forward and slid one of the *Missing* posters from the stack on Thad's desk. He focused on it, eyes flitting as he read the meager text, even though he'd approved the copy before Thad had hit print.

"I know you've been through some things recently. The missing kids..." He held up the poster for a second before placing it gently back on the pile. "Plus Detective Reasoner harassing us about these missing kids. And now my... visitor insulted you. I'd say his behavior was unforgivable if I wasn't in the forgiving business." Guy gave him a little smile, tilting his head to one side as if to gauge the success of his witty comment.

Thad tried to smile back, appreciating Guy's effort to cheer him up, to help him get past the inappropriate outburst.

Both smiles faded a moment later.

Guy stroked his mustache with one finger, tracing the whiskers to where they merged with his trim, dark beard. It was a sensuous move and Thad once again considered how handsome Brother Guy was. The lean, fit body. The expensive, tailored suits. The fierce, dark eyes. He shook himself. Speaking of inappropriate. Brother Guy was probably straight, although he hadn't mentioned a wife or girlfriend. Was he celibate? He'd founded the sect, so who knows what rules he'd invented for himself? But most importantly, Guy was his boss and you just don't go there. Even without the community relations training, Thad knew that was a very bad idea.

Thad knew himself to be a bit lonely. Maybe even a little desperate. It had been several months since he and Clint had broken up and in the interim, all he'd done was work, stagger home to catch some zees, then return in the morning for early B-ball practices. He rotated his shoulder where this morning's practice had left him stiff and sore.

"The detective is just doing his job." Repeating the phrase made the barrage of accusations a little easier to take. He was the last person who'd harm a child. "It makes sense he'd pursue everybody who works here since all three missing kids were enrolled in our programs."

Guy toyed with the small sundial he wore on a chain around his neck. The gold glinted against his brown pinstripe suit. Thad watched Guy's pale hand, almost mesmerized, as his boss turned the sundial over so the gnomon faced outwards.

The gnomon, Guy had explained during Thad's job interview, was the part of a sundial that cast the shadow. That's why his particular sect was called the Church of the Gnomon.

It struck Thad as odd since it was pronounced "no, mon." The Jamaican kids thought it was hysterical.

"I don't disagree with you, Brother Thaddeus. I just think with all you've been through, you should take a break. Why not leave these posters 'til tomorrow? Go somewhere. Have fun. I know you work late almost every day. Even weekends. And I appreciate it. I can't say that often enough. You know I had the funds to hire an assistant for you so you wouldn't have to work so much, but then the pipes burst in a basement..." He held up his hands in a gesture of helplessness. "I'm afraid even our Church is not exempt from acts of God."

Thad tried on a smile and it surprised him by sticking around. He relaxed a tiny bit, his inner conflicts pushed back down once again. "I knew what I was signing on for when I applied to work here. And I'm still grateful for this opportunity. Not many places would hire a guy right out of college and let him run his own show."

"I'm a very good judge of character. You have to be in my line of work." Guy patted the sundial pendant again, the gnomon slipping between his fingers like a tiny fin. "I felt you needed us as much as we needed you. Call it divine inspiration, if you will."

Thad chuckled politely and looked away. He wasn't religious, not after the upbringing he'd had. His grandparents had tried to beat the fear of God into him, but instead, they'd beaten it out. Still, he worked for a Church so he had to be respectful. To change the subject before Brother Guy invited him to attend a service—again—he asked, "Who was the silver-haired man in your office?"

"Oh, an old acquaintance who felt I owed him a favor." He narrowed his eyes at Thad. "And I think I might have found a way to *repay* him."

A shiver trickled down Thad's spine at the way Guy said "repay," but he told himself it was just a draft. The building's ancient furnace was given to blasts of heat and cold at unexpected intervals.

"Well, I'd better get back to work. Think about what I said about taking a night off. Spend some time with your... significant other." Guy raised an eyebrow.

Was he fishing to find out if Thad had a boyfriend, or was he wondering if he'd gotten the phrase right? The politically correct terms kept changing.

"I'm not seeing anyone at the moment," Thad surprised himself by saying. He'd kept his business private up 'til now. "My last relationship didn't end well."

Brother Guy was so easy to talk to. Thad guessed that in his line of work, he'd need to be.

"Well, Brother Thaddeus, do something you wouldn't normally do. Shake up your life a little. Go out dancing or shoot some pool. Just something different than what you've been doing here for the last few months. It'll be good for your soul." He pushed back the chair and stood. "Take care now. See you in the morning. And remember what I said about going out and having some fun."

Not willing to commit, no matter how right Guy might be, Thad lowered his gaze to the posters again, adding a friendly, "See you."

Once Guy's footsteps could be heard clicking away down the hall, Thad reached for his coat. He picked up the stack of posters, grabbed a staple gun and headed out.

If there was a chance of getting Jaden Raines and the other lost boys back, he'd do everything in his power to make it happen.

But was there any reason he couldn't find a nice, quiet place to get a drink afterwards?

CHAPTER 3

END OF AN EROS

THE WIND CUT THROUGH Thad's light jacket. Spring couldn't seem to make up its mind to stay. It had been warm yesterday, but today his hands cramped with cold as he put his weight behind the staple gun and shot the last staple into the last poster. He shoved the staple gun into his pocket and rubbed his aching hands together. He'd run out of posters before he'd run out of lampposts, so it was time to pack up.

He'd been at this for a couple of hours and the sun had long since set. The streetlamps made his shadow stretch out eerily before him. Somebody had played target practice with the next couple of streetlamps, so his shadow gradually disappeared as he walked along, merging into the darkness until he couldn't distinguish it at all.

As a child, he'd thought of his shadow as his brother. It was certainly more like him than the wrinkly pink adults he'd been foisted upon. His shadow had the same flat nose and generous lips. It was many shades of brown, as light sometimes as his belly and often as dark as the creases in his hand. It had the same cap of short, curly hair. It seemed to be the only one he was truly related to.

He hated it when they'd locked him in the closet and it'd been too dark for even his shadow to keep him company.

"Enough!" Thad said aloud, putting his mental foot down. "No more wallowing. No bad memories. Go make a new memory. Brother Guy must know what he's talking about. He's a spiritual advisor, right? I'm going to find a place to have a drink and maybe even have some fun." Of course, he immediately felt guilty that he dared have fun when three young boys were missing. He shouldn't go out. He should just go home and—

He spun around, thinking he heard footsteps behind him. But he saw nothing. Still, he felt he was being watched. He wondered if Detective Reasoner was staking him out, checking to see if Thad was out snatching up young boys. Well, the righteous detective could watch all he wanted. Whether the boys had run away as Thad believed, or been kidnapped as the Detective believed, Thad wasn't involved.

He glanced around again, but if someone was shadowing him, he was doing a really good job of staying out of sight.

Thad turned his feet toward home, thinking he'd seen a little neighborhood bar a few blocks from there. He'd planned his poster route so that he'd end up in his own neighborhood.

"A neighborhood on the cusp," a recent magazine article in The Barriesville Examiner had called it. It had been a rough neighborhood but was slowly gentrifying. Builders and other yuppies were buying up older homes and renovating or restoring them.

A row of old houses, purchased but not yet updated, stared unblinking eyes at him. Square, curtain-less eyes. It was downright unnerving and who knew who had taken up residence until the developer returned?

Thad jogged along Pine Street, hoping the brisk lope would both warm him and get him to the bar that much faster.

He passed shop after darkened shop, metal gates already chained in place for the night. A few entertainment joints were just opening.

A flash of rainbow caught his eye. Literally flashing, as an on-again-off-again neon sign announced a bar, The Closet, across the street.

It wasn't the bar he'd been thinking of. This was new. And apparently gay. How convenient. Perhaps even a sign, as Brother Guy would say. A neon sign, in fact. Thad walked to the crosswalk and, after checking for traffic, made his way to the bar. "Just what the preacher ordered," Thad mumbled, hurrying to get out of the cold and away from his imagined stalker.

Inside, The Closet seemed friendly, decorated with light wood paneling, subdued lighting and even a few plants. Thad had never been a big fan of bars, but Clinton had liked them so they'd gone to quite a few when they'd been together. This one was interchangeable with all the others.

He climbed onto a stool at one end of the bar. He rarely drank, only the occasional glass of wine with a meal, but tonight he ordered a beer. The first icy sip sent a chill down his back. Should have ordered a coffee instead. Or tea. Would the bartender have turned his nose up at a guy ordering tea? It was a gay bar, after all. Then he chastised himself for buying into stereotypes. He huddled into his jacket, waiting to warm up.

The bar was sparsely populated. A few groups of men sat at tables, mostly talking. Dance music played in the background, although not loud. Nobody inhabited the small dance floor at the moment, although things probably got jumping later in the evening. Thad knew he'd be long gone by then. He had an early morning meeting with the local high school coach the next day.

"'You should shake things up'," Thad quoted his boss, mocking himself. Truth was, he had no idea how to shake things up. He just wanted to go home. Or back to the community center. That was where he belonged. That was where he felt safe. He ran a thumbnail under the label, peeling part of it away from the cold bottle in one long strip.

A blast of cold air hit him as the door opened. A tall man pushed it shut behind him, smiling apologetically at everyone and no one. He stomped his feet like he had snow on them, although the last snow had departed a few weeks ago. If only it had taken the cold wind with it.

The newcomer followed the same path as Thad had, bellying up to the bar and ordering a beer. He looked over and did the raised chin nod—more acknowledgement of his existence than actual hello.

Thad mirrored the move in response.

The beer arrived and the man paid for it, sliding half-off the tall bar stool to retrieve his wallet. Tall, slim, fit. As a lifelong fitness fan, Thad couldn't help but assess everyone he met. His gaze traveled up the lean form.

The newcomer was dressed in black jeans and a black leather jacket that looked great but probably wasn't warm enough for this weather. He took a sip of beer and caught Thad checking him out. A genuine smile split his face. Deep laugh lines cut grooves through his five-o'clock-shadowed cheeks, bracketing his generous mouth.

Thad smiled back, running his hand over his chin. His facial hair was sparser, slower to grow back courtesy of his half-black ancestry. He didn't have to shave every day and for that, he was glad. Ingrown hairs were also a legacy of his father's heritage and those shaving bumps were painful.

The man in the leather jacket picked up his beer. He put it to his mouth and took a sip while meeting Thad's gaze. There was nothing overtly sexual about the gesture, nothing crude, yet it was decidedly sensual.

Thad felt his insides flutter and wasn't sure if it was arousal or panic.

Probably both.

Thad tried to keep making eye contact, but his gaze went to his own hand where he picked at the beer label. *I should just go over, but I've never been good at meeting men in bars.*

Luckily the other man was. He grabbed his beer and slid

onto the bar stool next to Thad, legs open just enough to indicate masculinity, dominance and invitation.

"Just get off work?" the man said, as if they were old friends.

"Actually, yeah. I had some... stuff to deliver and I ended up here." He traced an arc in the air with his beer bottle to indicate the bar.

"Yeah. Nice place, I guess. My first time here." He thunked his beer down on the little coaster the bartender had provided and stuck out his hand. "Jack."

"Thad." Should he have given a fake name? Jack could be fake. "I, uh..." He paused. Then he laughed at himself. "I'm so bad at this. Help?"

Jack laughed, too. "You're cute when you beg. What exactly is it you're so bad at?"

"This." Now Thad waved the half-empty beer back and forth between them. "Making small talk. Meeting new people. I'm supposed to be able to talk to people, get them to open up. But I kind of suck at it. At least with people over seventeen." He raised his gaze from beer bottle to new acquaintance. Then his own words echoed back through his brain. "Oh, wait. That sounded bad. I'm not some sort of perv who hits on young boys. I'm a counselor. I work with at-risk youth. And a sports coach." His cheeks grew warm and he hoped between the dim lighting and his darker complexion Jack wouldn't notice.

Of course he did. "Blushing, huh. How can someone as cute as you be shy? You're not just coming out, are you? 'Cause this is the place for it."

Thad's forehead wrinkled. "Oh, The Closet. I get it." He gave another nervous laugh, the label lay in pieces on the bar now. "No, I— It's just been a while, s'all."

"Bad breakup?"

"Yeah, actually. That was pretty insightful." He'd gotten pretty good at sussing out what other people weren't saying. It helped when he counseled the kids. Maybe it came with age.

Jack looked about thirty-five, ten years older than Thad. Theatrically, Thad placed his hand over his heart and put a country twang in his voice. "He took my heart, my dog and my big screen TV."

The corners of Jack's mouth twitched. "Not the dog! That's harsh."

"Well, to tell the truth it was his dog anyway. He brought her into the relationship and so I guess he got to take her away again. It's just when you've scooped three years' worth of poop, you sort of get attached, right? I don't even have visitation rights."

"You should get another dog. Something that suits you. I think a basset hound is just your style. You've got those big sad eyes." Jack reached out.

When Thad flinched, Jack stopped and lowered his hand.

"Oh, hey. I was just going to see if your skin was as soft as it looked. Sorry, if I startled you. Your ex didn't hit you, did he? 'Cause there are ways to deal with that."

To Thad's great embarrassment, his eyes burned. "No, no. Not Clint. It's— Uh—"

"Let's get out of here," Jack said, reaching slowly for Thad's hand and gently clasping it. "I don't think you're bad at this at all."

"Uh, Well..." Thad lightly bit the inside of his cheek, a childhood habit when he was nervous.

"Let's go to your place." Jack said. "You live closer."

"Wait. What?" How do you know where I live?" Thad pulled back. What was up here?

"Oh, no. I meant, you *probably* live closer. 'Cause, I live, like, on the other side of town. Out by the highway." He squeezed Thad's hand. "I don't bite. Unless you want me to."

Thad barked out a laugh at the campy, flirty old line, pushing his doubts away. It felt so damn good to laugh. To be touched.

Brother Guy was right, although he probably hadn't meant a gay one-night stand when he suggested Thad shake up his life a bit. Thad did need this. He needed to de-stress or he'd explode.

"Yeah, okay." But he still waited for Jack to slide off his stool and take a few steps from the bar before following. Something didn't sit right. But he figured it was the last vestiges of his grandparents' narrow-mindedness: sex outside of marriage was a sin, being gay was a sin. He sighed and pushed the echo of their voices away. How old would he have to be before he could put their misguided teachings behind him?

As they covered the few blocks from the bar to Thad's new apartment, Jack kept up a running monogue, recounting an amusing story about his job in a copy shop. It sounded like the sort of job Thad had worked to pay his way through college, since he'd left his grandparents' home by then. Clint had been an advertising sales rep and wore suits every day.

Well, this isn't Clint. Don't compare and don't judge.

They ambled along. Somehow, Thad felt warm, from the beer, from the excitement, from the company. Jack tossed easy questions at him. Personal, but not too personal. Thad found himself opening up despite his better judgment. He'd had no one to talk to for months. Clint had been his world and had taken, along with Thad's heart and the dog, most of their couple-friends. Between moving and spending nearly every waking hour at the center, he'd let the few friends he'd had slip away.

He told Jack about Clint, about work, about the missing kids. He said nothing about his mother or his grandparents, though. Half-black baby dumped on white grandparents by a drug-addict mom was just too pathetic a story for a first date... or whatever this was.

Instead, he told a few stories about Clint's yappy little dog. "I'd love to get another one, rescue a hound from the pound.

But I work such long hours, it just wouldn't be fair." He stuck the key in the lock and shoved the door to his building open.

A jerky ride up the smelly elevator brought them to his floor. "Third door on the left," Thad instructed. He unlocked the door when they reached it, stepped back, letting Jack into the little foyer. Jack gave the place a quick glance and said, "No roommates or houseguests, right?"

The way he said it chilled Thad worse than the cold wind. He shook his head, hand on the heavy staple gun in his jacket pocket.

"Good." Jack stepped up close. "Oh, the things I'm going to do to you..."

"Maybe we should just—"

Jack shoved Thad roughly against the hall wall, hands spanning his waist through his open jacket, over his Pride T-shirt. "I can't wait to get you naked." He yanked the shirt out of the waistband of Thad's jeans.

Thad stood there, numbly, hands resting on Jack's leather-clad shoulders. Not sure how to reciprocate until Jack gave him a crooked smile and nipped at the soft place just below his ear. Thad whimpered, gasping, knowing his self-control had just grabbed his good intentions and left the building.

Jack pulled back, leaving Thad feeling chilled all down his front.

"C'mere, you." Jack drew Thad over to the small couch like he was the one who lived there. "Take off your jacket." The gentle orders sent arousal spiraling down Thad's spine to lodge in the pit of his belly. There were times when he liked to be in charge, but this wasn't one of them. He'd gladly surrender to this warm and handsome man for a night.

Or possibly longer. He seemed really nice, but...

Jack stripped off his own jacket and plunked down on the couch. The springs squeaked a little under the weight.

Thad yanked off his own coat and hung it on the back of the

door out of habit. He approached the couch and Jack asked, "Hey, before you sit, would you mind getting me a glass of water?"

"Oh, uh. Sure." Thad stepped across the small living space to the narrow galley kitchen. He'd just purchased new drinking glasses. Clint had taken their dishes and silverware. Nothing a trip to IKEA hadn't fixed. He let the tap flow until the water ran cold.

"This is the first time I've had anyone over since I moved in here," he called through the kitchen pass-through. "I mean to fix it up a bit." His gaze roved over the place. Secondhand furniture and a sports poster taped to one wall. "Maybe paint it, too. It's only been a couple of months since Clint and I split, and I've been working a lot of long hours and..."

Babbling. You're babbling. Be cool. He took a deep breath and adjusted himself through his jeans before picking up the glass and walking back into the living room.

Jack sat on the couch, an undecipherable look on his chiseled features. His hands were loosely clasped between his knees. Was he nervous? Bored? He didn't radiate excitement anymore. Had he ever? Thad hadn't felt a telltale bulge against his hip when Jack had pressed him against the wall.

"Just set the glass on the coffee table, babe and c'mere."

Thad did as instructed and sat next to Jack. All of the heat that had been between them a moment before seemed to have evaporated. Movement drew his eye to Jack's hands, where the stranger was fiddling with a small glass vial of white powder.

"Oh, hey. No. I don't... You can't—"

"Relax, dude. It's for an upset stomach. Herbal remedy. Not even over-the-counter. I've got an ulcer and I just want to put this in the water." He dumped some of the powder out onto his right palm. It shimmered.

He'd never heard of anyone drinking cocaine or crack. But then, most of his knowledge of street drugs came from watching the news and from reading *Counselor Monthly,* so what did he know? Street drugs had held no appeal for him ever—losing your mom over them can have that effect on a guy. *I should really ask Jack to leave.* But once again, he heard his mother's voice: *hush and wait. Hush and wait.*

Thad decided to wait another few minutes just to see where this was headed. If he still felt uncomfortable, he'd ask Jack to leave and hope it didn't get confrontational. Jack seemed like a reasonable kind of guy. Maybe they could date a bit. Get to know each other.

"What's in it?" Thad asked.

"I don't actually know. I get it from this guy. For all I know it's baking soda and toothpowder, but it works." He leaned over his hand and sniffed it. "Smells like icing sugar. Does it smell like that to you?"

Thad leaned over to take a sniff just as Jack drew in a deep breath and blew on his hand, sending the powder all over Thad, up his nose and in his eyes.

"What the hell, man? What do you think you're doing?"

Why roofie me when I was going to sleep with you anyway? was Thad's last coherent thought. His brain spun and whirled, impossible to hold onto an idea. *Wait. Why what?*

He tried to sit down but discovered he already was. He grabbed the edge of the couch, trying to stay on the spinning cushions, but his hands were sweaty and he couldn't make a fist. He slipped to the floor, the loud clunk was probably the sound of his head hitting the coffee table. He lay there, looking up, dazed, unable to move. "What the fuck..." was all he managed.

Fear clenched his belly. Was this man going to rape him? Kill him? Steal his IKEA glassware? His mind cleared a little, but his body remained unresponsive.

"Whaaa?" He lay on his back, watching the ceiling swirl above him.

Jack's face appeared over him, all fish-eye lens-y. It

disappeared again. He heard the front door open, then close. A second set of footsteps. Was this gang rape? Bashing?

His stomach heaved and he knew if he threw up now, he'd aspirate his own vomit. He swallowed hard. At least his basic bodily functions still worked. What if this was permanent? What if the white powder had done brain damage? Nerve damage?

Tears of terror and frustration filled his eyes. He tried to speak again.

To scream, to shout.

To beg and plead.

Nothing. Just a semi-mute vocalization, like trying to scream in a dream.

Hush and wait. Hush and wait, his mother crooned softly in his ear.

Gee, thanks, Mom. What choice do I have?

Two pairs of shoes now tramped across his creaky hardwood floor. From the corner of his eye, he saw the coffee table being moved, being pushed out of the way, he guessed. He heard the shriek of wood on wood as the old couch was shoved back. They needed room.

Room for what?

He heart raced and his vision blurred. Bile rose in his throat. He choked it back again.

"Better turn 'im over." Jack's voice. "No reason for the fag to choke on his own vomit."

Fag. That word again. But hurtful words were the least of Thad's problems. Jack clenched his fingers around Thad's bicep, tight enough to bruise, and used it to lever him over onto his stomach. Thad's other arm lay trapped beneath him.

A pair of expensive men's loafers swam into view as well as a sort of roundish pot swinging on a chain. It looked like the black metal pots that cartoon cannibals boiled explorers in, only doll-sized. Strange smells wafted from it. Spicy, like, seasonings.

Oh, my God, were they going to eat him? Part of him?

A hand dropped into his line of sight, sprinkling something in the little pot. The hand wore a black leather glove and an oddly rough looking fabric slid down to cover the man's wrist. It reminded Thad of the canvas sacking his grandmother had bought potatoes in.

The little pot began to smoke. Thad's brain wasn't working well enough to figure out smoke without fire, so he gave up. If the drugs he'd inhaled weren't already numbing his thinking, fear certainly was. He choked again, acrid saliva clogging his nose and mouth.

A voice began to sing. No, not sing. Chant. He couldn't tell if it was Jack or the new arrival. He tried to pay attention, tried to make note of identifiers so he could report this if—when— he recovered.

Something glinted in his peripheral vision. Oh, God. Oh, God. A knife! Some kind of antique knife with a wicked blade curved at boomerang angles, serrated with vicious teeth and a tiny, shiny notch near the handle.

The slow, creepy chanting continued like a dire soundtrack, keeping time as other tools, horrific in their ordinariness, joined the knife in neat rows on the apartment floor: hacksaw, tin snips, wire strippers.

Brutal hands held his head although he couldn't have moved it if he tried.

And he tried. Oh, did he try!

The knife nicked his skin, as they sliced his shirt, then peeled it back. Lower, he felt cold metal against his skin as they scissored through his leather belt and jeans, yanking them down and off. Boots, taken off almost gently, were plopped on the floor nearby. He lay on his tattered clothes, naked, vulnerable. Terrified.

He expected to feel hands on his ass next, rough, cruel. But when they stabbed him instead, he wished it were rape they were after.

The knife slid into his neck—not like butter, not so sharp that it took him a moment to feel it. But horribly, gruesomely dull. Thad felt it that second, and every Goddamn second after that, slicing through skin, tendon, muscle, grinding against bone. They started at the nape of his neck, just below his hairline. Slicing him, cutting him open.

Pain tore from his neck down his back, butt, the backs of his thighs. Pain so great it overcame his paralysis, his legs drumming on the floor in agony, as they ripped the bones, sinew, muscles from his calves and ankle.

"No! No! For the love of God, No!" he screamed. Or tried to. All he could do was make underwater noises that barely registered on his own eardrums.

When they reached his feet, they ripped his life out his soles. Darkness claimed him.

CHAPTER 4

WRITHE AND SHINE

THAD AWOKE IN STAGES, mind still muzzy from whatever the hell drug they'd given him. His entire body ached. A line of caustic fire burned along his spine where they'd flayed him. He was surprised he hadn't bled out right there on his apartment floor.

He tried to move, to sit up, to writhe, to flail. His body barely jerked, remaining sluggish and uncoordinated. His fingers spasmed—just his left hand. Oh, God. He couldn't feel his right hand, no, his entire right arm. Had they severed nerves when they'd sliced him open? He jerked his head toward his right side, and on the second try he could see his shoulder, but not his arm.

Oh, no. Oh, no. They'd amputated his arm. Sweat prickled everywhere, his skin instantly soaked.

In his shock and horror, he managed to flop about a bit. *If I can move,* he tried to reason through his mind-numbing panic, *then maybe they didn't rip out my spine after all. Just my freakin' arm!*

Thad tried to twist around. His ankle hit something. His arm? No, his boots, discarded on the scratched parquet floor. He lay on something awkwardly.

Oh, there was his right arm. Still attached after all. He'd just been lying on it so long it had gone completely numb. Relief coursed through him, his breath leaving his body in a weak sob.

Although the motion made the room spin, he managed to roll himself onto his side. Slowly, with half-remembered yoga exercises, he worked the kinks out of his muscles and the rust from his pain-fused joints until his arm was free. It flopped like a dead fish. Or a dead limb. But at least it was there. He'd never been so glad to see his own hand. He sob-laughed, a grating sound offering no comfort at all.

Had he lain upon it so long that gangrene had set in? He sniffed, fearing the smell of rotting flesh. How long had he been there? The sun gleamed in the window, so at least overnight. He sniffed again. The only thing he could smell was ammonia. Where his head had been, a little puddle of puke coagulated.

He used his left hand to heave himself up, but crashed down again. Two more tries and he managed to brace himself against the arm of the sofa. His mouth tasted like bile and felt sticky with thick, half-dried saliva. A glass of water sat on his coffee table within reach. Surely the first man—Jack, if that was even his real name—hadn't asked him put it there so he could have it handy when he awoke. You don't bash a person in their own apartment and then make sure they don't get dehydrated.

His back burned and itched, but there was absolutely no blood on the floor. His T-shirt and hacked-up jeans flopped loosely, still joined here and there. No blood on them either. What had they done to him? There'd been a knife. He'd felt it. Oh, how he'd felt it. He shook his head to clear it, which only sent the room spinning.

Once the room settled back in its rightful location, he groped around his waistline. As far as he could tell, they hadn't taken a kidney like the urban legend.

So what had they taken?

He desperately needed to pee, which he could do while taking inventory of his body parts. Then he needed a drink and to brush the foul taste from his mouth. He also needed to call 9-1-1.

First things first, he began to haul himself along, half crawling, to the bathroom.

His right arm began to tingle, blood returning. The tingling increased exponentially until it felt like fire ants crawling under his skin. It grew painful enough to bring tears to his eyes, but it was nothing compared to the horror and agony they'd laid on him last night. He needed to see what they'd done. Having reached his destination, he used his left hand to heave himself up, grabbing first the toilet and then the sink.

The room spun again as he tried to twist around. But he persisted, panic spurring him on as he tried to see his back in the medicine cabinet mirror. There was something there, but it was hard to focus. He twisted one way, then the other, the movement making him dizzy and nauseated again. He sat heavily on the closed toilet, lowering his head between his knees.

"In-two-three.   Hold-two-three.   Out-two-three." He repeated the breathing exercises he'd learned in first aid training. It had left him lightheaded then and it left him lightheaded now. Raising his head gradually, his entire body fragile, he began to strip off his ruined T-shirt. They'd sliced the back up to the collar and left the short sleeves intact, so he still had to pull it off over his head. A herculean task if ever there was one.

He kicked off the sliced up belt, along with what was left of the jeans and underwear that had trailed behind him, still attached at one ankle. This time he ignored the mirror in favor of his bladder. No signs of blood colored his stream. A tiny frisson of relief traveled down his spine.

At least he still had a spine.

That taken care of, he washed his hands, cleaned his teeth and splashed water on his face. Then he drank two glasses of water. He searched the medicine cabinet for painkillers, even though he knew the cupboard was bare. He probably shouldn't take anything without a doctor's say-so, in case it didn't mix with whatever they'd roofied him with, or with anything the hospital might prescribe.

Grasping the sink for support again, he slowly, gingerly, bent down, rooting under the sink for a hand mirror he thought he owned. There. It had a crack down one side, but would work well enough. Once more, he hauled himself upright.

Turning slowly, he braced his bare butt against the chilly counter edge and tried to tilt the mirror so he could see his own back. There was something there, a shimmering, ghostly trail the dusky grey of a cat in the night.

Or a shadow.

What the hell? It had burned and ached so much. Even now, he could feel the echo of the wrenching, tearing pain. How could it be that there was hardly a mark? Of course, he should rush immediately to the hospital, but it was only a smoky line. They wouldn't see how awful it had been. They wouldn't realize what he'd been through.

He began to imagine scenarios where the hospital staff sent him away, snarking at him to man up, to not waste their valuable time that could have been spent with more important patients, more needy patients. He wrapped his arms around himself, feeling cold and shaky.

Thad's stomach rumbled. He hadn't eaten dinner last night and now it was... What time was it? He had a meeting this morning with the local high school coach to coordinate their efforts and try to keep kids in school. He needed to know if it was even still morning. The tiny, windowless bathroom held no clue.

He pushed off from the sink, beginning to feel a little better. He was rocky and his head throbbed, but he felt the picture of health compared to the way he'd been when he'd first opened his eyes.

Maybe he shouldn't eat. What if they needed to do surgery

or pump out his system? His stomach rumbled again. How long had he been out?

Maybe he was lightheaded because he was hungry. Maybe the pounding behind his eyes was his caffeine addiction demanding a coffee fix. He'd get something to eat, then call in the attack, whatever it had been. Maybe the police had received similar reports. Maybe he was part of some sort of serial attack. It was his duty to report the crime. He could add a clue or two to their profiling, he hoped.

Gingerly, he crossed the living room, arriving at the kitchen without keeling over or having to hug the wall. He hadn't been to the grocery store in a while. He shopped exclusively organic, although sometimes the prices were prohibitive. But everything took time to prepare. He suddenly wished he'd stocked a couple of fast-nuke dinners for emergencies. Not that this was anything he could have planned for.

He pulled out multi-grain bread, artisanal cheese and a locally grown apple that was only a little wrinkly.

He finally remembered to check the microwave display for the time. *I must still be muzzy from that drug.* The digital display read 9:50. Well, he was never going to make that meeting. He'd better call Guy and ask him to apologize and reschedule. He'd call the cops, too.

He located his iPhone in his jacket pocket, clicked on the contact info for Guy's direct line and hit the icon to connect. He took a big bite of cheese just as the line connected.

"Church of the Gnomon. This is Brother Guy Boniface speaking. How may I help you?"

"Oh, Umph. Sorry." Thad swallowed the wad of cheese. The edges of his throat tingled at the sharpness. "It's Thad calling. Uh. Brother Thaddeus. Listen, I—"

"Hello? Is someone there?"

"Yeah, hi. I—"

"Hello? Hello? Are you trying to reach the Church of the

Gnomon?"

"Hello! I'm here! We must have a bad connection. I'm going to hang up now and call b—"

The call clicked off.

Thad hit the redial icon and waited, only to have the same thing happen twice more.

"Damn it. On top of everything, I can't get through." He finished his breakfast, downed two more glasses of water. If they wanted to pump his stomach now, they'd have something to work with.

"Okay. I'll email him instead. He checks his mailbox pretty often." He paced the few feet to his desk and it occurred to him to see if he'd been robbed after he'd passed out. He knew they hadn't taken his phone, but maybe something else? He quickly surveyed the apartment while his laptop booted up. Nope, nothing taken. Except his pride, his dignity and possibly some internal organ.

He stretched, but felt no tightness around what he thought of as his wound.

He dashed off a quick email to his boss, then remembered he had Detective Reasoner's card in his wallet from one of his several *interviews,* as Reasoner called them. "More like interrogations," Thad had grumbled to Guy, who was receiving the same accusatory treatment. "All that was missing was the blinding light and a thug to work me over." Well, he'd certainly been worked over now.

He dug out the card. "Call me if you think of anything that can help the investigation," Reasoner had said, handing Thad the card, an accusing expression on his face. *Like a confession,* Thad had thought at the time, although he hadn't said it aloud.

He dialed the number on the plain white Police Services card, but his call went straight to voicemail.

"Uh, listen. It's, uh, Thad Wright calling. We met about the missing boys last week. But now I've been attacked." Was the attack related? He hadn't thought of that before. "Anyway, last night this guy—"

And the message cut off. He pulled the phone away from his ear and stared at it. How much information could you leave in ten seconds? Just the facts, ma'am, he guessed. He dialed back and left his name and number.

Should he shower? Head to the hospital? Run to work? Go in person to the cops?

Thad still wasn't thinking clearly, but health came first. As his head cleared, he realized he should have left for the hospital when he first woke up. He wanted a shower more than anything, but he'd watched enough forensics shows to know he might be washing away evidence. Pulling clean jeans and another shirt from his closet, he found moving had become a little less difficult as his muscles loosened up. Whatever drug they'd given him was working its way out of his system.

Or maybe he felt okay because he was still stoned.

CHAPTER 5

MEMORY SHTICK

THE ROUTE TO THE HOSPITAL took Thad back along the path where he'd put up the *Missing* posters for Jaden last night as well as the one featuring the other two missing boys, Hector Gonzales and Stanley Greenberg. He passed several and was heartened to see that a few of the little *Call this number* tabs had been ripped off. He passed one where some idiot had drawn a mustache and horns on Jaden's picture. Thad ground his teeth and looked away, jamming his hands tighter in his jacket pockets. This was serious stuff, people. But if it drew attention, then he guessed it was okay.

He walked briskly, the chilly, overcast day suiting his mood. His thoughts cycled through panic and depression like a tilt-a-whirl of emotional anxiety. First, he practically ran a block, then his feet turned to lead and he could barely force himself forward.

Eventually, he reached the hospital, entering via the *Emergency* entrance. He'd been there a couple of times before with kids who'd gotten injured playing basketball and one who'd gotten beat up.

He reached the reception desk just as the previous patient left, so he didn't have to wait for once. Maybe his luck was picking up.

"Uh, hi. I need to get looked at. I got attacked last night in my apartment and I don't know what they did to me."

The woman behind the counter looked up at him, a kind and caring expression on her face. He was glad he'd come and relaxed a bit. "Are you hurt, dear?" she asked.

"That's the thing. They roofied me and I know it hurt at the time, but I can't figure out what they did."

"Were you raped?" Her tone was both gentle and matter-of-fact. This was a person who belonged in health care. She took some of the embarrassment out of the lousy business of reporting his attack.

"I don't think so. I think they cut my back. They sliced up my shirt and it hurt like a son-of-a-bi— It hurt a lot." He was trying to curtail his swearing, what with working with kids at a Church-sponsored community center.

"Have you spoken to the police yet?"

"I left a message for this detective I met, but haven't talked to anyone. I'm having trouble with my phone." Maybe they'd done something to his phone last night. On TV, he'd seen tracer devices and spy gadgets that could be inserted into phones, but who would care what he was up to? Was it a case of mistaken identity?

He couldn't help wondering, now that he'd thought about it, if his attack was actually related to the missing kids.

So many questions, but at least he'd begin to get answers shortly.

"So you're not in immediate distress then?" The nice lady asked. "I'm afraid I have to prioritize my patients by severity of injury."

"Yeah, triage. I get it. I'll go wait over there."

"Here's a form to fill out and a pen. Bring it back to me when you're done and we'll get you in the queue."

"Thanks..." He glanced at the little fake brass nameplate resting on the counter. "Indira." He accepted the battered clipboard from her, along with a pen. The pen featured a chipped gold logo and a pharmaceutical company name.

He sat far away from the man with the barking cough and began to write. His phone worked well enough for him to copy his doctor's phone number out of his address book.

Emergency Contact stumped him though. Only a few months ago, he would have listed Clint, but now he really didn't have anyone. His grandparents would probably order him unplugged, even if he wasn't on life support.

That wasn't fair. Many a night his grandmother had sat with him when he was ill.

He shook his head, clearing it of conflicting thoughts. *How did I end up here?* He spent way too much time at the community center. He needed to find a new social circle so that he wouldn't be so desperately lonely that he'd abandon all good sense and bring home a stranger again.

Thad felt like an idiot. First, he'd let the guy come home with him, and then, even when he got a bad vibe, he'd hushed and waited. If he'd gone with his impulse to ask Jack to leave, he wouldn't be in this situation. Maybe *hush and wait* wasn't always the best plan. It had worked yesterday afternoon— thank God he'd put down the baseball bat, and not gone charging into Brother Guy's office and done damage to the aging parishioner.

And thinking about Guy, he pulled up his boss's contact info and copied his number onto the form. He should have asked first, but he was pretty sure the kind and helpful man wouldn't turn him down.

He signed the form, checked it and brought it back to the counter. The reception lady glanced his way and tapped her headset, indicating she was on a call. She finished up and smiled at him. "Hi, there, how can I help you today?"

He held up the clipboard. "I filled this out, like you asked."

She reached for the form, brows knitting in a confused look. "You were here earlier? Sorry, I see so many patients in a day." She glanced down at the form and looked up, puzzled. "You need to fill it out and then bring it back to me."

"But I did fill..." She held up the clipboard, showing a completely blank form. "It was filled out a minute ago." He felt his temper flaring. He'd been through so much, even something this minor seemed insurmountable. But he choked it back down. This woman had been nothing but helpful to him. "I guess there was something wrong with the pen. I can do it again." He shaped his mouth into a vague upwards arc, hoping the smile looked less forced than it felt.

She pawed through her store of pens, selecting a different brand and tried it on a little notepad before handing it to him. This one advertised a new type of anti-anxiety med. Thad thought he should order a bucketful.

He headed back to the hard plastic waiting chair and filled it all out again before returning to the receptionist.

"Hi, there, how can I help you today?" she asked brightly, if a little tiredly.

"I filled out the form again."

She took the clipboard from him, looking puzzled once more. "How did you... Oh, sir. You need to fill out the form before handing it in. What seems to be the problem?"

"But I did fill it out. The ink must be disappearing or something. Or maybe I'm still high from whatever drug they slipped me and I'm hallucinating about filling out the form." His stomach churned.

"You were drugged? Do you know what they gave you? Were you raped?"

"I..." How could she have forgotten already? He was the only person to have come to her counter in the last twenty minutes. "I told you."

"Sir, I deal with a lot of patients in a day. Now when did this happen? Have you filed a police report?"

She turned away to answer the phone. When she turned back, she gave him a tired smile. "Hi, there. How can I help you today?"

"I— But— I was just here. I told you twice that I'd been roofied and attacked last night."

"Calm down, sir. I'm going to need you to fill out a form and then we'll see what we can do. Were you injured or raped?"

Thad took the clipboard and a new pen with yet a different logo on it. He stepped to the side of the counter and wrote his name at the top of the form. He waited a minute and watched bug-eyed as the ink began to fade. There wasn't even an impression left behind on the paper.

"It's the ink. If this is a joke, it's highly inappropriate."

Indira looked at him. "Hi, there. How can we help you today?"

He left the clipboard sitting on the counter and stormed out. What the fuck was going on?

His anger carried him the few blocks to the community center, where he headed directly for his boss's office. He began to cool off as he paced along the hallway, non-slip soles squeaking on the tiles. When he reached Guy's office, he halted in the doorway, rapping on the door with one knuckle. The hollow-core door echoed his knock a lot louder than he'd intended.

"Oh, uh. Got a sec?"

Guy looked up, his usual smile melting to a look of concern. "Is everything okay with you, Brother Thaddeus?"

"Well, uh. No. No, it isn't." To his embarrassment, his voice cracked.

"Come in. Come in and close the door."

Thad shuffled into Guy's office, wishing he didn't have to deal with any of this. Couldn't he just make with the ostrich routine and go back to his own desk? "I had a meeting scheduled for this morning with the local high school coach. I'm so sorry I wasn't here to see him. I sent you an email. Did you get it?"

"Email? I don't think so." He spun his chair right and wiggled his mouse to wake it up.

Turning back, he said. "Hey, Thad. When did you get here?"

Before Thad could respond, Guy continued. "You missed a meeting with the high school coach, but I handled it. We had a nice chat and I told them you'd be in touch to reschedule. I know you're very reliable. I assumed you had a good reason and now, looking at your face, I can tell that you do." He clasped his hands and bounced them against his chin once before laying them on the table. It was a little like praying.

"I got roofied last night. I mean, I took your advice. Well, no. I'm not trying to blame you. You were right. I need to get out more and then I brought this... person home and I know I shouldn't have and then I got attacked. They... This person..." Thad sighed and gave up his attempt at gender-neutral terms. Why bother? Guy already knew anyway. "Him and another guy. They must have planned it."

"Have you filed a police report? Have you been to the hospital?"

"Yes. No. I don't know." Thad buried his face in his hands, eyes burning, muscles in his jaw jumping. He chewed the inside of his cheek until he tasted blood. "I got attacked last night. In my own apartment. They don't seem to have taken anything. I don't think I'm permanently injured, although they hurt me like hell last night."

Thad heard Guy's chair squeak and drew his hands away. His boss's face was dark and angry in a way that Thad had not seen before in their few months of working together. "Do you have any idea who did this?" Guy demanded. "Did you know these men?"

Thad felt a tiny glow of warmth in the pit of his stomach. It was good to have this man on his side. He cared so much. "No, I'd never met them before. But I'd know the one guy again if I saw him. The other guy, I never saw. I think he was wearing a

robe or something. He had, like, a little cauldron with him and...
it was like they were doing a spell or something."

"So nothing was taken and you seem okay. They didn't...
uh..."

"Rape me? No. I'd know if they had. There wasn't any blood
anywhere but they did something. I know they did. I just don't
know what yet."

"Did you contact the police?"

"I left a message for Detective Reasoner, but I'm having
trouble with my cell phone. I'm going to try again from my
office."

"You should go home. Take the rest of the day off. I'll let
Sister Collins know that you're to still be paid for the day when
she does the books. You've put in enough overtime to have
earned it. You've had an awful experience and there's nothing
here that's more important than your health."

"Yeah, I— I think I might do that. I really need a shower."
Thad gusted out a big breath. "Thanks for listening. The gal
at the hospital was, I dunno. Playing games or losing it herself
or something."

Thad rose to leave. He had an urge to shake Guy's hand, to
make a human connection, but he felt unclean. Like he was
tainted or something. Not worthy of this caring theologian.
Instead, he turned toward the door and walked away.

Reaching his office, he left another message for Reasoner,
then packed up and headed home. He needed groceries and
stopped at the local convenience store. They were pricier than
the supermarket, but they carried local produce. He knew the
owner well enough to say hi.

He took his purchases up to the cash and chatted a bit. The
clerk turned away to check a price, when he turned back, he did
a reset on the conversation like he hadn't just spoken with
Thad. Weird. Just like that receptionist at the hospital. Was it
national Pretend-To-Forget-Thad-Every-Time-You-Look-

Away day?

He stopped at the pharmacy for some Tylenol. He usually avoided drugs, but right now he needed something—something for his stiff muscles, his throbbing head and his overstressed nerves. The same thing happened there as well.

This wasn't funny anymore.

His stomach began to clench with panic as he rushed out into the street, clutching his groceries the way a drowning man would a hold life preserver.

He ran up to a guy leaning on a mailbox, having a smoke. "Can you see me?"

The guy peered at him. "Is this some kind of a joke, dude? Course I can see you."

"Hey, isn't that Bill Murray?" Thad pointed over the man's left shoulder. The smoker flicked ash and turned to look where Thad indicated.

"How 'bout now?" Thad asked when the man turned back to him.

"How 'bout now what?" The guy looked at Thad like he was crazy.

"Can you see me now? My name is Thaddeus."

"Of course I can see you, Dude. Thaddeus. What's this about?"

"Isn't that Bill Murray, the actor?" Again, Thad pointed away. Again the man looked.

"What's my name?" Thad demanded when the man turned back.

"How the hell should I know? I've never seen you before."

"Not a moment ago? When I told you my name was Thaddeus and pointed to Bill Murray."

"Bill Murray? Where? I love his movies." The smoker looked at where Thad pointed.

"What's my name?" Thad demanded, nearly hysterical. Hardly able to breathe.

"How would I know? I've never met you before."

Thad punched the guy in the arm, hard.

"Hey, dude. What was that for?"

"Oh, look. Isn't that the actor Bill Murray?"

When the man turned back, Thad smiled at him. "Does it hurt where I just punched you?"

The man stared at Thad. "What are you talking about?" He flicked ash and turned his back and started to walk away.

"Hey, there. Can you help me?" Thad called, running after the guy.

"Sure, dude. What's up?" Thad punched him in the arm again and walked away, shoulders slumped, heart hammering. What did it matter? He'd lost his ability to make any sort of lasting impression—even for a few seconds.

He rushed back to the community center, this time he barged into Guy's office. "Guy, Brother Guy. Can you see me? Do you remember me?"

"Well, of course I can see you. And remember you. You're quite memorable and you've made a very worthwhile contribution since you've been here. Are you all right? You know you missed your meeting with the high school coach this morning. Were you ill? You don't look so good."

"You don't remember me coming in here half an hour ago and telling you I was attacked last night?"

"You were attacked? That's horrible. Did you call the police? Seek medical treatment?"

Thad stepped back into the hallway. Then reentered the room. "Hi, Brother Guy. How's it hanging?"

"Brother Thaddeus! You missed a meeting with the high school coach this morning. That isn't like you. Are you okay?"

"Never mind," he said. "This *Groundhog Day* stuff was a lot funnier when it was happening to Bill Murray."

CHAPTER 6

GET A HALF LIFE

THAD STAGGERED TOWARD HOME, stopping every now and then to re-test the theory that he'd lost his memorability. Everyone he spoke to could see him and speak with him, but the moment they looked away, it was as if a reset button had been pushed.

He watched other people's interactions. Nobody else faded from memory—just him.

He passed an electronics store, one of those that thought a camera facing passersby was great marketing. You could watch yourself watching yourself on the various TVs in the window. Thad glanced at it as he passed.

Oh, God! He didn't show up on the TV screens!

He checked again. Was it some kind of camera trick? Maybe a promotion on funky lens equipment?

The street behind him, the cars passing by on the road, they all displayed just fine. A prerecorded loop wouldn't feature the Joe's Contracting truck driving by that very second. He released his death grip on the grocery bag, and as soon as it was no longer connected to him, it appeared on screen. Of course it immediately dropped out of frame, hitting the pavement and scattering his organic oranges.

His knees crumpled and he followed the bag to the sidewalk, needing to sit down before he fell down. Bracing his back against the store's dirty brick wall, he put his head between his knees as he had in the bathroom earlier. He slowed his breathing until he thought he'd pass out from that instead.

How was this possible? It wasn't just the face-to-face communication he'd lost. He got it now. The ink disappeared, the email never arrived. The phone didn't register his voice. He didn't show up on camera. What the hell had they done to him?

He'd never believed in superstition or voodoo or any of that crap. He even had his doubts about God but wasn't prepared to say them out loud.

The journey home seemed to take forever, his knees trembling and threatening to deposit him on the cold sidewalk again. Rain began to splatter down, big, fat, icy drops that seemed to seek out the back of his neck. Like he wasn't shivering hard enough already.

Thad tried to hurry home, but he couldn't force his numb legs to go any faster.

Finally, he made it into his apartment, promising himself he'd figure it out after he'd showered. He dismissed his earlier concerns about washing away possible clues. Any trace evidence would probably go the way of the ink on the hospital admissions form.

He dropped his misshapen and torn bag of groceries on the little kitchen counter. They could wait. All he wanted was the Tylenol. He dug it out of the bottom of the bag and carried it into the bathroom.

Grimacing, he grabbed the bottle, cursing at the amount of packaging he had to break through to get to the actual medication. He left the cardboard and plastic on the counter to be recycled and pitched the huge wad of fluffy white cotton into the wastebasket near the sink. He tossed two caplets into his mouth, washing them down with a glass of rusty tap water.

He stripped down, using the hand mirror to check out his back again. Whatever smoky residue had been there earlier had drifted away. He retrieved his ruined clothes from the garbage and sniffed his shirt, trying to figure out if they'd used herbs or pharmaceutical grade chemicals. A faint odor of burning... sage, maybe? He'd once known a woman who believed you could cleanse a room of bad vibes or something by burning sage. He'd think twice next time he scoffed at those kinds of practices.

Staring into the mirror, he frowned at his reflection. He didn't even feel silly when he checked his incisors to make sure he hadn't grown fangs. He'd been out in the daylight, so at least he felt he could strike vampire off his list of possibilities.

Which brought him back to witchcraft, which was so much saner, right?

Witchcraft. What was witchcraft, after all, but a brand of chemistry? Eye of newt and wing of bat probably broke down to multi-syllabic chemical names and interacted just like any other chemicals.

But right now, he intended to focus on the chemical properties of soap and water. Shaking, terrified and confused beyond words, Thad reached into the shower and forced his stiff fingers to turn the creaky old taps. He leapt backwards and closing the stall door before the icy spray could soak him.

In some past renovation, the landlord had taken out the original bathtub and replaced it with a shower stall. He'd missed soaking in a tub, but was mighty glad for the walk-in shower now. He didn't think he had the wherewithal to climb into a tub without falling. Maybe that's what had happened, he'd hit his head and this nightmare was exactly that—a nightmare. He tried the standard pinching but just left himself with another bruise.

When the cheap plastic shower door finally misted over, he pulled it open, a welcome blast of steam hitting his chilled body. On second thought, he turned back and locked the bathroom door, turning the bolt for the first time since he'd lived there.

The old pipes shuddered and banged, but they produced a decent amount of hot water. At least some technology worked for him, just not anything that allowed him to leave an impression on the world. Some of his fear and tension washed away. He always felt calm here. He could usually sort out his problems in the shower. Clint had gifted him with a small waterproof notepad and pencil that you could write with in the shower. They stuck to the glass partition with little suction cups. He tried making a note on it, but even the special pencil and paper failed to retain any indication that there'd ever been anything written on it.

What had they done to him and how could he undo it? Would it wear off in time? Or would it get worse? Would he fade from the world altogether?

Hush and wait. Hush and wait. His mother's voice sing-songed in his ear again.

Well, if he had to wait, he could do that. Waiting was something he'd learned and learned well.

He'd do an internet search as soon as he left the shower. He scrubbed his skin, closing his eyes and letting the hot water ease his tense muscles and pounding head.

As therapeutic as the shower might have been, he was too antsy to linger long. His skin glowed almost sienna when he stepped out and began to towel off. He rubbed his short curls roughly, regretting it instantly as his head began to pound again. So much for the shower alleviating his headache. He couldn't catch a break.

Now it was his grandfather's voice that echoed in his mind: *You deserve vat happens to you. This is punishment for your sinful vays.*

Thad wanted to shake the voice right out of his head but knew that would only cause it to throb worse than ever. Why couldn't *his* memory be erased? He'd just as soon forget that ugly, accusatory refrain.

He draped the wet towel around his neck and checked himself out in the mirror again.

I've changed. But how? Something's definitely different.

A drop of water caught his gaze as it slithered down his chest, his well-defined pecs funneling it right down the center. He followed its progress until it disappeared into the fine line of dark curly hair leading to his belly button.

But what? What's different?

Maybe Google could help. Lord knows you could find anything on the internet. If that even still worked for him. He'd been able to dial his phone and check his contacts on it. He just hadn't been able to make any impression on anyone or anything. Interact, yes. Communicate, no.

As he finished toweling off, he churned search parameters and key words over in his mind. Then he reached for the light switch over the sink to flip it off.

And froze.

Wait. No. How could it be? It wasn't possible. It contravened every principle of physics and Einstein and Jesus. Fuck!

He held out his hand, moving it slowly in various directions: forward, back, right, left, up down. Other objects weren't affected, until he touched them. Then they changed, too.

Well, at least now I know what they stole.

And somehow, knowing the answer, knowing why they'd come, knowing what to google put an end to his panic and anxiety. Instead, he felt determined. Now he had a goal. He was good with goals.

Thad stood straight and tall and headed for his computer to research *shadow theft.*

POWER TO THE PEEPHOLE

AS IT TURNED OUT, Thad could still work a computer as long as he didn't try to communicate with anyone. In other words, he could bring info in, but he couldn't send anything out that reached another person. Or post to Facebook or his website or anything that whatever controlled this shit might think of as communication. He was like a ghost... sort of.

At this point, the best he could do was interact with a search engine, but that would serve his purposes. He'd worry about contacting people later.

He began by typing "missing shadow" in the search bar. At first he got excited—the little summaries beneath the links contained words like "wizard" and "sorcery." But clicking through to the relevant websites revealed other terms like "role playing," "gaming" and "Skyrim." Another day that might have interested him, but not today.

With grim determination, he began to pursue variants. "Stolen shadows" pulled up info on a film about AIDS, which he found highly unsettling. He shifted his weight, causing his cheap desk chair to creak. Only ten minutes in and already his right butt cheek had grown numb. He was better with physical activity.

He pulled a cardboard carton he'd never gotten around to unpacking from under his desk and rested one bare foot on it. The number of shoe prints on its surface testified to the fact that he'd done this many times before.

On and on, he googled, trying *purloined shadows, loss of shadow, shadowless state.* Next he inserted *abducted shadow, kidnapped shadow, pilfered shadow, plundered shadow, ransacked shadow* and finally *swiped shadow.* Between the online thesaurus and Google, his browser endured a hefty workout. Mostly, his searches garnered him games, music, fiction and works of art.

So the state of being without a shadow must reside in the collective artistic subconscious, but it sure didn't reside on the internet.

He discovered that while *unmemorability* wasn't a word, he still had to wade through 2,500 hits on Google. *Immemorability* had twice that. Also not a word.

The further afield from stolen shadows he roamed, the more esoteric the results. But the hits just kept on coming.

Hours later, he still had a big, fat nothing. Nada. Zip. Zilch. Nothing he could use. Nothing about having one's shadow brutally stripped from one's body.

But it made sense, of course. If a shadowless individual had ever tried to post their circumstances to the net, or even to write it down, it would just fade away as if it never had been.

Had nobody ever recovered their shadow and lived to tell the tale?

Thad scrubbed his hands over his face. He no longer felt faint or nauseated or any of the other symptoms of panic. He felt a cold, slow anger blossoming in his belly. Somebody had done this to him. He would find those people and make them undo it. He wouldn't *hush and wait* this time, no matter what.

The only problem was where to start. He watched a lot of cop shows on TV. Maybe something he'd learned there would help.

He rose and stretched, popping his spine, really glad they hadn't absconded with that, too. Who knew a shadow could be so important?

The old apartment building wasn't that weatherproof and goose bumps dotted his arms. He still wore only the damp towel. A glance out the window showed him a dull, drizzly day. He was glad he didn't have to be anywhere, although if he did get a lead, he'd be off like a shot.

He decided to dress in case he found a clue to follow. At the very least, he could head back to The Closet and ask around about the man who'd called himself Jack. He'd said he'd never been there before but maybe he'd lied about that, too.

Once he had the coffee brewing, he returned to the one bedroom of his one-bedroom apartment and pulled on a pair of clean jeans and a sweatshirt with the community center's sundial logo on it. Before clocks and timepieces, how had people told time on dull days like today? Or at night?

The old coffee maker chugged slowly through its cycle. He couldn't afford one of those fancy one-cup-at-a-time brewers. Plus, all that packaging generated too much waste.

He passed the time by doing a few chin-ups on the bar he'd installed across the kitchen entrance. It felt good to stretch out his muscles after hours at the computer. The kitchen's doorway faced into a tiny foyer that led to the door out into the common hallway. It also featured a big pass-through into the living area. On sunny days, light would stream in from the sliding doors to the balcony off the living room and paint the kitchen all yellow and warm. Today the apartment was dull and bleak.

The doorframe wasn't wide enough for him to get his preferred grip, but he'd managed to execute five or six pull-ups when a knock on the door sent his heart into overdrive.

Hands suddenly slippery, he let go of the bar and sprang toward the apartment door. Not wanting to be caught off guard again, he assumed a fighting stance he'd learned from a couple of karate classes he'd taken. If only he'd stuck with karate— he'd be black belt by now, or at least a belt of some sort instead of a poser. He chewed the inside of his cheek again. It grew raw and sore under the sporadic assault.

Another knock sounded.

He felt silly. It was probably just the super or someone soliciting door-to-door, but caution was his new mantra. If he'd been more cautious last night, none of this would be happening. He crept up to the door and peered out the little peephole.

A man in his early twenties stood there, peering back. He might have been cute, but it was hard to tell with the mostly nose, fish-eye view. He had sandy hair with a bit of a wave and straight, white teeth. Thad could see his teeth because he was grinning. He probably grinned a lot, enough to have earned him the deep laugh lines spanning out like ripples on either side of his mouth.

Nobody Thad knew. No way was he opening the door for a stranger. Possibly ever again.

The coffee pot dinged readiness at the same moment as a warm, rich voice called through the door. "Hello? Thaddeus Wright? Do I have the correct apartment?" The words had a clipped, British accent.

In addition to the battered self-esteem and questionable religious beliefs his grandparents had drummed into him, they'd also instilled in him basic good manners. He answered the man before he even really thought about it.

"Go away. I'm not seeing anyone today."

"But I've come an awfully long way, Mr. Wright. And I think you might want to see me."

The accent was charming—not that Thad was in the mood to be charmed. It wasn't *Downton Abbey*, but it wasn't *Coronation Street* either. Not that he was all that familiar with British accents. This sounded like that actor who'd played *Doctor Who* last time he'd caught an episode. *BBC-English* someone had once called it.

"What do you want?" Thad yelled through the door,

becoming concerned that it was a very thin door. He stepped to one side in case the Englishman had a gun and decided to fire through the cheap wood.

"I can help you."

"What makes you think I need help?"

"Lose something lately?" The reply came back with just the hint of a smirk in the tone.

That did it. *Hush and wait* be damned. Thad had had enough. He wrenched the door open and hauled the Englishman into the apartment by his sweater-front. Shoving him up against the foyer wall, Thad leaned into him, pinning him there with all his strength—the mirror image of last night's promising pose when Jack had shoved Thad up against the same wall.

This man was a little shorter than Thad and a lot more wiry, whereas Thad was 180 pounds of solid muscle. Thad could feel lean, hard pecs beneath his knuckles but refused to let that distract him.

"What do you mean *lost something?*" he snarled.

The man did smirk at him now, which seemed to Thad like an unhealthy stance to take when being mauled and threatened. "Been there, lost that. If you'll let me go, I might be able to help you reclaim your shadow."

Thad unclenched one hand from the Englishman's green sweater and checked him for weapons. His unsensual groping turned up nothing more than the latest model iPhone. The phone's solid black case featured an unfamiliar logo of a bird-lion creature and the initials BOO, whatever that meant. Keeping his gaze on the guy, Thad let him go and backed up a couple of steps.

"Explain," he ordered, his hands loose by his sides in case he had to... he wasn't sure exactly what he'd do, but at least he was ready. If what this man had said was true, then there might be a way to re-attach Thad's shadow, provided they could find it first. "I'm listening."

The man took a tentative step away from the wall, keeping his hands raised in a placating gesture. Then he lowered his right hand out and thrust it toward Thad.

Thad leapt backwards like a terrified cat.

"Oh, so sorry to startle you." The visitor dropped his hand.

"You didn't," Thad lied, cheeks burning when he realized the guy had just wanted to shake hands, not karate chop him in the solar plexus. "Who are you?"

"Good morning, my name is Batique, Peter Batique." This time he gave a royal wave and kept his distance. "I'm an agent for an international paranormal policing agency known as Borderless Observers Organization. We investigate, and set right, things that have gone wrong." He reeled it off effortlessly, like he said it all the time.

"How can you possibly know that something has gone wrong here unless—" He kicked the apartment door shut and strong-armed Peter back against the wall. Peter's head cracked against the plaster. "Ow," he said, looking displeased.

Good. "How can you know what went wrong unless you were in on it?"

"Here, now. Listen to me, please. I'm here to help. I'm not the one who did this to you."

"Prove it," Thad ordered, without any clue what kind of evidence he'd accept.

"Why would I be here if I were in on it?"

Good point, but Thad kept his hand splayed against Peter's chest.

"I have ID," Peter said.

Thad rolled his eyes, fingers digging into Peter's sweater.

Peter's grin put in a return appearance. "Yeah, I get that a lot. What's the point of proving I'm a BOO agent if you've never heard of BOO?"

"BOO?" Thad felt his forehead wrinkle up. "What kind of a

name is BOO?" He let go of Peter's sweater and stepped back.

"We used to be The Royal Society for the Investigation of Natural and Unnatural Phenomena, but saying 'I'm an RSINUP agent' was rather odd. And difficult. I wasn't there yet when they changed the name but frankly, I think it was someone's idea of a joke. I'm a BOO agent. *Boo!*"

He leapt toward Thad as he said the final "Boo," hands up like claws and teeth gnashing.

Thad jumped away again, nerves on edge and fraying.

Peter laughed hysterically for a bit, then sobered up as if someone had flipped a switch. His mouth twitched at the corners, but mostly he was solemn. Thad began to suspect that the self-proclaimed *agent* was nervous too.

"I know what you're going through," Peter continued. "I was lost for a very long time before BOO found me. I can help you. I'm the only one who can. You need me."

"Need you? How?" Thad raised an eyebrow.

"Let me show you." The sandy-haired man smiled again. He seemed a little volatile to Thad, like a child, jumping from happy to angry and back to happy all in the span of a minute.

"How?" Thad repeated.

"Step away. Like, uh..." The man cast a glance around the apartment. "Is that a bedroom? Go into the bedroom for a moment."

"What? No. You'll disappear."

"Ah, but you won't. At least not to me."

Thad stared. The man opposite him was a little older than Thad's original estimate, but not by much. If he was all of twenty-five, Thad would be surprised. He wore a green sweater under a khaki-colored leather jacket, blue jeans and streamlined brown leather boots that looked a little girlish to Thad and were probably custom made. Nothing like the heavy-duty hiking boots Thad favored in this weather.

"Okay, yeah. But I'm not going into the bedroom. I'm going

to step out into the hall."

The keys hung from a hook by the door. He snatched them up, clenching them in his fist so hard it hurt. Stepping out into the hallway, he closed the door behind him. "Ten, nine, eight..." He counted back from ten as if he were re-booting his router. It hadn't taken any time at all for people to forget him this morning, but he wasn't taking any chances now.

Suddenly it occurred to him that he was doing exactly what he'd done last night—trusting a strange man in his apartment. He shoved the key in the lock and charged back in. The stranger—Peter—had made himself at home in Thad's kitchen, helping himself to a cup of coffee.

He took a sip, staring coolly at Thad through the doorway. Then he threw his free arm up, back of his hand pressed to his forehead. "Oh, who can this be? I have totally forgotten the very existence of Thaddeus Q. Wright. What will become of you?"

Peter dropped his arm before taking another sip of his coffee, his features arranged in a devilishly smug smile.

Instead of asking why or how, Thad responded with, "My middle initial isn't Q." He'd had so many shocks lately he wasn't even making sense anymore.

"I know, my new friend. It's D for Dennis." His grin widened. "And we've got some work to do. But first, you want to know why I can continue to see you and nobody else can. Am I right?"

Thad felt an impulse travel from his reptile brain to his fist, telling him to punch the shit-eating grin off Peter's face. The reaction shocked him. That wasn't his way. Quickly, before his mother's voice could croon at him again, his more civilized mind ordered his clenched fingers to stand down. He needed the information this man offered and violence never solved anything. Not for him.

Besides, now he took a moment to check, Peter had a very attractive face, boyish, almost pixie-like. He tried to see if

Peter's ears were pointed, like that guy with the bow in *Lord of the Rings*. The word *elfin* floated up through his brain, as if this morning's endless searches had left him plugged directly into thesaurus.com.

He shook his head to clear it. The move caused no pain—the Tylenol had done its duty.

More to the point, though, was to never trust a pretty face. He had done so last night and look where it had gotten him. Not that Jack would be described as pretty. He'd been more ruggedly handsome like Clint, whereas Peter had a unique fae look and style that was all his own.

"So you can see me. Continue to see me. Why?"

"Because, I too had my shadow stolen once upon a time. And it took me a hundred years to get it back."

"A hundred years?" Thad managed to include both disbelief and mocking in his tone.

"Oh, at least." Once again, Peter sounded childish. He looked to be mid-twenties, but he acted about twelve. One minute he was insisting he was a century old, the next he stared down at his feet, face scrunching up like he might cry. "I don't actually know... I— I don't remember."

"You don't remember how you lost your shadow?"

"I don't. Well, at least the first time. Jacqueline thinks I might have been born with a defective bond because my shadow kept coming off at the slightest tug. I know. I know. You suffered horribly when yours was detached. Most horrible experience of your life."

He gifted Thad with a rueful grimace, but it didn't make up in any way for the fact he was making light of Thad's pain. Thad narrowed his eyes, but Peter plowed on.

"That's because the shadow-thieves don't know what they're doing. Shadow detachment is painless. I think." He screwed up his face. "If that happened to me, I'm grateful I don't remember." He looked serious for a moment. It didn't last. "Oh, you'll love this. One time a dog snatched it."

"A dog took your shadow. Did it also eat your homework?"

A half-laugh, half-scoffing noise escaped from Peter. "I'd be careful what I mock, now that you're a shadow-free zone, Mr. Wright. I may call you Thaddeus, mayn't I?"

Peter pushed off the wall and skipped around the room. Actually, he walked, but there was a skipping quality to it, as if he felt joy with every step. Turning back to Thad, he said, "When you don't have a shadow, you don't age. I was a boy for over a hundred years. Now I'm trying to grow up, but immaturity is a hard habit to break."

Thad was about to give the guy the heave-ho when Peter's earlier words sank in. What right did he have to be skeptical when his shadow had been stolen? He kept his comments to himself, trying for an open mind. Maybe *hush and wait* was the best strategy once again.

"Okay, so you lost your shadow—"

"For a hundred years," Peter insisted.

"Okay, right. So how did you get it back?"

Peter executed a hell of a leap and plopped himself onto Thad's sofa, booted feet resting on the scarred coffee table. "Wendy sewed it back on. Or maybe it was Wendy. The other Wendy. I forget. It's so difficult to remember. I think if you're unmemorable long enough, even you start to unremember you."

That had a weird logic to it. And a scary promise of the future for Thad.

"But this last time, Jacqueline, that's my mother, my most recent mother, anyway. She sewed it back on. Because you know soap doesn't work, of course. Did you try soap? Anyway, Jacqueline, she's kind of scary with the scarification and all, but she understands me and, more importantly to this conversation, she can sew. I think all girls were taught to sew back in her day." He nodded once, as if pleased with his explanation.

Which, to Thad, clarified nothing. Lacing his hands together, Peter cradled the back of his head and stared upward. "That's quite a crack you have in your ceiling. Perfect place for a fairy to hide."

He jumped up and once again bopped around the room.

His antics made Thad want to remain as calm as possible, as if there were a one-maniac-per-apartment limit. The counselor in Thad kicked in and slowly, non-judgmentally, he asked, "Are you on something, Peter?"

"I was on the couch." He pointed behind him, his expression puzzled, like he thought it a weird question. "Before that I was on the island of Azunya. It's nice there. Warm and sunny. A lot like Neverland, I think." He shrugged, returning to the kitchen for his half-finished cup of coffee.

Thad's mouth hung open, eyes wide with disbelief. *Neverland?* Holy crap. Wasn't that the name of the place in that kid's book? And wasn't the kid in that book named Peter? *Have I slipped into some other dimension of reality where books come to life?*

He snapped his gaping mouth shut. Impossible. This guy had to be delusional. Wasn't there some sort of mental disorder where people thought they were someone famous? Or in this case, fictional? Thad pictured all the cartoon images of mental institutions that featured some guy in a Napoleon outfit. It wasn't a stretch to picture this energetic young man in green tights and a tunic. The fact that he wore green seemed to support Thad's personality disorder theory.

No way. Shadow-extraction. Being trapped outside the world. These he'd been forced to believe in. But that Peter Pan was an actual person? No way.

"He based the book on me, you know. Very unflattering, thank you very much. And why he kept describing me as having little teeth, I'll never understand. My teeth are just like everyone else's. See?" He drew back his lips and grimaced.

Thad stood his ground this time, tired of leaping back from this delusional and possibly dangerous man.

"Hey, wait. How did you know what I was thinking?" Was the delusional and possibly dangerous man psychic?

"No, sadly. I'm not, unlike my mother. And Tom. No. It's simply that after years of trying to inform people of my true identity, I know that's what any sane person would think. No doubt you have now lay-diagnosed me with some sort of personality disorder." He sighed and scratched his eyebrow. "You don't have to believe me. But I'll tell you now, so that later, when you come to see it for yourself, you won't feel as if I'd kept it from you. Jacqueline counsels against surprises of the paranormal sort."

Before Thad could ask about Jacqueline, whom he didn't remember from the kid's book, someone else knocked on the door.

It startled the hell out of his jangled nerves.

Peter glanced at his wristwatch. "Speaking of Tom, he and Adrian have arrived. They were on their way to handle their own case, but I asked them to meet me here."

Peter bounced toward the door, but Thad threw himself into the kitchen doorway to block Peter's path. "Listen, buddy. I don't know you. Your story sounds nuts and after last night, I'm sure as hell not letting more guys into my apartment. I shouldn't have even let you in."

"Okay. Right. That sounds reasonable. Except..." He leapt high in the air and dove through the pass-through that opened between the kitchen and the living area. It was almost as if he flew.

He might as well have saved himself the trouble. By the time he dove the five or six feet from the living room to the entryway, Thad had stationed himself at the door, blocking it closed.

"We have ID," called a deep voice from the hallway. "We are who we say we are."

"Like that'll help. Anybody with a printer can make up fake IDs, Adrian." A second masculine voice from the hallway countered, surprising Thad by arguing his case for him.

"Well, you try saying something that'll convince him, Tom. I'll wait over here," the deep bass—obviously not Tom's voice—rumbled.

Thad half-turned toward the door, craning his neck, trying to see the new arrivals out in the hallway through the little peephole without quite turning his back on Peter. Again, the fish-eye lens presented him with a distorted version of reality. A thirty-something white guy with a buzz-cut stood staring at the door, as if his fierce disapproval could will it open. Another white guy, younger, with longish, curly brown hair paced the hall close behind him. "We should have brought Delilah, man. She could have sprung that lock in a second."

"If we'd known we'd need a metal-head, then we would have invited her. In the meantime, why don't you work your charm here and get this guy to open up so we can do what we came for and go deal with our own assignment. The airport's at least an hour from here. It's not like *we* can fly."

"More like two, but traffic's a bitch at rush hour, especially in this shitty downpour. Maybe we should grab a hotel for the night." The longhaired guy waggled his eyebrows. The military looking guy, apparently Tom, rolled his eyes but couldn't quite keep the fond smile off his face. It appeared huge to Thad, thanks to the distorting lens.

Thad sighed. It sounded like a lover's conversation. He missed that easy closeness he'd had with Clint. If only...

"Okay. Let me try."

"Door's this way, babe," Tom said.

"I'm not going to shout at the poor guy through his door. He probably already thinks we're crazy. And he has met Peter."

Both men nodded ruefully.

"What're they saying about me? Budge over." Peter pressed

himself up against the door, and up against Thad. Thad refused to relinquish his fish-eye view of the hallway. He felt torn between pressing closer to the warm, lithe body and pulling away in case delusional thinking spread by contact.

The longhaired guy pulled an iPhone from his leather jacket pocket and punched at it. Beside Thad, Peter's pocket began to play Alphaville's *Forever Young.* Seemed appropriate. The guy acted sporadically adult and childish.

"Yo, Adrian," Peter answered, clearly demonstrating the childish part with the famous *Rocky* quote.

Thad rolled his eyes before turning his attention back to the peephole. As Thad watched, Adrian moved away from the door, head down over the phone, murmuring softly. A bright, woven backpack hung from his shoulders. It looked like something sold at those world market stores. Sort of an Aztec-y print or something from the rainforest.

Thad could only hear Peter's side of the conversation, which consisted mainly of, "Yes." "Alright." And "But—" repeated in various combinations. Eventually he pulled the phone away from his ear.

"They agree you're correct to not let strangers in and suggest we could meet in the lobby or at a coffee shop."

Thad considered this for a moment. "Gimme the phone." He held out his hand. Peter smirked again. "What?"

"They won't be able to hear you, you know. Haven't you figured that out yet? And even if you yelled at them through the door, they wouldn't remember it for longer than half a sec."

Thad ground his teeth in frustration, realizing he was dependent on Peter to function as interpreter. Like a TV vampire with a "day guy," except Thad would need Peter to be his all-the-time guy. For how long? Peter was annoying already and they'd only just met.

But also a bit endearing.

"Okay," Thad said. "Tell them to go to the Coffee Bean on

the corner and call from there. I'll be able to tell where they are from the background noise." Peter opened his mouth to speak, but Thad cut in. "'Cause I can hear them even if they can't hear me, right?" Peter closed his mouth and nodded. Thad wondered if the smirk was permanent.

Peter relayed the message and pocketed his phone. Thad strained to hear the couple's faint steps on the threadbare hall carpeting. The elevator dinged and rumbled open, then closed again. No guarantee the two men had actually entered the elevator.

The coffee shop idea was a decent solution. He wondered which one of them thought of it.

Peter flitted about the apartment. The man had no sense of personal space. He picked up Thad's belongings, examined them and dropped them back in entirely different spots.

"Peter, about this BOO agency. Are those guys agents too?" He hooked his thumb over his shoulder at the door behind him, even though Adrian and Tom had left.

He hoped.

"Why, yes. Tom's been an agent for a while. Before that he was some kind of soldier." Peter's shoulders rose and fell, but on him, it was more like a shimmy than a shrug. "American military, of course. Black Ops. Very hush-hush. He's an amazing psychic and something else. I'll tell you later. Adrian's new. They were on their way to their own assignment. They probably told me what it was, but I'm afraid I didn't pay attention. Anyway, my mother thought they could help me with my fir— With my assignment. So I called them. They were changing planes here in Barriesville anyway…"

Thad gave up. Trying to get Peter to explain things in ways that were actually enlightening wasn't working. He still wasn't comfortable with this stranger being in the apartment, so he kept one eye on the guy while he retrieved his jacket. By the time he was ready to go, Peter's phone rang again. Thad held out his hand for it.

He took the phone from Peter and held it to his ear. Definitely café noises in the background. He tried anyway. "Hello? Hello?" Nothing. In fact, he heard Adrian's deep bass asking the same thing. He slapped the phone into Peter's outstretched palm. "I heard Adrian's voice. Tell him to put Tom on now."

Peter did so. Thad wrapped his fingers around the phone, which of course included Peter's hand. He positioned his head next to Peter's so they could both listen. They were practically cheek-to-cheek. He could feel Peter's cheek lift, no doubt in yet another grin as he hit the button for speaker, so when Tom came on, his few words blasted them.

"On our way, gentlemen." Peter clicked off the call.

Thad checked the peephole again before unlocking the door, and even then, he stayed poised to defend himself. There was no guarantee that more men weren't lurking around his hallway. *Fool me vunce, shame on you. Fool me tvice, shame on me.* His grandmother's voice echoed across his brain.

They encountered no one between the apartment and the street.

The rain had eased off to a fine mist. Thad and Peter strode quickly up the street to the nearby coffee shop. Peter walked forward, pointing, commenting, then turned around to face Thad and walked backwards, while still pointing and commenting. The guy was a whole power station full of energy. Thad hoped Peter would order decaf when they got to the cafe.

It dawned on Thad that maybe Peter was trying to distract him. Trying to help him. He'd been through this, he'd said. Maybe he knew how freaked-out Thad was by not being able to interact with the world.

Deep inside, somewhere in the vicinity of his heart, Thad felt the tiniest seed of trust begin to sprout.

CHAPTER 8

SLEIGHT OF MIND

THAD PUSHED HIS WAY into the café, the hubbub of conversation practically deafening after the quiet of his apartment. Body heat coupled with steam generated by the bubbling brewers and simmering carafes coated the windows in a layer of drippy condensation.

Tom and Adrian had snagged a table in a corner. Thad hoped it would be quieter over there, because at the doormat it was too loud to think, let alone hear what others were saying.

A piercing blast sent him rocking back and crashing into Peter, who had entered the café behind him. "Problem, my friend?" Peter yelled over the crowd, half shoving, half supporting Thad back to his feet.

"Just startled," he yelled in the direction of Peter's ear. "That steam machine is really loud, don't you think?"

Peter patted Thad's shoulder. "It's completely understandable. Your nerves are so frayed that the very sound of milk being frothed is terrifying." With a sympathetic frown that may or may not have been completely false, he stepped around Thad and gestured for him to follow.

Peter wove his way around patrons and between tables. When he reached Adrian and Tom's back corner, her drew out a chair and floated into it, graceful as a dancer.

Thad joined them, peering around for other potential conspirators. He knew he was being generally paranoid but couldn't see any downside, so he kept up his suspicions.

It wasn't any quieter in the corner. Between the shouted conversations around them and some indie band blasting over speakers in need of an upgrade, they'd have no choice but to shout. Which meant no privacy at all. Maybe he should have let them come into his apart—

"We got a plane to catch," Tom said. "Let's get on with this. Peter?" He reached over and wrapped the fingers of his left hand around Peter's wrist. His right hand clasped Adrian's left. A half-drunk black coffee sat before Tom, while Adrian used his free hand to dunk a tea bag of some sort, herbal or green. A bracelet made of leather and brightly colored cord bounced on his wrist with each dunk. It matched his colorful backpack, which now rested on the floor at Adrian's feet.

Tom wore a bracelet too, which surprised Thad. The former soldier looked like the sort of man who didn't bother with adornment. He was handsome enough in the rugged-jawed way of Marines. Maybe the two of them had just come back from a nice vacation in Costa Rica or something.

"Let's get on with it," Tom ordered. He'd probably been better at the *hurry up* part than the *wait* part of being in the military. A tiny smile tugged one side of Adrian's mouth up. He took a hurried sip of his tea, placed the cup out of the way and let his hand lay on the table, palm upwards.

Peter nodded gravely in Tom's direction, as if the tall man had said something important.

"Okay," Thad shouted over the café cacophony, eyeing Adrian's upturned hand. He was so not doing anything kinky with these guys. So maybe holding hands in public wasn't kinky, exactly, but still... "Now what?"

Peter grabbed Thad's wrist. It was like tuning into a radio program in progress. Adrian's voice echoed in his head. "We gotta tell him, man. Everything."

"Too much detail's confusing." It was Tom's voice, although

the man's lips hadn't moved. "Strictly need to know, you know?"

"What the—?" Thad yanked his hand away from Peter's warm grasp. The voices ceased.

Adrian gifted him with an encouraging smile, saying aloud, "I know it's weird, man, but it's okay. This is how we talk sometimes." He wiggled his fingers, beckoning Thad to hold his hand. Thad rubbed his suddenly sweaty palms on his thighs. He brought them back up to the table, clasping them before him, well out of Adrian's reach.

"Right, then." Peter rolled his eyes. "No answers for you. I'm going to fetch myself some java. You chaps okay? Adrian? Tom-Cat?"

Both men had beverages already and Peter hadn't asked Thad. He probably figured Thad wouldn't accept anything he hadn't prepared himself. Peter leapt from his seat and made his way toward the busy barista.

"No patience, that one." Tom took a sip.

Thad almost laughed at the irony. *Ve're quick to see our faults in others*, his grandmother used to say.

Who were these men? What was going on? And then it dawned on him that Tom hadn't spoken aloud, that his lips hadn't moved. He realized that Adrian, while still holding Tom's hand in his left, had gradually shifted his right so the backs of his knuckles touched Thad's bare wrist. Thad started to move away, then with steely resolve, he grabbed Adrian's wrist. Hard.

It must have hurt, but instead of wincing, Adrian laughed. "You got it, dude!" Again, Thad heard the words clearly but Adrian hadn't spoken. "But FYI, holding tighter doesn't make for a clearer connection."

Thad lightened up on his grip. "O— Okay. Then. Let's. Try. This," he said in his mind.

"You. Don't. Have. To do that, Thad." Adrian's voice, more

teasing than snarky. "Just think it like you'd speak it. Or think in pictures. We'll get the picture."

Tempted as he was to roll his eyes, Thad thought Adrian looked pretty pleased with himself at this weak play on words.

"Yeah. I guess it was weak," Adrian responded.

Thad snatched his hand away again. He hadn't meant for Adrian to hear that. Or any more of his private thoughts.

Adrian beckoned Thad to give him back his hand. And he said something—at least his lips moved. Another blast of steam rendered hearing impossible. Left without an option, Thad let Adrian take his hand.

"This all takes a lot of getting used to. I know. I'm a recent convert. You should see some of the other folks we work with. If you can think of a mythical being, we probably have at least one on staff."

Thad pushed his skeptical and probably insulting thoughts down and asked, "So who are you guys?"

"Didn't Peter tell you? Man, that kid cannot be trusted with anything." Adrian, who looked only a few years Peter's senior, was obviously the spokesperson for this duo. Tom merely watched, like a big cat. Thad hoped he wasn't currently assigned the role of mouse.

"He mentioned an agency. You're, like, secret agents?"

Peter picked that moment to return, placing a coffee in front of Thad. He'd purchased a hot chocolate for himself. Well, a little less caffeine than coffee, but too much sugar.

"Oh, right then. You'll hold Adrian's hand but not mine. I'm cute too, you know." The handsome Englishman put his fists on his hips and turned first left, then right, gifting everyone with the wonder of his profiles. Then he snickered and sat.

Thad laughed, assuming the petulant performance was for show, although he was quickly realizing that with Peter, you never knew. Just to make peace, he wrapped his free hand around Peter's wrist. Maybe having a closed circuit helped.

What did he know? "This may make communication easier," he thought, trying to cover his nervousness with humor. "But it's not great for drinking coffee."

The others laughed, a bit out loud and a bit in his mind. Some of the day's tension began to lessen.

"So," Adrian began, "BOO is an internationally recognized group of people—and beings—with special talents."

Thad could practically feel his mind closing. *Beings?*

"Yes, beings. Deal with it. We have internet guys, and I mean *internet guys*, who monitor the globe looking for patterns. When they spot someone we can use, we *acquire* them if we can. Sometimes a guy can be on their radar for a long time. Like Tom here. BOO had to wait until he was done with his military career before approaching him. He's so stubborn."

Tom slit his eyes at his partner. Thad could see the stubbornness shining through. Along with love and admiration.

"Sometimes they get taken by surprise. Like with me. Nobody had any idea of my talent, least of all me. It took a nightmare expedition in the jungle to bring it out."

Jungle? That explained the rainforest accessories. "And Peter?" Thad asked aloud, already forgetting he could just think his question.

"Well, Peter, now. He's a whole different story," Adrian continued mentally. "He'll tell you, or maybe give you the book to read."

"I shan't be doing that. It's a horrible betrayal of my sterling character. It makes me sound so immature."

"So he really is..." Thad couldn't even bring himself to ask such a crazy question, even in his thoughts.

"'Fraid so," Adrian answered. "All that impossible shit he's dumped on you? One hundred percent true, man."

Thad turned to Tom for final reassurance. The quiet, imposing man just tipped his head and raised his eyebrows as if to say, "I couldn't believe it either."

"Well, one should." Peter's thought was accompanied by a haughty look. "My recollection's sketchy at best, but it seems at one point during my association with the Darlings, before I lost my shadow yet again, I met a children's author in the park and told him my story. Have you read it, by chance?" Peter asked. He tried to sound casual in their odd way of conversing, but Thad could tell this was important to him.

"Nope. I guess I saw the movie or something, but I really don't remember. My grandparents weren't big on television."

"Oh, good. Well, just remember the various creators took a lot of liberties with my biography. A. Lot."

Peter let go of Tom's hand long enough to raise his hot chocolate to his lips and take a sip. His tongue swept out to deal with the hot chocolate mustache. Thad slid his eyes away, hoping the others hadn't registered the small frisson of interest that glimpse of pink tongue had aroused.

Adrian had let go of Tom and pulled out his cell phone without taking his eyes off Thad. When he reconnected skin to skin, he was all business. "So enough about us. Let's talk about you. We already knew there was a problem here with missing boys, but we had no idea it was paranormal in nature, and therefore falling into BOO's area of responsibility. Tom and I have our own assignment, but since we were changing planes here anyway, Jacqueline suggested we pop over and see if we could provide any help. And when Jacqueline makes a suggestion, it's really an order." He shrugged. "Jacqueline never takes credit for orchestrating convenient coincidences."

Tom nodded, backing up his partner with a flow of wordless approval through their connection.

Tom seemed like the strong, silent type. Not Thad's type at all. Thad liked gregarious, upbeat people. But he found himself glad that Adrian and Tom had found happiness together. He liked to see happy couples and missed being half of one. At least he'd thought he'd been happy. Now that he'd had time to reflect on his past relationship, he wasn't so sure.

Maybe after all this shadowlessness was behind him, he could try to meet someone new. He cut his eyes away quickly when Peter caught him staring.

Realizing his thoughts were probably clear to his tablemates, he quickly re-focused on the problem. A thousand questions raced through his mind, but he went with the most important one. "Is this, what's happened to me, connected with the boys' disappearance?" Thad gripped the hands he held tightly. "You don't think I had anything to do with their disappearance, do you?"

"No, we know you didn't. And if we weren't sure before, we sure are now." He raised their joined hands. "All your secrets *are belong to me.*"

Thad laughed at the popular but grammatically grating internet saying. He felt he could really like these guys. Under entirely different circumstances.

"But it's all connected." Adrian's hands jerked as if he usually gesticulated while talking. Instead, he only succeeded in jerked on Thad and Tom's hands, nearly spilling Tom's coffee. With a grimace, he let his arms relax again before continuing. "You've had your shadow stolen. You've figured out that part. And Peter has experience with losing and reconnecting his shadow. He might be the only person in the world with that particular skill set. It allows him to remember you."

Peter preened. Now that Thad was getting to know him, he saw that in addition to the self-interest was an awareness of that self-interest. Peter seemed amused at himself. A weird, likeable wryness accompanied his behavior.

"Now Tom 'n' me. We were briefed, but the moment we look away, we'll forget you again."

"But you've taken your eyes off me. Tom's been surveying

the café like he expected an enemy attack." Thad swept his gaze around the room. "You don't, do you?"

"Force of habit," Tom thought back as if he'd invented succinctness.

"We were briefed on what to expect, so we're prepared to keep forgetting you. And now that we're physically touching..." Adrian raised his hand, drawing Thad's arm up with it. "...we can look away and not lose you. We won't be able to remember you once we've left here, though. We'll only know that we helped Peter with some case." He shrugged apologetically. "So we're here to help you get your shadow back. Or at least Peter is. We're just going to do what we do best, then take off. You'll be fine in Peter's tender care." Adrian rolled his eyes at his own words, but Thad found the accompanying warm smile reassuring. Adrian gently extracted his hand from Thad's, breaking the circle once more. Without taking his focus from Thad, he picked up his iPhone.

"Switch chairs with me, Thaddeus," Peter said, also letting go and standing up. He drew his vacated chair away from the table like an old-fashioned gent.

When Thad hesitated, Peter added, "Please," in a whiny voice as if asking nicely pained him.

Thad moved over one. Tom wrapped calloused fingers around Thad's wrist. "Think about last night. Think about the man who stole your shadow from you."

The last thing Thad wanted to think about was Jack. How he'd hoped to have met someone special. Maybe not Mr. Right. Which made him think of Clint's old joke, that Thad was his Mr. Wright. Thaddeus Wright. Look how well that had turned out.

He'd never even told Clint that Wright wasn't his birth name, that he'd legally changed it. As soon as he'd been old enough, he'd lit out on his own to escape his judgmental grandparents. He'd worked long hours to pay his way through school, changing his last name from their long, complicated surname with the vowels all out of order to plain, simple Wright, after a favorite coach he'd had in high school. The man had been a much more supportive parental figure than his grandparents had ever been.

"The guy last night..." Tom silently prompted, raising one eyebrow.

"Sorry," Thad mumbled. He concentrated on Jack, the bar they'd been at and their walk home together. He skipped over the part where Jack had shoved him up against the wall in an entirely different manner to the way Thad had shoved Peter that morning.

Adrian barked out a laugh. "You threw Peter against a wall? And I missed it? Damn." He held onto the iPhone but didn't look at it, keeping his focus on Thad.

The next part was particularly painful—the white powder, the drugged-out attack and the horrific pain of having his shadow ripped from his body.

Too much. Too much! It was as if he were reliving it. He yanked his hand away from Tom, gasping. Tom stared at him with compassion. The depth of empathy in his eyes made Thad's heart clench. He and Tom understood each other. They'd both suffered at the hands of magic.

Magic. Oh my God! It really had been magic. Bad magic. Black magic. He hadn't thought to google magic, but now he wished he had.

Up 'til that moment, he'd been skimming the surface of the concept. Like a skipping stone, he'd only let his mind touch down on the idea a bit here and a bit there. Now it socked him in his face, his heart and his very soul. That's what it was. Magic.

Spells. Psychics. *Beings.* All of a sudden fairy tales were real and magic part of his life.

How could he get back to the way things were? He bounced

his gaze from Tom to Adrian to Peter, hoping for an answer. But they couldn't know what he was thinking since he'd jerked his hands from theirs.

Thad glanced around. The café had cleared out a bit while they were communing. The late lunch crowd had gone back to their jobs or classes. It was possible to communicate the old-fashioned way now. Still keeping his laser-focus on Thad, Tom asked aloud. "You get that, Adrian?"

Adrian was holding up the phone so that from his perspective it would be right in front of Thad's face. But he wasn't snapping headshots. Seemed like an odd time to check email.

Without thinking about it, Thad reached across the table and grasped Adrian's free hand.

"Thanks, man. Now I can actually look at the shots I'm editing," Adrian explained. It struck Thad as a strange thing to say since Adrian wasn't tapping any icons or maneuvering any little sliders. "There. Done. This your guy?"

He turned the iPhone around so the screen faced Thad. On the little display was a photograph of Jack.

Thad snatched the phone, staring at the picture of his assailant as he ground his teeth.

"There's more," Adrian said.

Thad swiped at the small screen, growing more and more alarmed as picture after picture of Jack slid into view: Jack smiling, Jack frowning, Jack betraying.

When he got to the pictures of the other person who'd been in his apartment that night—a gloved hand, an expensive loafer, the little black cauldron—Thad began to freak. "How the hell?" He leapt to his feet. "The only way you could have gotten these shots was if you were in on it. You were there! You were part of it! Give me back my fucking shadow!"

The café's remaining patrons grew quiet, staring at the raving man.

"Relax, man. We weren't there. Hell, we weren't even in this hemisphere last night and we have the stamps on our passports to prove it. We're trying to help you get your shadow back. Look at the phone again." Adrian pointed to the device Thad clutched. "Notice how all the pictures are from your point of view, even after you were, what? Lying on the floor? There's no way we could have taken these pictures without being there on the floor with you and you would have seen us then, right?"

Peter cut in now. "And we're trying to get those kids back, too."

The kids. Jaden and the two other missing kids. That brought Thad up short. "What do you mean?" He realized they'd mentioned the kids earlier, but he hadn't made the connection. "Oh, my God. You took those kids' shadows, too. There not missing, they're shadowless!"

"Wrong and right," Tom sat forward. Something about his quiet strength grabbed Thad's attention. For a second, he thought he saw a black furry tail twitching behind the man's chair, as if a giant cat sat in Tom's chair.

"There a problem here, guys?" A young hipster with a black cotton apron tied around his waist appeared beside Thad, but he addressed his question to Tom.

"No, we're good," Tom responded, still keeping his gaze on Thad. "Our friend here was just about to sit down, weren't you, Thad?"

Thad sat, embarrassed at having caused a scene. He hated drawing attention to himself like this. *Hush and wait* drifted across his brain.

"Great, then." The café manager beamed, "But just so you know, I'm switching you all to decaf." He tossed a cotton bar towel over his shoulder and turned to go, chuckling softly at his own joke.

Thad wasn't in the mood for laughter. He leaned back in his seat, trying to put distance between himself and these, what?

Magical beings? Secret agents? It sounded so crazy. He couldn't believe he'd begun to buy into this load of crap. "So you had nothing to do with the missing kids?" he whispered, accusation dripping from his words.

Tom leaned farther forward into Thad's space. "You're right. The kids are missing because you can't remember seeing them. But you're wrong about us being involved. We're here to fix it. Okay?"

"But those pictures. How did you..."

Adrian flushed, looking oddly embarrassed. "That's *my* talent, man. My gift. It's not a big, magical gift like Tom's. He's a shape-shifter and a psychic. No, forget the shape-shifter stuff for now. I know we're already stretching your credibility beyond, well, belief." He reached for his phone, but Thad wasn't ready to surrender the evidence yet. "So you know what a psychic does, right? They can read minds. But Tom can do more than that. He can facilitate mind reading in others, right? You just experienced that. Like input and output."

Thad just stared, reluctant to agree with anything these people were saying despite what he'd just experienced.

"And me? I can take pictures with my brain. Yes, go ahead. Look incredulous. It's a new talent. Something that's only just arisen in the history of the supernatural. I'm the first one they've found, anyway. There's probably others. Remember I said sometimes us recruits are a surprise to BOO. Well, believe me. An agency with a bunch of seers and psychics is hard to surprise, but they had no idea I could take pictures with my brain until I did it." He pawed the air next to him without taking his eyes off Thad, finally finding Tom's hand on the third try. "That's right, isn't it? Jacqueline didn't have a clue?"

"How would I know what Jacqueline knows or doesn't know?"

"Only the shadow knows," Peter intoned, referring back to the old radio program. "Oh, was that tactless? Terribly sorry."

He didn't sound sorry at all.

"So," Adrian continued. "You think about this guy, Jack. Tom transfers it to my brain and I, uh, mentally digitize it and upload it to a memory stick or a digital device. Like an iPhone." He held out his hand and wiggled his fingers again. Thad handed the phone back to him. "Do you want another demonstration?"

Mutely, Thad agreed. He let Tom take his hand again.

"Think of your, I dunno, your favorite pet or teacher."

Like everyone who encounters a magic trick, Thad thought he'd try and trip them up. His grandparents had never let him have a pet, and he'd had the good fortune to have several favorite teachers and coaches who encouraged him to combine his desire to help kids in trouble with his love of sports. So instead of concentrating on either of Adrian's suggestions, he closed his eyes and tried to think of something completely unrelated. Something only he would know. Something he knew had never been photographed.

He meant to think of something unimportant, something meaningless, something harmless, but instead, his mind betrayed him and dredged up his oldest and most private memory.

Thad had been maybe four years old and his mom had still been alive. She'd not been high for once or at least not too high. She sat on the floor with him on a bright sunny day. The room had been awash in bright primaries. And in retrospect, none too clean. But to his child-self, it had seemed normal. Mom stoned, dumpy apartment a mess. Dust motes danced in the sunbeams. He was coloring on white paper with broken crayons, his mother looking on, encouraging, loving.

A deafening, remembered crash sent shockwaves through him, he re-experienced it as a four-year-old would—terrified, but sure Mommy would protect him. He cut the memory off there, winding it back to the happy part. White paper, broken crayons. Mommy. His eyes misted and he let go of Tom's hand.

"There," he said aloud, drawing his hands in close, picking at a hangnail even though it hurt like hell to do so. "Show me that."

A moment later, Adrian passed him the phone. Sure enough, a bright, if somewhat blurry picture of a government housing facility. Of course, he hadn't known that then. It had just been the latest in a series of apartments they'd occupied. A pretty white woman with his grey eyes appeared off to one side, laughing. But the focal point of the picture was the crayon scribbles. It was exactly how he remembered that day.

The last time he'd ever seen his mom alive.

He slammed his fist down on the table. The cups and spoons jumped noisily. "Okay. I get it. It's just a lot to take in, you know."

"Oh, jeeze. Do I know." Adrian rolled his eyes and put one hand on his jacket over his heart. "I mean these guys." He jerked his chin first at Tom and then in Peter's direction. "They grew up with magic. The paranormal was, well, normal to them. But you and me... Pow!" He mimed shooting himself in the temple. "It's a brave new world, Thaddeus Wright. And welcome to it." He held out his hand.

Thad peered at Adrian's hand for a long moment before making his decision. The two men shook.

"Thanks," he whispered. "What do we do next?"

"For our next brilliant trick, my new friend, we shall require a dove, a top hat and a volunteer from the audience. Ow!"

Tom had thunked Peter on the head without taking his eyes off Thad. "Adrian'll email the photos back to BOO's tech people. They'll run it through facial recognition software and try to get more info on this son of a bitch."

"Done!" Adrian's phone pinged a message. All four men leaned over the tiny screen to see what BOO had replied. "Jack Stabler. Our sources say this guy's name is Jack Stabler." Then

Adrian asked. "Why do we want to know this?"

Tom looked up, running his steely gaze over Thad. "Who're you? How did you get here?" Turning his focus on Peter, he demanded, "Who is this guy and why is he at our table?"

Adrian laid a hand on his partner's arm. "This must be the shadowless guy Jacqueline told us about."

Peter nodded. "Gentlemen, may I present to you—again— Mr. Thaddeus Wright." Tom leaned back, still looking suspicious.

Thad's gaze jumped from Tom to Adrian, who was looking at him curiously, to Peter, whose usually frenetic movements had gentled. His face conveyed nothing but pity.

"Is this my life now?" Thad asked.

Nobody answered him.

CHAPTER 9

WISH UPON A BAR

THE FOUR MEN HAD EXITED the café together, making it impossible for Tom and Adrian to keep an unbroken focus on Thad. They forgot him over and over.

It wrenched Thad's gut that he had only just connected with this kind and fearsome duo and that the entire experience was lost for them. It reminded him in some oblique way of the time he'd run into Clint on the street with some other guy. Clint had treated Thad like a casual acquaintance instead of the partner who'd shared his life for three years.

"Okay, then. I guess it was nice meeting you." Adrian gave him that twisted half-grin again. "Sure wish I remembered."

Tom just watched.

How could Thad go on like this? He turned and took a step away, knowing they wouldn't even remember saying goodbye to him.

With a disproportionate amount of sadness at losing his connection with relative strangers, he turned back to watch them climb into a taxi and drive away.

"Never mind," Peter said, grabbing a handful of Thad's jacket sleeve and dragging him along. "You've still got me, don't you?"

"If that's supposed to be comforting..." Thad drew in a breath. "No, sorry. I'm glad you're here. I'm just worn out by all this."

"You think you've got it rough. We're going to get *your* shadow back posthaste. But when I rejoined society, I had to learn an entire century's worth of history. Did you know they had these carriages that didn't require horses? Some that even flew. I'm telling you, my friend, I do know what adjustment is like."

Thad wasn't sure if Peter was joking again to cheer him up, or if he was co-opting Thad's misery. Tiredly, he asked, "What's our next step? Can your people locate the missing boys?"

The kids were still top priority. At least now he knew what had happened to them. Now he and Peter just had to make sure they were all right.

And get them their shadows back, too.

"We retrace your footsteps," Peter suggested. "Take me to the bar you visited last evening and we'll see if anyone knows this Jack Stabler. He's our connection to your shadow."

Thad couldn't get over how fast the BOO computers had come back with information based on the pictures Adrian had leeched from his brain. They had a name, previous addresses in other cities, but nothing current. And nothing local.

"This way," Thad called after Peter who was striding down the sidewalk in entirely the wrong direction.

"I knew that," Peter answered with a grin, spinning back toward Thad.

Despite the dire circumstances, Thad found Peter's smile infectious. He grinned back and pointed across the street.

"The Closet. Such a clever name." The sarcastic tone and exaggerated eye-roll told Thad what Peter really thought. Thad hoped it was actually the name that Peter found distasteful, and not the fact that it was a gay bar. Having co-workers like Tom and Adrian who were obviously gay didn't negate the fact that Peter could be mildly homophobic. Thad found himself hoping that wasn't the case. He wanted Peter's approval, wanted Peter to like him.

They crossed the street and pulled open the heavy wooden door.

Weak mid-afternoon sunlight and a couple of dim overhead bulbs did little to brighten the place. It looked the same as it had the previous evening. Thad stomped his feet on the mat to shake off the last of the rain and mud that clung to his boots. Peter just charged up to the man cleaning the counter and shoved his phone in the guy's face.

"Know this man?" he asked with an authority Thad hadn't heard before. It was a little like Tom. Perhaps the younger man had studied under the former soldier.

"Who wants to know?" came the unoriginal reply.

With his other hand, Peter fished a badge from his jacket, flashed it at the barman and pocketed it again. "Peter Batique, Special Agent, Borderless Observers Org."

The man looked like he was about to say, *Special Agent of what?* But the picture on the phone must have caught his eye. "I guess it can't hurt to tell you. I saw that guy the other night. Uh, last night, in fact. He came in alone but he left with... that guy." He pointed at Thad.

"We know that, thank you very much indeed. What we need to know is where we can find him."

"Why? He get you pregnant?" The barman laughed long and loud at his own joke, sobering and looking squinty-eyed at them. "Can't take a joke? Then I guess I can't help you." The man went back to wiping down the bar. "Never saw him before last night, cutie. Now if you're not drinking, you're leaving, right?"

Movement behind the bartender caught Thad's attention. In typical watering-hole fashion, a long mirror covered the wall behind the bar. Glass shelves protruded from the mirror at intervals. Half-empty bottles and supposedly clean glasses lined the glass shelves. If it hadn't been for the mirror doubling up the flicker, Thad might not have noticed the little light fluttering around the shelves. *Must be a trick of the gloom.* It was far too early in the season for fireflies.

"Are you quite sure you've never seen the man before?" Peter waved his phone in the air, screen toward the barman. "Because lying to an international agent is bad luck. It might cause a localized earthquake, which would be very bad for business. And your glassware."

A glass jumped off its shelf behind the bar and crashed to the floor.

What the hell? Thad thought.

"How the...?" Before the barman could even finish his sentence, a second glass slid off the shelf and hit the floor.

Next, the tiny light fluttered to the liquor shelf. A pricey bottle of vodka began to inch toward the edge. The barman caught it just in time. "I don't know how you're doing that, but I swear I don't know the guy. If he'd paid by credit card, I'd tell you. But he didn't and I don't know where to find him."

Peter produced a business card, sliding it across the damp wood toward the barman. "If you see him again, please call us. It's very important."

Us, Peter had said. Thad found himself inexplicably pleased at that.

The man picked up the card, actually looked at it before asking. "Why? What did this guy do?"

"He may have some information on those kids that went missing," Thad said.

"When did you get here?" the barman asked, looking at Thad, eyebrows nearly meeting. "Anyway, I don't like to see kids get into trouble any more than the next guy. If I hear anything, I'll be in touch."

Another glass hit the floor.

"However you're doing that, please stop. All right? I barely make a living here as it is."

Peter nodded at the mirror and the next glass ceased its little dance toward the edge.

"Let's go." He beckoned to Thad and they left the bar.

"You didn't mention telekinesis," Thad said, halting Peter in the bar's parking lot.

"I'm a man of many talents." He bowed from the waist. "But I'm afraid telekinesis isn't one of them. Speaking fairy, however, is."

"That's not a very politically correct term these days, you know." Thad was always very careful to use the most sensitive language, even among friends. "We prefer gay or even queer."

"And if I'd meant it in any other way than literally, I'd agree. But no, that particular bar has an actual fairy. You probably saw her light."

"I... Yes, I saw a little light."

"You wouldn't have been able to before, but now that you've had contact with magic, you'll be able to see things you previously couldn't."

Thad decided to keep an open mind—at least until he had another explanation for all this woo-woo stuff. "So that was a fairy? Like a pixie?"

"Yes, she was a fairy. No, nothing at all like a pixie. What do they teach in schools these days? And she was having the time of her life being my personal earthquake. Fairies aren't very mature, you know." He grinned.

Neither are you. And I kind of like it. Out loud, Thad asked, "What next, International Man of Magic?"

Peter pursed his lush lips, "I don't actually know. I'm hoping something will come to me. Maybe if we stake out the bar tonight, he'll return."

"I don't think so. Based on the things he said after he'd roofied me, I'm sure he wasn't actually gay. I think he followed me in and faked a connection to get me alone. I felt like I was being watched before I even went in."

Peter nodded. "Then I don't know what. Maybe one of the missing kids knows."

Thad felt his temper heat again. "One of the missing... If we knew how to find them, then they wouldn't be missing..." He trailed off, realizing that he needed to change his thinking. "Right. Find the missing kids who aren't really missing."

Peter's smirk lasted long enough for Thad to add, "How do we do that?"

"Where did you see the kids last?"

Thad paused. "I saw Jaden about a week ago, before he went missing. No, wait!" An image formed in his brain, overlaying whatever false memories magic or whatever had installed there. "No! I saw him in my office just yesterday. He came to see me. He said he had several times before." Thad pressed the heels of his hands into his temples. "Gah! I can't recall. There's memories laid on top of memories. I can't tell which are real. I saw Jaden and before that, I spoke with the two other boys— Hector and Stanley. Oh, my God, they've been trying to get my attention all along."

"Right. We'll have to find them. Or rather they'll find us." He walked over to the *Missing* poster Thad had stapled to the telephone pole yesterday. It was the one with horns and a mustache drawn on it.

"They can call us!" Thad said. "You can hear them. Hell, even I can hear them, right? Because we've all lost our shadows?"

"That's correct, but they'll have no way of knowing that. I would guess that by now they've given up trying to use electronic devices. So we're going to go old school. I'm going to write your address on a bunch of these posters. Then we just have to wait for the boys to come to us."

Thad and Peter spent the last few hours before dusk checking out places the boys might be and writing Thad's address on the posters.

Of course, it had to be Peter doing the writing. Thad's kept fading away.

CHAPTER 10

KISS MY ASSET

"THERE'S NO SENSE IN BOTH of us sitting around your flat in hopes the boys show up. I can wait here," Peter said, executing another impressive leap onto Thad's couch. "You go check the boys' homes. Maybe they've returned there out of habit."

"It's worth a shot," Thad agreed. "Although I wouldn't hold out much hope. The boys were all in foster homes. Hector and Stanley lived together in one of those places that takes in a dozen kids. Jaden's foster mom was pretty hard on him."

"Ah, I see. The shadow thief seeks out children whom nobody would really miss. They'd report them and forget them. Assume they'd run away. Too bad, so sad." He twisted his head around, meeting Thad's gaze.

Thad looked away. Would his grandparents have done much more if he'd gone missing as a teen? Probably would have rented out his bedroom before he'd been gone a week.

"I'll try anyway. I'll drop by the Center to get their addresses." He added a scarf to his damp ensemble. It hadn't rained hard, mostly just sprinkled during the day, but it was chilly now that the sun had set.

It occurred on him that he'd been so distracted by everything that had gone down that he'd never asked a key question. "Peter, why is someone stealing shadows? Why did someone steal your shadow?"

Peter swung his legs off the couch, boots barely clunking

when they hit the floor. Thad walked over to stand before him, the coffee table between them.

"As I have mentioned, as far back as I can remember, my shadow wasn't firmly attached. Perhaps I was born that way, like, say, a cleft palette. Or perhaps it had been stolen, retrieved and not re-attached properly. Regardless, it came off with just a tug. I remember trying to stick it back on with soap once."

"Soap? Wouldn't that make it more likely to slip off?"

"Cake soap was a lot stickier back then, made from animal hooves, same as glue, or something. Besides, I was a child. What did I know?"

Thad wanted to ask a thousand more questions but held his tongue while Peter answered the theft question.

"After Wendy, the first Wendy, grew up and had children of her own, the next Wendy came to visit. You know..." He tapped his lip with his index finger, eyes staring at the corner of the room but probably seeing back in time. Thad wished Tom was still here so he could see firsthand what Peter had been through. Magic was starting to seem less menacing and more useful—except in the wrong hands, obviously. But that was true of technology, too.

"I always assumed the next Wendy was the first Wendy's daughter. But she was probably John's or Michael's daughter since her last name was still Darling. For a woman to keep her last name after marriage wouldn't come into vogue for another half century." Peter seemed to come back to himself, refocusing on Thad. "So the last time I escorted her home, she managed to detach my loose shadow. She told me she'd keep it in a box for me. To make sure I returned."

Peter sprawled, messy boots once again plunked on the couch. Thad hoped the dirty water spots would come out with a little fabric cleaner. But then he thought he had bigger problems to worry about than stains on his second-hand furniture.

"That meant," Peter continued, "that I couldn't contact the world and that I didn't age. I had these other talents..."

"Like the ability to talk to fairies?"

"Exactly. I don't know if that was also something I was born with, or if I developed it on the island. Nature or nurture, as they say."

"What *do* you remember?"

"My first memories are of the island. I must have found it when I grew tired of people forgetting me. Others came to the island, a tribe of redskins, what you'd call First Nations or Native Americans today. A boatload of pirates. It was a magical isle, so they could see me with or without my shadow. Eventually they all died or left me. As did Wendy and the lost boys."

The nape of Thad's neck prickled. He had just about decided that this Peter was actually *that* Peter, but suspicion still niggled at the back of his mind. It was all so improbable. He stared out the living room window, unable to meet Peter's gaze.

His lack of belief was starting to feel like a betrayal of the dedicated young man before him.

Peter seemed to interpret Thad's unease as confusion. "Forgive me, my friend. I'm telling this all out of order. It wasn't until after I was alone that the next Wendy took my shadow. But being without a shadow kept me from aging and trapped me on the island because, after a while, you begin to forget yourself. I forgot all about Wendy and my shadow and just lived on the island day to day. Alone for decades."

Peter's story was breaking Thad's heart. Even if he didn't quite believe it 100 percent, he could tell Peter believed it. It was also serving to leave Thad even more confused. He'd get the story straightened out later. Right now, he had three young boys to rescue. "But why is someone taking the kids' shadows? And mine?"

"Oh, right. Perhaps I should have led with that. There's a

black market for shadows."

Stunned, Thad lurched around the coffee table to the couch. Peter moved his damp boots at the last possible second, smirking. "You're sitting in the wet spot, you know."

Thad glared at him. "Explain."

"Well, when two or more people really love each other..."

"No, I know that. I mean... Jeeze." Fire crawled along Thad's cheekbones at Peter's silly innuendo. "No, I mean explain about the shadow black market."

"Oh, right. There's this belief that a shadow holds the weight of your sins."

"Like a soul."

"Assuming you believe that, then yes. When you get to the pearly gates or Valhalla or whatever, they're going to weigh your shadow."

Thad remembered a semester of world religions he'd taken, hoping for an easy credit. "Weighed against a feather? Isn't that something out of mythology?"

"Yes, quite a few mythologies, actually. Which may mean they steal from each other, or it may mean it has some grain of truth at its basis."

"So you're saying that if someone leads an evil life, as long as they replace their sin-heavy shadow with an innocent, weightless shadow, then they'll get into heaven no matter what?"

"Exactly. So people sin, get a new shadow. Sin some more, get another new shadow." Peter counted these cruel activities off with his fingers. "Then if they die suddenly, they're golden."

"Or if someone knew they had a terminal disease or something, they just go out and buy a new, innocent shadow."

"Yes, exactly. That's why they take the shadows of young people."

"I wondered. Because these three particular boys, Jaden, Hector and Stanley, were all really good kids. Even though they were orphans bouncing around the foster system." Thad frowned, picking a loose thread on his couch. "They weren't into drugs or shoplifting or any illegal activities. No immoral activities like bullying or fighting either, that I knew of. They'd have pure, sin-free shadows."

"Exactly."

"But why mine? It's certainly not pure." He felt his cheeks staining red. "I mean..."

"No details, please. I am starting to like working with you. Best we keep the true confessions to a minimum."

Peter liked him? The blush that had begun to recede flooded back, burning hotly. "Okay. Guess I'd better get going if I want to check out the boys' foster homes tonight." He stood, keeping his head down, and moved over to his desk where he began poking through the little drawer. "Ah! Here's an extra key in case you have to go out." Peter caught the tossed key one-handed, dropping it on the coffee table with a clang. "Call me if you do leave or if one of the kids shows up."

They'd already ascertained that even though Peter could remember Thad, the phone still wouldn't work both ways— Thad could hear Peter, but not vice versa.

"Make yourself at home." Knowing Peter would do exactly that, Thad pulled the door closed behind him without waiting for a reply.

Trudging along, he expected to feel sorry for himself. Instead, he found himself buoyed up by the thought of doing something to help the missing kids. He'd dedicated his life to helping these kids and had felt so frustrated and useless when he couldn't.

But now he could. He also had the backing of a powerful international organization—a weird, unbelievable international organization. Plus a guy who could talk to fairies.

Thad decided he had nothing to lose by buying into this secret BOO organization. Besides, if there was magic, and of course the inevitable mis-use of magic, there would logically be a magic police, right?

A rough-looking pair of men approached him along the sidewalk. Their behavior broadcast attitude. Thad kept his head down and didn't make eye contact. The last thing he needed was some punks wasting his time. He had young boys to save.

As they drew abreast of Thad, the closest one deliberately shouldered him into the gated storefront at his side.

"Hey! Watch it, asshole!" snarled the first punk, a white thug with dirty, spiky hair. "You ran right into me!"

"Yeah, fuck-tard." The other man was Hispanic, a faded bandana tied around his shaved head.

"Sorry." Thad righted himself, rubbing his shoulder.

"Sorry? You're sorry? Damn right you're gonna be sorry. I'm gonna whup your sorry ass until... What? What are you pointing at?"

The plan was for Thad to make a quick exit as soon as they forgot him, but instead of looking away, the white guy shoved him up against the gate again, one huge hand wrapped around Thad's throat.

Turning back, the white guy said, "I'm not falling for that, asswipe. That's the oldest trick in the—*Oof!*"

Screw *hush and wait.* Thad clocked the guy in the throat with a right hook. He'd never really fought before, but some things were instinctive. The guy stumbled back, now gripping his own throat instead of Thad's.

"You'll pay for that!" the bandana-guy screamed, leaning back to get momentum behind his incoming fist.

Thad looked over the man's shoulder and shouted. "Help! Officer. Help!" Again, he pointed across the street.

"We're not falling for that again." Bandana said, sneaking in a quick glance anyway.

This time, the throat-punched guy looked, too.

By the time they turned back, Thad was ten feet away, striding along with hands in his jacket pocket.

"What?" Bandana-man asked, sounding puzzled and angry.

"What *what?* Why the fuck are you asking me?" The white guy rasped, hands still cradling his throat. So much rage and nowhere to spend it.

Thad began to whistle as he continued on his way. Grunts, groans and the sound of flesh connecting with flesh faded into the distance behind him.

There just might be some advantages to this disappearing act.

He arrived at the Gnomon Church and Community Center and found the door unlocked. He peeked in, relieved no one lurked in the hallway past the gym and down to his office. Then he realized it really wouldn't matter. He'd make no lasting impression on anyone he might meet.

Stepping inside, he could hear the screech of sneakers and smack of basketballs on the high gloss gym floor down the hall. They probably shouldn't be in there unsupervised, but what could he do? If he went in there, they'd forget him every few seconds. A whistle shrieked and Guy's voice called a foul. It appeared the good Brother was covering for Thad. Whether out of the goodness of his heart or concern about their insurance policy, Thad didn't care. The kids would be supervised until Guy realized Thad wasn't coming back and recruited a replacement.

Or maybe Thad and Peter could find the shadows tonight and set everything back to normal.

Reaching his office, he opened the filing cabinet, quickly pawing through his files. He had consent forms signed by each boy and counter-signed by a guardian—no parents with these three. Grabbing a pen, he jotted down the addresses. But of course, the first one began to disappear before he finished copying out the third. Just to be sure, he tried a pencil next.

Even the pressure marks faded away.

Advantages, yes, and disadvantages, too. If only there was a way to detach and re-attach a shadow at will.

Next, he laid the forms on the desk and tried snapping a shot with his iPhone. But when he searched through his photo stream, only the pictures he'd taken before yesterday displayed. The new photos vanished, just like his shadow.

Left without an option, he shoved all three files into a bag and started for the door, nearly smacking into a dark figure blocking his doorway.

"Going somewhere with those files?" Accusation dripped from Detective Reasoner's words. He held out his hand for the bag. Thad passed it over.

Drawing out the files, Reasoner sucked in a noisy breath. "Hector Gonzales, Stanley Greenberg and Jaden Raines. Aren't those the missing kids?" He narrowed his eyes at Thad. Of course he knew exactly whose files they were.

"That's right. I might have a lead on them."

"A lead? Which you were planning on calling in to me, right? No way were you going to play vigilante detective, right, Wright?" Reasoner looked a bit flustered at the way his threat had ended on a silly note. It undermined his intimidation factor.

"Yes, I was just about to head to the precinct. In fact— Oh, wait. Did you hear that?"

The detective spun around, peering down the hallway first right, then left. By the time he turned back, Thad had ditched his coat and seated himself at his desk. "Well, I'm glad you found those files helpful. I'm just going to put them back in this locked drawer where they belong." He held out his hand.

Confusion painted the detective's features. He hesitated but handed the files back to Thad, who opened his file drawer, put them at the front and locked it again. "Was there something else I can help you with, Detective? Brother Guy is in the gym if you need to speak with him."

The detective waved him off, muttered something that might have been "G'night" or possibly "Don't leave town" and headed toward the gym.

Thad waited until he heard the smack of the gym door settling into place before he quickly unlocked the cabinet, grabbed the three files and locked it again. He tossed his jacket over his shoulder and charged down the hallway in the opposite direction, toward the parking lot exit.

CHAPTER 11

TOSSED AND FOUND

THAD DRAGGED HIMSELF BACK to his apartment, so tired he practically staggered. It wasn't as if being roofied had gifted him with a restful night's sleep. Plus, he'd been through emotional hell. He tried to review the excessive weirdness he'd experienced that day but just assembling it into a mental list was exhausting, so he gave up. Fear and worry chewed at him just as hunger gnawed at his empty gut. He needed to take care of the basic human needs before he could think a single constructive thought.

Rooting through his pockets for his keys, he listened at the door for boyish laughter or yelling or crying, anything that might indicate he had an apartment full of the missing boys. He heard laughter and began to shake, only to realize Peter had the TV tuned to some laugh-tracked sitcom.

He sucked in a deep breath and shoved the key in the lock. It refused to budge. Would keys even work for him now? He jiggled it while drawing it in and out a millimeter at a time. The lock had always been quirky. The key finally turned. Thank God. At least that hadn't changed, but then opening a door didn't involve leaving an impression on the world. It might re-lock behind him, but he was too tired to deal with that now.

The warm smell of pizza surrounded him and his mouth watered as he stepped into the little foyer. He tossed his keys into the bowl on the kitchen counter as Peter leapt up from the little table, balancing a slice and trying to swallow.

"Look who showed up." Peter gestured grandly toward the three young men seated on Thad's couch watching a *Fresh Prince* rerun and chowing down on pizza.

As if Thad needed to be directed to them.

"Oh, my God! I'm so glad to see you guys!" Thad dashed to the couch, running his gaze over the kids, checking each boy in turn. "How are you? Everybody okay? I see Peter ordered pizza and—*Oof!*"

Three pairs of warm arms wrapped around him. Or tried to as the boys jockeyed for position. Young, shorter Stanley got one side, arms around Thad's middle, cheek pressed against his coach's chest. Hector, a little taller got the other side, trapping Thad's right arm as he hugged Thad tightly around the shoulders. Eldest, tallest and shyest, Jaden stood a foot away, eyes shining. He hesitated, probably not sure where he fit in, and finally just stepped up and wrapped his arms around everybody.

"Oh, man, Coach. We are so glad to see you." Jaden stepped back, a little embarrassed probably at his unmanly outburst of emotion. No doubt, he figured fifteen was too old to be hugging his coach. "I, uh. I found these guys and then, you know, got your address off the posters. Thanks for looking for us, Coach." He stared at the floor. His spiky hairstyle made him look like a troubled hedgehog.

"You did good, Jaden. Taking care of the younger boys. And you're all okay?" He tried again to get a read on the boys' health. He glanced at Peter, now standing near the sofa. The Englishman gave a tiny nod. Thad felt every nerve in his body relax. Here, safe, healthy. Thank God.

Hector pulled back now. He was the most gregarious of the three. Not as good at basketball as Jaden—Jaden was the star player of their after-school program. But pretty good. Even though he was younger, he was the team strategist. "Too smart for his own good," his current foster dad had said when Thad had tried to track down the missing teen.

"At first it was so scary, Coach. Nobody could remember us. But then, Jaden found me 'n' Stan and made sure we got enough to eat and a warm place to sleep. Then we figured out how to get stuff for free 'n'—*Ow!* Why'd you do that?" Hector had been staring at Jaden with admiration as he rattled off their exploits. Now he glared at him. "Whaddya swat me for, dude?" He rubbed his ear, managing to look severely injured by what had only been a light tap.

Thad wanted to say something about the theft—that all crime was wrong. But this was not the moment. These kids had been through so much. Instead, he leaned over Stanley, who was still clinging to him like he'd been stuck on with magic glue, and ruffled Hector's dark, curly hair. The boy's curls were soft and loose, not like Jaden's or Thad's own tight, kinky spirals. Hector's Hispanic background was easy to read in his swarthy complexion and warm brown eyes.

"Yeah, Coach. Jaden was great. Hector, too." Stanley finally let go of Thad, although Thad could have stood a few more minutes of being tightly hugged. It had been a while since anyone had hugged him. Jack Stabler's fake advances couldn't have been more different from Stanley's open affection.

Stanley moved over to stand beside his adoptive brother. Hector's dark features only looked darker next to Stanley who had frizzy red hair and freckles that stood out like connect-the-dots against his pale, pale skin.

"So, no broken bones, then?" Thad asked. He'd meant it as a half-joking way of checking, but it dawned on him that a serious illness or injury for any one of them—himself included—could be a real problem, even lead to death. How do you get someone to treat you if every time they turn away, they forget why you're there? He shuddered, recalling his attempt to check in at the ER.

How had Peter survived all alone on an island for a century, if that was true? All the more reason to fix this right away. But, man, that pizza smelled delicious. He hadn't had anything to eat except that cheese sandwich at noon. "Any pizza left?"

"The one on the left's vegetarian." Peter grabbed a fresh slice from the box on the right. "I knew you ate healthy, so..."

Bypassing both paper plate and paper napkin, Thad downed half a slice in the time it took to say *pizza*. "Oh, man, that hits the spot," he mumbled, barely intelligible around a mouthful of cheesy goodness.

A line of on-screen dialogue cut through the happy reunion. Will Smith said something poignant about missing his mom. The room fell silent, even the chewing slowed. Each one of the five people in the room coughed, shifted, looked away. This they all had in common, Thad realized. Peter might not be able to remember his mother, but he could surely remember the ache caused by missing the most important person in a child's life. Thad's heart clenched as he looked at Peter. It was mind-boggling that the young man had survived at all, let alone become a personable, if somewhat unpredictable, adult.

Swallowing hard, Thad grabbed a second slice and, balancing the floppy, saucy triangle, deposited himself into a chair at the small two-seater table in the corner. It was more kitchenette than dining room, but it barely fit in the tiny apartment as is. It dawned on Thad that this was not so different from the government housing projects he'd spent his first few years in with his mom, only much cleaner. And drug free. Or at least it had been until Jack had arrived, bearing his evil white powder.

Peter picked up a sweaty plastic bottle of water, unscrewed the top and brought it to his lips. Thad watched, tired yet mesmerized, as Peter's Adam's apple bounced with each slow swallow. *Lord help me, but I find that sexy as hell.*

He ducked his head at the inappropriate thought. Not the

thought, actually. Peter was sexy as hell, but given the circumstances, the timing was lousy.

But it struck Thad that there was a hint of deliberateness to Peter's actions. Was the man flirting with him?

Peter thunked the bottle back on the little tabletop with an "ahhh!" that sounded just like the sigh a man might make during intimate moments.

No, no, no, Thad told himself, trying to will his hardness away. *This is so not the time. And it's probably all in my head. Peter's given no indication that he's interested in men, let alone interested in me.* Peter hadn't said outright that he was straight, but that was the default, right?

To cover his embarrassing arousal, Thad cast about for something to say. "So, Peter... I guess this explains why I didn't have any luck locating these guys at their homes. How long have they been here?"

"I tried to call you, but you didn't answer." He responded sulkily, like a kid accused of something he didn't do.

Thad pulled out his phone with stiff fingers. He was still so chilled he hadn't yet taken his jacket off. "Battery's drained. Guess in all the excitement, I forgot to charge it."

Peter looked delighted to be off the hook. "So you forgive me?" His tone held just a little too much hopefulness to be strictly the one-liner he probably intended it to be.

"Yeah, sure. How long they been here?"

"About an hour and a half. Long enough to order pizza. They showed up at the door together."

Something on TV made the boys chuckle. The warm sound of their laughter began to thaw something deep in Thad's chest. He finally pulled off his jacket. "Who's paying for this delicious repast?" Although joking, Thad was pleased to have a chance to show Peter that he, too, had a pretty decent vocabulary. He took another bite. It was good pizza.

"BOO. Jacqueline gives all her agents carte blanche to cover expenses when on assignment." Peter licked his index finger, using it to rescue pizza crumbs from his plate. His pink tongue flashed in and out, drawing the bits from his fingertip into his mouth.

Damn that was hot. Thad shifted in his chair, making things a bit more comfortable. He was really glad mind reading wasn't one of Peter's self-proclaimed abilities. But he wondered what, exactly, was. Again, he reached for something to say to break the awkwardness. "Have you worked a lot of assignments?"

"I've assisted before. This is the first one I'm lead investigator on."

Thad didn't ask who he was leader of, but he found he was damn glad to have Peter here. The agent's ingenuity with the posters had brought the boys to them safe and sound. Plus, he'd bought dinner, although if he had carte blanche as he claimed, couldn't he have sprung for Thai instead?

"Now all we have to do is get their shadows back." Thad sighed, rubbing his forehead tiredly. "Any new thoughts on that?"

"Oh, yes. I suppose I should have led with this. Jaden knows where Jack Stabler lives."

"What? How?"

"They all got attacked and drugged and de-shadowed, just like you. By the same duo. And also just like you, they were lured away by Jack and never saw the other man's face."

"I kept coming back to the community center," Jaden joined the conversation, leaning one elbow on the back of Thad's sofa.

If a little tomato sauce dripped on the fabric, Thad bit his tongue and said nothing. These kids needed a break in a big way.

"'Cause all of us," Jaden gestured to Hector and Stanley who were still glued to the TV. "We all hung out there. That was the clue, right? So we waited and then saw him follow another kid. I distracted him and the kid got away with his shadow.

Then I hid, 'cause Stabler couldn't remember me, and then I followed him home. Stabler, not the kid. He lives in an old apartment building on Chester." Jaden had carried his empty plate over to the table as he talked. He piled three more slices on it before re-joining Hector and Stanley on the sofa and handing each boy one of the new slices.

How many slices had each boy had? Four? Eight? Fifteen? Peter had ordered a party size and the box was nearly empty. Who knew where and when these boys had been eating? Hector had said Jaden had kept them fed, but they might have been dumpster diving or they might have been executing the perfect dine and dash maneuvers. He'd have to ask carefully. They'd done what they had to do in order to survive. No way was he going to make them feel unworthy or guilty.

Like his grandparents had made him feel just for existing.

"That was brilliant, guys. Rescuing the other kid and tracking Stabler. Just amazingly clever. Thank you."

"I can't believe how calm they are," Thad said to Peter, keeping his voice low. "After what they've been through."

"On second thought," Peter said, piling two of the last pizza slices on Thad's plate. "I probably should have led with this last bit of news. Apparently, our boys here didn't experience the same degree of pain you did upon shadow extraction. I'm guessing the white powder Stabler used to drug all of you was less effective because of your greater body weight. The boys were unconscious during the process."

Thad dropped his current slice on the pile, sighing hugely. He'd refused to let himself even think about that particular aspect of the situation and now he didn't have to. "That's a relief. But Jaden's report about the kid who escaped proves that the shadow thieves are still collecting shadows. We have to stop them. Right now!" He pushed his plate away, even though he could have eaten the rest of the pizza. "If you could stay here with the boys, I'll go have a talk with Mr. Stabler." He stood, wiped his fingers on his jeans and pushed his chair back. He was so tired he lost his balance and had to grab the back of the chair for support.

"Tomorrow." Peter wiped his own hands on a paper napkin bearing the name of the pizza joint. "BOO was able to get an eye on him by possessing a local surveillance camera. Yes, possessing. We can do that. Deal with it. Our surveillance tells us Stabler is already in bed for the night and, therefore, not going out seeking shadows. We'll get an alert if he suddenly gets up and dresses for paranormal activities. And you, my friend, need some sleep. It's nearly midnight and you've been at it since well, whenever you woke up on your floor shadow-free."

Thad yawned right through his protest. Peter was right. After a certain point, it didn't matter that he was fit and ate right and avoided anything stronger than beer. He was just too exhausted to be of much use.

"I gotta get the boys settled for the night." He rubbed his eyes. "Let's see. The couch opens out into a double bed and I got a single air mattress in the closet, along with sheets and towels. No extra pillows, but they can use their jackets or something."

Peter rose and grasped Thad's elbow. "I shall look after the lost lads. It certainly won't be the first time I've done so, although this is a new crop of lost boys. Now you, Mr. Wright, go lie down before you fall down. Don't make me put you to bed." His smile flickered at the corners as he caught Thad's eye, then his gaze shot away.

Was he nervous about the bed reference? He needn't worry. Thad had self-control. He nodded, the motion using up the last of his reserves. "Okay, I'll just..." Thad found himself propelled toward the bedroom by his collar, not roughly, just guided. Peter pushed him gently to sit on the bed, then crouched down to deal with his hiking bootlaces. "No. No. I can do that." He yanked his foot out of Peter's hands. The Englishman toppled forward, landing practically in Thad's lap, face dangerously close to Thad's crotch.

Thad had thought he was too tired to get seriously aroused, but he'd been wrong.

A bit of hope blossomed in his chest. Peter was certainly a handsome man. His cheekbones alone would have made him a fashion model. And the mercurial tendencies might prove interesting in bed...

Then the door closed and Thad was alone. Oh, well. Wrong time, wrong place, probably wrong guy. He finished untying his laces, pulled off his hiking boots and damp socks, shoved his jeans down to his ankles and stepped out of them right into bed. Normally he kept the place pretty tidy, but tonight, nobody would rag on him for leaving his jeans in a heap on his little bedside rug.

His mind swirled with everything that had happened to him in the last twenty-four hours. For a moment, he thought it might keep him awake. But just for a moment and then he was out as if he'd been roofied again.

THAD HAD NO IDEA how long he'd been asleep when the shift of the mattress roused him. "Wha—?" He cried, half sitting.

"It's just me, my friend. I've had a long day, as well. Flying in from Azunya this morning was taxing, even if I did fly commercial for once. I'm sure you don't mind a little company."

"'Kay," Thad muttered, not quite surfacing. When he awoke the next morning, he wasn't sure whether or not he'd dreamt that Peter had held him all night long.

CHAPTER 12

THE RUDE OF ALL EVIL

WHATEVER POSITION THEY'D SLEPT in overnight, by morning Peter was drooling on his side of the bed while Thad lay on the other, thinking, *Lord help me if I don't find that adorable.* He tried ordering his erection away, but it wasn't having any of it. Not until he recalled what he'd been through and what he needed to do today. Then his traitorous dick faded away like a man without a shadow.

He snuck from the room and into the bathroom, realizing too late that he should have brought a change of clothing with him.

In case anyone else wanted the bathroom, he took the world's fastest shower. And he might as well have lingered for a half-hour power shower for all interest the boys showed in waking.

Thad could relate, though, with maybe a touch of envy. As an adolescent, he'd always felt like sleeping 'til noon, but his grandparents, having emigrated as adults from an Eastern European farming community, believed in rising with the sun—even on Saturdays. Of course, Sundays had been for church. They'd washed, brushed and dressed him in Sunday best, only to sit in the back corner, eternally ashamed of their black bastard grandson.

The corner of his mouth tilted upward in grim amusement. Imagine what they'd make of the 100-year-old secret agent currently snoring in his bed, of an ex-soldier who could read minds and his partner who could output his thoughts as photos to electronic devices.

And other kinds of *beings,* they'd said. And who—and what—was Jacqueline? They spoke of her with respect. And maybe a little fear. Even Peter, who'd said she was his 'most recent' mother, whatever that meant. Oh, sure, the flippant agent had tried to sound casual about it, but really he spoke of her with a level of deference he'd shown for little else in the time Thad had known him. Thad hoped he didn't have to meet her. He had enough to deal with.

He snuck back into his bedroom. Peter snoozed on, so Thad dropped the towel and battled with his boxer briefs. It's never easy to pull up lycra-cotton blend over damp thighs.

"Ah, brilliant. Here's you in all your morning glory. At least I'm not the only piss-proud bugger in the room," Peter muttered, sounding only half-awake.

Thad bent from the waist to cover himself, yanking on the fabric harder, for all the good it did. He had no choice but to stop, unroll the briefs and start again. Sweat beaded on his forehead and Peter smirked from the bed, watching Thad's attempts to cover himself.

"Enjoying the show?" Thad snapped, confused by whatever Peter had said. It was the first time Peter had sounded like someone who'd lived a hundred years ago. What had that even meant?

"Highly entertaining, friend Thaddeus. But we mustn't allow ourselves to become distracted. We'd best get a move on. Busy day and all that." Peter pulled back the covers to reveal his own briefs, not the least bit ashamed of his morning wood. Thad envied that—the confidence, not the woody. He felt something completely different towards that.

"Enjoying the show?" Peter teased, turning Thad's own line against him.

Thad blushed and averted his gaze, embarrassed he'd been caught staring. Peter's chuckles trailed after him as he left the bedroom.

Thad finished getting dressed and headed into the living room to rouse the boys.

The kids groaned and protested at the unreasonably early wake-up call. In typical teenager mode, they wanted to sleep in, shadowless state notwithstanding.

He gave up and went to make breakfast, hoping the smell of turkey bacon frying would give them a reason to rise and shine.

The plan only worked on Peter, who seemed to feel a worn-thin beach towel was adequate breakfast wear. Thad peeked at Peter's semi-nakedness. He was wiry but not skinny, having a lithe, well-defined body with the kind of long, ropy muscles earned from regular exercise. Well, he had said he lived on an island. Perhaps he swam a lot.

Peter laughed when he caught Thad checking him out and sat back to pose blatantly. And get toast crumbs on his flat stomach.

"Er, uh. I should wake them," Thad said to cover his embarrassment. He very much wanted to brush those crumbs away. Possibly with his tongue.

"Leave them sleep. This could be the first good night's sleep they've had. Who knows where they've been residing? They might have had to sleep with one eye open or been cold and hungry."

"But we need them to show us where Jack..." Thad cut himself off as Peter waved his words away.

Of course they'd given Peter the address, otherwise how could BOO's surveillance people have located the camera and "possessed" it? He wanted to ask exactly what that meant but feared another tangent, so he put it on his mental list of *Things That Need Explaining* to deal with later.

If only Tom and Adrian had stuck around. He felt he could

have gotten more decipherable info from those two grown-ups. Peter's charming boyishness had its drawbacks.

Peter, on the other hand, had no problem asking tangential questions. "What exactly am I eating here, my friend?" he asked, a theatrical note of fear in his voice.

Thad grinned. "Healthy stuff, *my friend.* You might not survive!" he snarked back, using Peter's apparent nickname for him.

At Peter's raised eyebrow, Thad listed: "Organic eggs, turkey bacon and multi-grain toast with locally produced butter."

Peter shuddered, but he undermined his own performance by shoving half a slice of toast into his mouth and taking a huge chunk out of it.

"Should one of us stay with the boys?" Thad asked.

"I doubt they'll move until noon and then only to gather sustenance. You and I will be back by then."

Thad thought that was likely only if things went smoothly. When did they ever?

Peter swallowed his last mouthful and said, "I know it won't take more than one hour."

Was Peter able to predict the future? Thad wished he could remember more about the classic book. He'd read it as a child, but hadn't thought about it since. He'd never seen the animated movie—his grandparents hadn't approved of television. Whether everything in the book was true, or even partially, it would be helpful. He could sure use an owner's manual for the mercurial Peter. And even if it were all nonsense, it seemed that Peter himself believed it.

Thad wished he had time to boot up his computer and see if it was on Project Gutenberg. Was it old enough to be in the public domain by now? There was something else about the Peter Pan character that poked at his brain, but every time he got near the childhood memory, it just flew away.

Peter disappeared to get dressed as Thad washed the dishes, setting them in the drain board to air-dry. After leaving a note for the boys, they pulled on jackets and footwear before heading out.

The air was crisp and the morning sunny, which only served to make Thad nervous. What if someone noticed his shadow missing? He kept close to Peter, hoping anyone passing near them might assume their shadows overlapped.

He kept so close, in fact, that he kept bumping into the Englishman as they walked along. Peter chuckled and shoulder-checked him. It was nothing like last night's confrontational shove from the thug. By comparison, it seemed almost... affectionate.

The warm sun, the companionable journey, knowing that the boys were warm and safe all conspired to make Thad feel better than he had in ages. Until each time he remembered their shadowless state and the bottom dropped out of his stomach anew.

The trip to Jack Stabler's apartment took them past the community center. It felt weird not to be heading in to work. He hoped they could fix the shadow problem soon. Then everything could get back to normal.

And Peter could wrap up his first lead assignment and leave.

A dark cloud passed over the sun, dimming Peter's shadow as if he were already fading from Thad's life. Thad's shoulders slumped and his hiking boots seemed to grow suddenly heavier.

Eventually they arrived at Stabler's building. As Jaden had reported, the building was old, probably built in the fifties. The aging lobby door rattled but remained locked.

"Damn," Peter grumbled. "Should have brought Delilah along."

Thad didn't ask.

Peter shaded his eyes and stepped backward, right into the street. The early morning traffic honked at him as he raked his

gaze along the front of the building. "I'm going to check around
back. Maybe that's open. Stay here in case your boyfriend
comes out this way."

"He's not my..." Why bother? Peter's teasing contained no
real sting.

Peter smirked back over his shoulder as he rounded the
corner and disappeared from Thad's view.

Three or four minutes later, the sound of the lobby door
opening drew Thad's attention.

"Told you I had many talents." Peter's grin was warmer this
time, less teasing.

"Back door unlocked?"

"Something like that," Peter answered, eyes actually
twinkling.

Thad could feel an answering grin spreading across his own
face. He quickly shut it down. *We're here on serious business,
not a date.*

They found the apartment on the third floor. Peter knocked,
standing in front of the peephole. Thad stepped to one side.
Jack would never open the door for him.

The door jerked open. "Yeah, what?" Jack-the-nice-guy had
obviously been an act.

"Jack Stabler?"

"Who wants to know?"

Do they script these guys? It was every police drama Thad
had ever watched. Every police comedy, too.

"I do. That's why I'm asking. May I come in?" Peter had one
hand shoved in his jacket pocket. He gestured with it. Was he
trying to imply he had a gun?

Icy sweat broke out over Thad's nape. Maybe he did. Just
because BOO agents had super powers didn't mean they
weren't also armed. The day suddenly took a scary turn. Thad
had a problem with guns since his mother had been shot to
death right in front of him.

Jack held up his hands in a *Look. I'm unarmed* manner. "Yeah, whatever. Don't expect coffee." He turned his back and confidently strode back into his apartment.

Thad told himself that maybe a gun was a good thing under the circumstances, but shuddered at the thought. Needing to know, to be prepared, Thad hissed, "Do you have a gun?" directly into Peter's ear.

Keeping his eyes on Stabler, Peter gave his head a tiny shake. "But let's keep that little fact from the bad man, shall we?" he whispered back.

With a sigh of relief, Thad followed Peter into the apartment, pulling the door closed behind them. No need to entertain the neighbors, or risk having someone call the cops.

The apartment was similar to Thad's own, including well-used furniture and a state-of-the-art entertainment system. Jack looked different this morning. More... ordinary. Thad figured he'd dressed up nicely and styled his hair in order to pass as gay. Or maybe they'd just caught him early. Either way, breakfast churned in Thad's gut as he realized he'd been attracted to this guy. Loneliness affects judgment. He vowed to get out and make some friends so he wouldn't be so desperate for companionship in the future.

His gaze slid to Peter, who looked all dangerous and adorable.

"Have a seat," Jack offered, waving toward the couch.

Neither visitor sat.

"I want to ask you a few questions. Do you recognize this man?" Peter jerked his chin in Thad's direction.

Thad crossed his arms over his chest and tried to look tough, even though that ship had sailed. Jack had already seen exactly what kind of person Thad was.

"Oh, shit. You! Uh, listen. You're okay, aren't you? I mean, we didn't actually do anything to you. You know that, right?"

"I know you roofied me," Thad began, not wanting to get

into the supernatural stuff right off the bat. Better to work your way up to accusing someone of shadow theft.

"Look, guys. Sit down. I can brew up some coffee. Listen, Brad. I'm sorry. I kind of got myself into something and I..."

Not exactly the blustering bad-guy rhetoric Thad had expected.

"It's Thad," Peter snapped. "Short for Thaddeus."

"Oh, sorry. I forgot, I guess."

The three of them stood there. None of this was going the way Thad had expected it. Peter looked surprised, as well.

"Why? Why are you stealing people's shadows?" Peter finally asked.

"Stealing what?" Jack's face scrunched up and he cocked his head to one side like a dog trying to understand what's being said to him. "No, see. This guy contacted me. Through a referral website for, well, not quite regular stuff, you know? A nice, clean reference, right? Paid me a decent bundle of cash to hunt down the people he asked me to. I'm to get them to someplace private and use that white powder to put them to sleep." He seemed to be running through a mental checklist. "Yeah, then the guy comes, does this *magic*—" He made those annoying air quotes around the word "—ritual and then leaves right after. He barely touches them. You." He peered at Thad, his expression solemn, almost begging for forgiveness. "So I figured it was okay. He wasn't hurting those boys. Or you."

"Except that I screamed and struggled during the spell, right?"

"I— Yeah. I didn't understand that. I thought maybe you were in on it and it was some kind of kinky thing. The boys didn't stir when he cut off their clothes."

"Kinky thing? With underage boys?"

"Well, it wasn't sexual like. He barely touched them. Maybe some *Who's your daddy?* thing, but the boys were okay when we left." He stood up a little straighter. "I never left the guy alone with the boys."

Oh, my God. Did Jack think that was, what? Noble? Caring?
Thad squeezed his fists so hard his nails dug into his calloused
palms. "Until they went missing," he growled.

"I didn't know the boys went missing until I saw the posters.
And by then it was too late. I was already committed."

"You spent the money," Peter said. Not a question.

"Well, yeah. That stuff's not the only white powder, man.
And it just knocks you out. No high at all. I know. I tried it.
Caught royal shit from the guy for using it on myself. Great
night's sleep, though."

"Who's this guy you keep talking about? Who are you
working for?"

"Dunno. We deal by email."

"Don't play stupid. He was in the room with you." Peter held
up his phone, screen toward Jack. He peered at it.

"What? Dude. You have a nanny cam or somethin'?" He
seemed affronted.

Thad knew he was dealing with a self-deluding idiot. Of
course dealing with a drug addict would be exactly like this. His
own mother had been like this—even to his four-year-old
memory. *Hush and wait. Hush and wait.*

"He always wore the robe. It came with a mask. Like
ComiCon, you know. I figured they were role-playing. Teenage
boys love that sort of thing."

"Yes, Jack. Teenage boys love to be kidnapped, drugged and
have their lives ripped away from them. Almost as much as I
do." Thad clenched his teeth hard enough to hear them creak.

"Hey, now. It's not like I did any of that. I just, you know,
put them to sleep."

"Like a dog?" Peter spat. "Let me see your computer. It's
been offline since yesterday at least."

"How'd you know that? You been watching me?" He sounded
suspicious and entitled.

Thad wanted to find out how to excise a shadow just so they could leave this numbskull in shadowless limbo. Except he'd probably use his unmemorability to rob banks or something. He could understand evil genius, maybe even admire it from certain angles, but this guy was just a waste of space. A waste of a life. An addict whose addiction led him down dark paths where he wasn't looking where he was going.

Jack was probably an idiot even before the drugs.

While Thad growled at Jack and considered suitable punishment for the asshole, Peter disappeared into the other room. Thad could hear the familiar sound of a PC booting up as Peter re-emerged. What? He turned it on and then just wandered away? Seemed hinky, but he'd come to trust Peter's method's enough that he let it go for now.

Peter sprawled on the worn couch just as he had at Thad's apartment, phone in hand. Thad and Jack stared at Peter as he stared at his phone.

Despite the obvious setup, all three men jumped when Peter's ringtone sounded.

Peter's side of the conversation was once again unenlightening, consisting of, "Hello. Yes. *What?*" and finally, "Okay."

He sat up and turned his attention back to Jack. "I need you to tell us everything you can about this guy you've been working for. Anything. Anything at all. Even the smallest detail."

"Like I told you. He wears a mask and a hood."

"Is he short? Tall? Definitely not a woman?"

"Uh, tall. Deep voice. If that's a chick, she's fierce, that's for sure."

"What about his race? Surely you've glimpsed his wrists above the gloves. Is he a black man? A white man? Mixed race like Thaddeus here?"

Jack re-focused on Thad, his mouth dropping open. "What

the hell? When did Brad get here?"

He took an aggressive step toward Thad, but Peter snapped his fingers in Jack's direction. "Focus, Jack. Focus. The question I just asked you?"

"What question?" The man grumbled, keeping his eye on Thad.

"The guy who paid you?" Peter said slowly, patiently, as if speaking to someone a little slow or high. Which maybe Jack was. "Did you see anything that gave you a clue to his race?"

Jack screwed up his face, a parody of deep thought. "Nah. Not that I remember. Maybe they're like, elbow-length evening gloves or something."

Thad drew his own phone from his pocket to re-check the pictures. Adrian had air-dropped both Peter and Thad their own copies. He didn't ask how Adrian had his contact info. Looking at the pictures yet again, Thad still couldn't tell who was the villain or the victim. Or whose hands wore the gloves. The only identifiable person was Jack.

"I don't suppose Tom can do his little trick by phone?" Thad asked.

"Sadly not," Peter replied. A knock sounded at the door. "Thaddeus, would you mind getting that, please?"

"What the fuck, dude? It's my apartment," Jack blustered, obviously losing patience. This kind of attitude made Thad wish the entitlement gene could be fished right out of the gene pool. "And hey. When did Brad get here?"

Before Jack could do or say anything else, or forget Thad again, Detective Reasoner strode in with two uniformed cops in tow, already singing the "You have the right to remain silent" refrain. He slapped handcuffs on Jack, then turned to Thad. "You sent me these pictures?"

"Yes, he did. He's anxious to help with the investigation," Peter said.

Thad knew he hadn't sent them, but figured Peter was up to

something. Making him look good, maybe, so he was less of a suspect? He could live with that. And appreciated it. His computer was password protected but his phone wasn't. Peter must have snagged his phone while he was in the shower. Sneaky bastard had only pretended to be asleep.

"Okay, I don't know who you are, but Wright here is going to have to join us at the station for a little pow-wow. You better come, too. What did you say your name was?"

"It's him. He did it! He's responsible for the missing boys," Peter shouted, pointing toward Thad. "Check Stabler's computer. You'll find the emailed instructions concerning which boys to hit were sent from Thaddeus's computer!"

"What? No! I'm a victim."

Peter's betrayal punched him in the gut like a giant, angry fist. The detective and one of the uniforms leapt toward Thad. He turned and ran out into the hall.

The last thing he saw was Peter thrusting a window open wide enough to squeeze through. What good would it do to escape to a third floor balcony?

Of course, as soon as Thad was on the other side of the fire door to the stairwell, the cops forgot they were chasing him. He was safe from interrogation and arrest, but how could Peter have done that to him?

His feet felt like lead as he plodded down step after step and out onto the street. He almost walked right back into the scene as a truck with "Police Services" screened on the side screeched up to the building. Men in suits with silver hard-sided briefcases rushed out. While the forensics guys wouldn't know him, they might have an APB or BOLO or whatever they called it out on him, so he slipped back into the stairwell and found a sign indicating a fire exit at the rear.

Why had Peter turned on him? Even Clint dumping him hadn't hurt this bad. At least he'd seen that coming, and truth be told, he probably should have ended it himself. But Peter...

He thought about Peter's warm arms wrapped around him while he'd slept. It hadn't been a dream. He just wasn't sure what it meant.

Thad reached the fire door. The sign said it was alarmed, but he bet it wasn't. Not in a decrepit building like this. Probably hadn't worked since the nineties. He pushed on the lock-bar gently, as if that might circumvent the alarm system. The building remained silent. He stepped out into the bright sunshine.

"What took you so long?" Peter fell into step beside him. "We have to figure out—"

"What do you—? Why did you—?" But of course, Peter had just used him to distract the cops while he climbed out the window. He and Peter couldn't very well continue their investigation if Peter was locked away. Thad tried not to smile the foolish grin that was bursting its way out of his face, but he failed completely. "I should have known."

"Sorry, but having just been informed that the emails to Stabler came from your office computer was on my mind, so saying you were guilty was the first thing I thought of. I needed to distract them so I could escape. They won't remember."

"Right. And you managed to climb down the fire escape while they were distracted." Thad glanced back, wondering why the cops hadn't followed Peter. Making a break for it usually indicated guilt on the cop shows he watched. "Peter," he said slowly. "There isn't a fire escape. How did you—"

"We need to figure out why the emails to dear Jack came from you," Peter cut in. "Who else has access to your computer?"

CHAPTER 13

CLUE UNTO OTHERS

"WE NEED SOMEWHERE we can work on this. Set up one of those evidence boards like they do on television, so we can see all our clues and leads laid out in a logical manner," Peter said.

Thad held off raining on Peter's evidence parade, not wanting to remind them they had very few clues and no leads at all. Instead, he said, "We need to check on the boys."

They compromised by heading back to Thad's apartment, where the boys were finally stirring, taking turns in the shower.

"Jaden barely got wet," Stanley informed everyone. "I think he's afraid of water."

Jaden blushed, his mocha complexion doing nothing to hide the high color along his cheekbones. "So what? I don't like water. It makes me feel... weird."

"Back off, Stan," Hector cut in. "We've all had bad experiences."

"But I— I know." Stanley dropped his gaze to his knees. "Sorry."

Thad's fists clenched as did his stomach. What the hell had happened to Jaden to make him afraid of water? And what had happened to Hector and to Stanley to leave them so casual about bad treatment? What was wrong with a world that treated its children this way? His own upbringing didn't seem so awful when contrasted with what these kids, and orphans everywhere, had lived through.

"I'm hungry," Jaden said. Whether he was changing the uncomfortable subject or just being a teen, Thad didn't know, but he was grateful.

"I'll cook you something," he offered. "Eggs okay?"

"You know," Stanley offered. "We can just walk into any store and walk out without paying."

"Or restaurant," Hector added.

Thad's "You're doing neither," overlapped Peter's, "Great, then."

"No," Thad continued, cutting a sidelong look at Peter. Having been a child on his own for a century hadn't given Peter much in the way of parenting skills. "Aside from the fact that stealing in all its forms is wrong, when you dine and dash, it comes out of that waiter or waitress's salary."

Stanley looked horrified, head hanging. "My mom is a waitress—was, I mean. I didn't know that."

"I knew that," Hector leapt in. "And stealing from mom-and-pop bodegas comes out of their bottom line. That's why I only took from big chain stores. They get to set allowances for a certain amount of unsalable goods in their accounting." He looked so proud of himself, as if he were the very essence of virtue.

Thad admired Hector's knowledge. He was going to make either a great accountant or a criminal mastermind someday. Thad was hoping for accountant. "It's great that you know that stuff, Hector. But stealing is still wrong," Thad told them. "I'll go for groceries and I'll pay for them."

"I hope you're not intending to use a credit or debit card," Peter said around a bite of the last wrinkly apple in the crisper. "Technology won't work for you, remember?"

Thad slumped. "Can you use your expense account?"

"Done and done. I ordered groceries online last night. They should be here..." He checked his watch, shook it, held it to his ear. "Anytime now. In fact—"

A knock on Thad's apartment door interrupted whatever Peter planned to say next. Didn't anyone use the intercom anymore?

After first checking the peephole, Peter flung the door wide. "Here they are now."

A deliveryman in a green jacket and cap stood at the door. "Where'd'youwant'em?" One hand rested on a dented cart handle.

"Uh, on the counter's fine." Thad stepped up to help the man.

The deliveryman's gaze passed over Thad and crew as if he didn't even see them. Somehow, Thad thought that was more to do with the man's attitude than that four out of five of the apartment's current occupants existed in a state of unmemorability. Thad hopped out of the way as the man wheeled the cart in and began dumping grocery-filled cartons onto the counter. Peter had bought out half the warehouse!

Thad rushed to help, nearly spearing himself in the eye with a crusty baguette.

Peter tipped the deliveryman on the way out, hopefully in American currency. If he'd paid the man in whatever BOO's local currency was, then the poor guy would end up shelling out more in bank fees to convert it than it was worth.

He left Peter and the boys to the task of sorting through the groceries while he crossed the room and booted up his laptop. Once it had started with its techno-gurgle routine, he jerked the top desk drawer open, digging through to find some markers and tape.

He grabbed a white cord dangling by its USB plug and shoved the tiny connector into his iPhone. Highlighting the eight new pictures that iTunes helpfully auto-uploaded to his PC, he set them to print, hoping that would work.

It didn't. He had to get Peter to come over and hit the print button.

While the printer spat out photos, Thad strode out to the middle of his living area and did a slow three-sixty. The expanse of wall between the window and the couch was blank except for a poster of his favorite basketball player. He carefully peeled the poster of John Amaechi off the wall, rolled it up and stored it in his closet. How ironic, since John had been the NBA's first player to come out of the closet.

"Now." Thad tapped the closed marker on his teeth. "What do we know?"

Peter came to stand beside Thad, as did Jaden. They stood staring at the blank wall.

"We know the dates we disappeared," Jaden volunteered. "Write those down."

Thad scrawled dates on the wall. Hector and Stanley confirmed theirs from the kitchen. The names and dates faded away. Without a word, Peter took over duties as scribe.

"We know he had access to your office computer," Peter said, brandishing the pen like a sword.

"I don't lock my office door if I'm just going down the hall to the gym, which is half the day. So lots of people had access, likely still do."

Peter checked his phone. "According to the analysis done by BOO's techs, some of those emails were sent in the dead of night. Three o'clock, two-thirty. One at four in the morning," he read off.

"Cleaning staff?" Thad offered. "Building maintenance?"

Peter wrote those possibilities down. In the meantime, the printer finished chugging out the pictures. Jaden helpfully began taping them in neat columns on either side of Peter's writing. Luckily, tape still worked for the shadowless and the pictures stuck. The wall grew cluttered.

"What else do we know?" Thad mumbled. "What else do we know?"

"The cape and hood! He doesn't want to be recognized,

which means he's recognizable. Someone we know," Hector said.

"Brilliant. You're one sharp customer, my good lad." Peter wrote down *Recognizable* and underlined it twice.

"Yes," Thad said. "But recognizable by who? You? Me? The entire city?"

While the others pondered this, Stanley added, "He's into weird stuff, practicing magic. So he'd be someone who's spiritual. Or religious."

Peter dutifully wrote *Religious* under *Recognizable,* but Thad had his doubts. He didn't believe a spiritual man would put the boys through such a horrific experience. He leaned close to the wall, examining the picture printouts. "Is there anything we can tell about this guy from the fabric?"

Peter pointed to one shot that captured the chest and a gloved hand of Thad's robed assailant. "It appears to be homespun."

"What's homespun?" Stanley asked.

"Homespun," Peter began, "...is the term for coarse, hand-woven fabric. Do you boys recall if he was wearing the same thing when you..."

"I was pretty out of it by the time the second guy showed up," Jaden said. "It wasn't like I was paying attention to the dude's fashion accessories."

The other boys shrugged, nodded, mumbled agreement and helped themselves to the various sandwiches and snack foods Hector and Stanley had dumped in a heap on the table.

"What's this?" Peter pointed to a slight bulge in the robe right in the center of the man's chest. "Perhaps our villain wears his regular clothing under his robe."

Thad leaned over Peter's shoulder, examining the next picture. "Damn. The hem of his robe almost brushes the floor. All I can see are his shoes. I can't tell if he's wearing jeans or khakis or a suit." He bit the inside of his cheek, releasing it quickly. It had grown raw and sore under the recent onslaught.

"But we *are* seeing shoes." Peter pushed up next to Thad, their shoulders pressed tightly together. "These appear to be loafers. A posh brand, I'd say from the quality of the leather and the construction of the sole, although I can't see any indication of the manufacturer."

Thad straightened up, gusting out a big sigh. "Yeah, well, that narrows it down. We know the guy wears shoes. Great."

"Black, expansive loafers, does in fact, narrow it down, my frustrated friend. How many people do we know who favor loafers?"

Thad plunked heavily into one of the little dining chairs. "Me, personally? Not a whole lot, but if you take into account public figures, like politicians..."

"And actors and, like, anchormen," Jaden supplied.

"Businessmen," Hector chimed in.

"Uh. And rabbis?" Stanley added.

Thad smothered an ill-timed chuckle. The youngest boy so wanted to contribute. Thad thought carefully about how to phrase his next statement so Stanley's feelings wouldn't be hurt. "I really don't believe men of the cloth get mixed up with magic spells, but thanks, anyway." He gave Stanley a one-armed hug and grabbed a sandwich from the pile.

Thad stared at their makeshift clue board while he munched, considering the evidence, hoping for a break. Any number of people could get in at night. Maybe a broken window or a duplicate key? Plus, there'd been dozens of workmen and contractors through the place during the conversion from dilapidated railway station to church and community center. And it wasn't like the Church had funds to blow on a state of the art security system. Burglar alarms and barred windows would be a low priority on Brother Guy's list of improvements anyway. The devout pastor was just too trusting. He'd never believe anyone would break in and do them harm.

Maybe it was one of the HVAC people who'd been in recently to fix the furnace. That foreman had looked pretty shifty. But he wore steel-toed boots, even when he'd just come in for a preliminary meeting, so not him. The bookkeeper's husband? The volunteer who tidied the grounds?

While Peter wrote down the last of their clues and Thad kept himself from jumping to conclusions, the boys finished the tray of sandwiches and snacks, and even attempted a bit of a clean up in the kitchen.

They began to argue that they were bored and should be allowed to go investigate with them. Thad and Peter decided the boys were safer in their sight than out of it. They all grabbed energy bars and the adults began pulling their jackets back on.

"I must check in with my superiors back at BOO. I'll meet you downstairs. I'm not getting enough bars here. No, not those kind of bars," Peter rolled his eyes as all three boys offered him energy bars. "Yes, indeed. Exceedingly funny," he said as he exited the apartment while Thad rode herd on the unruly teens.

Peter had included new toothbrushes in his grocery order and there was much fighting over the sink and some frothy spit in Hector's dark hair. Eventually, the three boys were ready to go.

The old elevator took forever to arrive, so they gave up waiting and hoofed it down the stairs instead. Thad and the boys reached the lobby just in time to see Detective Reasoner shoving a handcuffed Peter into a patrol car.

"Wait! Wait!" Thad cried.

"You can't arrest him. We're not missing!" the boys yelled and jumped up and down, but if Reasoner heard them, he didn't pay attention. Besides, he wouldn't remember them anyway.

"Now what?" Jaden looked at Thad as if he had all the answers.

Thad wished he did.

"I don't know. Peter was the special agent. I'm just a victim like you—" He cut himself off. That wasn't what these kids needed to hear. They'd been through so much already in their short lives, even before their shadows had been ripped away. Orphaned, abandoned, stuck in foster homes. Compared to them, he'd had a blissful childhood.

They needed him to step up and be a leader.

"Let me think," he said. It was almost pleasant standing there in the bright sunshine. His gaze traveled over the boys and the sidewalk, his stomach wrenching anew at the lack of shadows. He needed to fix this and fix it fast.

But what to do first? Rescue Peter or go check out shoes to see if he could find the pair that matched the ones in the photo? He choked back a bitter laugh. Peter Pan or Cinderella? Those were his choices. Who'd have ever thought? And then he did think—and came up with a plan.

"First, we need to rescue Peter," he said slowly. "Because we're going to need all the supernatural experience we have when we take down the shadow thief. I'll just go down to the local precinct and get him released."

Thad had no idea where that was and found it a little unsettling that all three boys did. These kids needed a stabilizing element in their lives. He was glad that in his role as coach and counselor at the community center, he was able to provide them with a decent role model.

"But why did they take Peter? They don't even know him," Stanley asked. The young redhead looked so lost and bewildered.

"That's exactly why!" Hector smacked his fist into his palm. "They always arrest what scares them and they don't know Peter."

"That may be part of it, Hector," Thad began, being careful to think before he spoke. "But there's actual detective work involved. Detective Reasoner and cops in general are good, trained, smart people." All three boys looked less than convinced. "No, listen. The one thing that connects you three is that you all hung out at the community center. So that puts the spotlight on anyone associated with the center, right?"

Jaden nodded. Stanley looked like he might cry.

"So that's you," Hector said. "And then you went missing, too."

"But they probably think I'm the bad guy, not that I've become another victim. According to all the TV shows we watch, a serial killer sticks with a single MO."

"So if this guy goes after teenagers, he doesn't suddenly go after an adult." Jaden narrowed his eyes. "So when you go missing, they figure you've made a run for it."

"Right. So they stake out my apartment. They don't remember seeing me going in and out, but they do remember Peter."

"They think he's your accomplish," Stanley said, tears forgotten.

"That's accomplice, dude." Hector punched the younger boy in the arm in a way that was more affectionate than aggressive.

"Right. So how are we going to get Peter out of jail?" Jaden looked about twelve instead of his actual fifteen. "If we just go down and announce we aren't really missing, it won't take. It'll just get more and more confusing."

"I know, guys. I know. We just have to open a window for him."

The boys had been through so much that it spoke volumes when they didn't even ask why.

CHAPTER 14

SMOOCH AND RESCUE

THAD STATIONED THE BOYS in a small park near the precinct after first making sure it was populated with toddlers and caregivers rather than crackheads and dealers. The sun rode high and the day had turned warm enough that they could sit outside for a while, although he'd made sure everyone wore jackets and scarves before they'd left his apartment. "If anyone asks why you're not in school or in the unlikely event that someone notices you have no shadow, just point behind them. By the time they look back at you—"

"Yeah. We know." Jaden interrupted with typical teenage impatience. "We've been at this longer than you."

"You're right. You have. I'm the newbie. It's my own newness that makes me worry." He shot the boys a weak smile. "I should trust you on this. Jaden, you're the oldest, so you're in charge, alright?"

Jaden sat up a little taller. The others just rolled their eyes. "C'mon, Stan. Let's go see what trouble we can get into on the swings," Hector said.

"I'm too old for swings, Hect." Stanley was already hurrying toward the swing set, even as he protested. Thad hid a smile and turned away.

He made a quick trip to the coffee shop across from the precinct to buy hot chocolate and cookies to keep the boys happy despite his normal disapproval of sugary snacks.

Unhealthy calories were the least of their worries at the moment.

Thad paid cash since his credit and debit cards wouldn't work. He tipped the barista generously. She didn't look much older than a teen herself. Wondering why she wasn't in school, he made a mental note to come back and talk to her about life choices once the shadow thing was settled. He found himself checking to see if she had a shadow. Of course she did.

Upon his return, he cautioned the boys again to stay put no matter what. They had plenty of experience flying under the radar, as all kids learn, especially ones in the foster care system. He left them reluctantly, hoping boredom and stress wouldn't drive them to act out.

After taking a deep breath, Thad entered the precinct, explaining he wished to speak to Detective Reasoner. He had to say it over and over again, as each subsequent person he dealt with asked about his presence and then promptly forgot.

Eventually, he was led into a waiting area. He put his jacket over his arm so he'd look like he belonged, grabbed a newspaper from a heap and walked, head down, along the corridors.

"What are you doing here?" he was asked repeatedly.

"I'm looking for the holding cells. Could you direct me there?"

He'd get either an accusation and an order to get out or a helpful response. Either way, he was able to then distract each person and move on.

Deceiving police officers and skulking in their hallways didn't sit well with him. His breakfast weighed heavily in his stomach while sweat beaded on his forehead. He wiped it away, figuring a professional investigator might notice and become suspicious of someone nervously prowling their halls.

Finally, he had the feel of the building. A diagram of each floor set near the fire extinguisher helped with that.

He made his way down to the holding cells in the basement.

Using his disappearing act twice more, he was able to snag the keys and find his way to Peter's cell.

"I knew you'd come," Peter announced, looking far too relaxed. The only other occupant of the room was a large, well-dressed man snoring loudly in the next cell. Where Jack Stabler had been taken, Thad had no idea.

"Thank God for outdated technology. If they'd had a computerized lock, we'd be screwed." Thad dangled the key in front of the cell before inserting it in the lock.

It clicked open. "The roof?" he asked.

"The roof," Peter confirmed, eyes sparkling. "I see you've figured it out."

"Special talents. Plural."

"Special," Peter agreed, laying his hand on his own chest in mock-modesty. "Plus, I can talk to fairies." He leaned over and pecked Thad on the side of the mouth.

Thad was so surprised, he didn't try and kiss back. "We'd, uh... We'd better get going," he said, thumbing the spot Peter had just kissed. Not to erase the kiss, but to cherish it. He warned himself not to get distracted. "You... Um. Well..."

Peter's customary smirk had developed a warmer overlay with a top note of nervousness. Was he worried about Thad's reaction? For once, Peter remained silent.

To break the awkward, yet promising silence and refocus them on their important task, Thad said, "Speaking of special talents..." He blushed. He hadn't meant that to sound flirty. Quickly he added, "Can't you just take off your shadow? You said it wasn't well connected or something."

Peter screwed up his face. "That was then, this is now. Unfortunately, as I've aged, it's gotten rather attached to me." He reached down yanked on it near his ankle to demonstrate.

Thad's eyes bugged out. "You just grabbed a handful of shadow."

"Talents, plural. Remember?"

"I hope those talents include acting like a felon," Thad said, borrowing a pair of handcuffs from a peg near the door and linking them loosely over Peter's wrists. "Act guilty."

"Not in my nature," Peter laughed.

"Like a cat," Thad said.

"No, that's Tom."

Thad did a double take and added it to the already lengthy *Ask Later* list.

Peter sobered up quickly when they heard footsteps down the hall. Shrugging his jacket back on so he'd have his hands free, Thad whispered, "Precede me."

He grabbed Peter by the elbow and scowled, hoping he looked like a plainclothes cop. It must have worked. They passed a uniformed officer in the hallway and she didn't even glance up. They were pretty deep in the bowels of the precinct. It was probably because she trusted their security systems to have dealt with intruders well before this point. Of course all the good intentions and high tech security meant nothing when you had no shadow.

"If someone's watching a security display, they're going to see you walking along alone in handcuffs."

"Better hurry, then."

The two men managed to find their way along the corridors without being challenged. Apparently having a prisoner in cuffs goes a long way to bestowing credibility within a police station. Plus, they weren't headed toward any of the exits.

The elevator took them to the top floor where, according to the fire safety map, they would find another door to a narrow maintenance access staircase that would take them to the roof.

Having located the access stairs, they dashed quickly up them, crowding together on the small landing at the top. "This door is alarmed," Peter said, chuckling. "I wonder if the railing is startled and the steps nervous."

"Careful," Thad instructed, trying not to smile or groan at

the bad wordplay. Even old jokes sounded new again with Peter's sexy British accent. "Unlike the one I dealt with in Stabler's building, this one will probably work. It'll sound as soon as you push on the bar to open it. You'll be okay?" Thad asked.

Peter beamed. "Done this a million times. Perhaps literally." He started to wave one hand around in imitation of a bird, but the cuffs brought him up short. He slipped the loose cuffs off his wrists, handing them back to Thad. "I'd take you with me, but you're a little on the heavy side."

"I'll have you know I just lost five pounds."

"Oh, vanity, they name is Thaddeus."

"Meet you at the apartment?"

"I hope you left the balcony door unlocked."

Thad didn't care about locks, or doors, or anything. He'd had his shadow stolen, broken a man out of prison and would soon be confronting some sort of magic-wielding arch criminal who preyed on helpless young boys. Yet what he was about to do took far more courage than any of that.

Ignoring the butterflies battering his ribcage, he gently placed his hands on either side of Peter's face, cupping his jaw and leaning in. "I don't know if you really are who you say you are, or whether this organization you work for really exists, but I never wanted to do anything as much as I want to do this."

He swept his lips over Peter's, giving the other man plenty of time to pull away. Instead of the half-expected brush-off, Peter opened his mouth slightly, sighed and leaned in for more.

Thad's mind whirled as he pressed against Peter, clasping him to his chest. When Peter grabbed his hips, the kiss accelerated from chaste to tongue-tangling, hip-grinding passion in less than a second.

"I've been dying for this," Peter murmured against Thad's mouth.

Thad thought he'd never hear another English accent

without getting turned on.

He pushed against Peter, who widened his stance and shoved back. Thad drove his hips against Peter again, this time harder, needing to pin Peter up against a wall, needing to really thrust against—

Horrendous clanging sent both men ducking and covering, palms cupped over ears.

"We set off the alarm," Thad shouted, stating the obvious.

"Oops." Peter gifted Thad with his usual smirk. "Talents, plural," he shouted over the clanging. Laughing, Peter pushed his way out the door, letting it slam behind him.

Thad adjusted himself hurriedly and made his way back out of the building, the alarms proving so much of a distraction that he hardly had to stop and sidetrack at all.

At the park, all three boys were pushing small children on the swings while mismatched caregivers gossiped in the welcome sun. He herded the teens back to his apartment, which wasn't the easiest chore now that they were out and feeling fine.

The caffeine in the hot chocolate and sugar in the cookies probably didn't help. They jumped around and laughed. Thad was never comfortable drawing attention to himself—what had happened with his mother had left him vulnerable in that respect. He didn't need therapy to know that. But the kids were so joyous that he couldn't help but join them. Besides, nobody would remember him in a few seconds, so he could lighten up for once.

After a boisterous trip home, they found Peter lounging on the balcony. Thad's heart fluttered and he could hardly keep the smile from his face. *Not the time or the place,* he ordered himself.

His dick, however, wasn't inclined to take orders from anyone.

CHAPTER 15

THE UNUSUAL SUSPECTS

"WHILE YOU CHAPS WERE TRAIPSING around the city, I had time to do a quick reconnoiter of the Community Center." Peter admired his fingernails, his usual smirk hovering over those tempting lips. *Now is not the time to get distracted,* Thad told himself yet again with the same amount of success as the last few times—which is to say not much.

"What's reckon loitering?" Stanley asked.

"Reconnoiter," Hector corrected. "It means to check out. Get the lay of the land."

"Lay," Jaden giggled. The other boys—including Peter—followed suit.

Thad rolled his eyes, but couldn't quite keep his own smile under control. Not that the silly innuendo amused him, but the boys' boundless good humor gave him hope that maybe they'd get out of this without suffering the weirdest PTSD in history. How could he counsel them for that? How could anyone?

It occurred to him that Peter hadn't yet revealed what he'd uncovered with his sleuthing. "And you discovered..." he prompted.

"It seems that your boss, the right reverend, favors expensive loafers."

"Yeah!" Jaden fisted the air. "Got 'im!" The other two boys chimed in with cheers of their own.

"Well, not quite. They're not the same loafers. The ones

Brother Guy wore today are oxblood, whilst the ones in the picture are black." At the confused expressions and "Ewww," comments, Peter clarified. "It means dark red."

"Does that mean we aren't going to get our shadows back?" Stanley asked, lower lip trembling.

"Oh, you'll get them back. I promise you that or my name isn't Peter P—Batique. Yes, Peter Batique. Even though he isn't wearing the same shoes, I suspect he's up to something. There was just something furtive—that means sneaky—about his movements."

"Or he might be innocent. Lots of people wear loafers." Thad crossed his arms over his chest. He knew he sounded defensive, but Brother Guy had been good to him, hiring him right out of school, trusting him with so much responsibility. He was willing to do the detective work, but not to convict without enough evidence. "We have to be sure beyond a shadow of a doubt."

"The key word there, my friend, being *shadow.*" Peter raised an eyebrow. "Oh, I forgot to mention, he had some old books on his desk. They looked to be S-P-E-L-L books," Peter spelled, probably going for the obvious pun. He seemed to feel there was no wrong time for levity.

"Or maybe they were B-I-B-L-E-S," Thad spelled back. "He does have those, you know."

Peter tsked. "Yes, of course. There would be many reasons why a loafer-wearing man of the cloth would have weathered old volumes on his desk. One of which is that he's the shadow thief."

Thad opened his mouth to defend his boss again, then gave up. The evidence pointing to Brother Guy was hardly conclusive. Thad wasn't yet ready to let go of his loyalty and join Peter in his suspicions.

"It's not looking good for the pastor, I'm afraid." Instead of the shit-eating grin he expected, Peter gave Thad a regretful look. "Sorry, Thaddeus. I know you liked the man."

"Whoever it is, he might be out to steal another shadow." Jaden flopped on the sofa. "You said he sells them, so he could be getting ready to make another sale."

"But we're the only orphans. All the other boys have homes and would be missed." Stanley again looked like he might cry.

Hector went over and stood near him. It would be a shame if they had to be separated. They were as close as brothers.

"We'll go back tonight," Peter announced. Then the self-assured and brash young man did something unexpected. He turned to Thad, a questioning expression painting his features. "Isn't the right, Thaddeus?"

Surprised and flattered to be consulted, Thad had been inclined to object, to defend his boss again. Now he took a moment to reconsider. Eventually he said, "I think that's a good idea. And I believe the boys should accompany us."

Peter nodded once. "Agreed. Now, we need to kill the rest of the afternoon until dark. Let's see what's on Netflix, shall we?" He did that leaping thing, which Thad now realized was actually a very short flight, and landed on the couch.

"But I don't have—"

"You do now. What good is having ethereal colleagues who live inside the internet if you can't get them to hook you up with free cable and Netflix?"

"I can't, in good conscious, allow illegal access to an entertainment service in my home." Thad knew he sounded sanctimonious, but he stood his moral high ground. He stopped himself from sticking out his chin and crossing his arms over his chest, though.

"It's a victimless crime," Peter tossed back over his shoulder as he hooked up the laptop to the TV.

"The key word there is crime," Thad might have stuck his chin out a little at this point. "What kind of example are we setting?"

The boys started clamoring, begging, arguing, threatening—using every technique in the childhood arsenal. And an adult one too, as Hector stated reasonable and logical arguments for why they should be allowed to break the law just this once. "We're living outside this world at the moment, so worldly concerns aren't relevant to us."

Hector was going to be a force to be reckoned with. Thad didn't know whether to be frightened or proud. Both?

Finally, the boys fell silent, allowing Peter the last word, no doubt hoping he'd have more influence on Thad than they were having.

"It's only for a few hours." Peter looked up at Thad, an expression on his face Thad never thought he'd see— uncertainty, coupled with a request for approval. "I'll take full responsibility if they grow up to be downloading miscreants."

Thad felt like he had four lost boys in his charge instead of three wise-beyond-their-years orphans and one hundred-year-old rebellious adult.

"Okay, but just this once." Thad knew he'd caved and done something against his better judgment. But inflexibility had been his grandparents' strong suit. He would prefer not to mimic their rigid and alienating parenting techniques. After a long sigh, which was drowned out by the boys' cheers, he headed for the kitchen to make dinner for five.

CHAPTER 16

HEXPERT WITNESS

"CAPTAIN AMERICA WILL JUST have to wait." Peter clicked off the remote. "Right now, we have a villain to thwart."

"Can we pick up some game consoles on the way back?" Jaden asked.

It seemed the boys had decided they liked living with Thad and Peter and expected to stay on, even once they had their shadows back. And Thad couldn't fault their logic. He hadn't asked them to do dishes or get up for school or anything. No wonder they liked living there. Plus, it wasn't like they had nice homes to return to. His heart clenched. He could relate to living in a cold and unloving household, yet unlike these kids, Thad had never had to worry that tomorrow they'd kick him out and he'd end up somewhere new. Maybe somewhere worse.

Thad had searched the internet while the boys and Peter watched back-to-back action flicks. He'd googled news sites regarding the missing-boys to see if Jack Stabler's arrest had been reported, and maybe the guy who'd stolen their shadows as well.

It infuriated him that the two foster homes where the boys had been living had made deals with the media for exclusive interviews. To these vultures, the boys were worth more missing than sleeping in their assigned beds.

He had no doubt that when they returned home tomorrow, if things progressed according to plan, they wouldn't be greeted with hugs and kisses. Maybe if they stayed away a while longer, the families would get another round of media attention for the return of the prodigal sons.

Thad rolled his eyes so hard he thought he saw gray matter.

A glance out the window showed the sun had set and darkness settled.

"It's time," Thad announced in somber tones. He wanted the boys to realize how serious this was. The only reason he was taking them along was because he wanted to reinstate their shadows the instant they found them. Assuming they found them, of course. Peter was convinced the culprit would return to the community center tonight. Having no better lead to go on, Thad signed on for the mission.

Declaring that he was going to *reckon-loiter* again, Peter left via the balcony. The boys raced out to watch, incredibly impressed that he could fly.

"Cool!"

"Awesome!"

"Teach us!" they demanded.

"Sorry, lads," Peter said, alighting on the balcony softly after executing a neat barrel roll and a few other showy moves. Thad, too, hoped flying was a skill Peter could impart.

"I'm afraid that ship has sailed," Peter said ruefully. "There isn't enough fairy dust left in the world to allow new people to fly. A hundred years ago, the world was full of magic, but sadly, today the world is full of video games and internet and other cool things instead. It's a trade-off, really." He reached behind him and hauled Hector off the shaky metal railing.

"I figure if I'm falling to my death, you'll have to teach me how to fly real fast to save me."

"Firstly, young man." Peter placed a hand on Hector's shoulder, probably more to keep him there than for comfort. "You are much too smart for your own good. And secondly, it can't be done."

"You can always learn to be a pilot," Thad offered, trying to cheer them up.

It didn't work and he really hadn't expected it to.

"I'll be off now. I shall see what I can see while you make your way over on foot. Ta-ta." Peter leapt into the air and disappeared into the night.

Once again, Thad herded the boys into jackets and scarves. The gang trooped the few blocks to the community center and found the doors locked earlier than usual. A piece of paper taped to the door apologized for the inconvenience, but offered no explanation. Everyone in the neighborhood was probably aware of the suspicious circumstances regarding the missing coach. Guy had probably stepped in the first night Thad disappeared only because it had been too late to cancel.

Thad had keys, of course, and let them in, leaving the door unlocked so Peter could follow when he was finished reconnoitering.

Thad warned the boys to be quiet and, for once, they obeyed him. Maybe the seriousness of the situation had finally sunk in. Or perhaps all the boisterousness and laughter had been nothing but a thin veneer over the deep fear gripping the three lost young men.

They'd gone no more than a few steps into the center when they heard chanting echoing down the empty corridor. Sound traveled oddly in the old converted train station, but Thad could tell it originated in the gym. "This way," he mouthed, barely making a sound.

The boys responded with exaggerated nods, their eyes big and round like anime characters. Silently, they followed Thad up the stairs to the visitors' gallery. If they'd had moms and dads, this was where the enthusiastic parents would watch them play their games. He doubted anyone had come to watch these boys play. Just as no one had ever come to watch his games while he was growing up.

Thad halted the boys outside the door leading to the gym's balcony. He whispered a warning about how sound bounced off all the hard surfaces in the gym. He mentioned, too, that if they leaned out over the railing, their head and shoulders would be silhouetted against the ceiling. The lights might be dim, but they were bright enough to reveal them if the chanting man looked up.

Thad drew the door open slowly, managing to circumvent the creaky hinges. The four shadowless victims made their way to the first bench and sat, peering through the Plexiglas barrier that ran the length of the balcony. Below them, a robed man continued to chant and swung a tiny cauldron on a chain back and forth over a child-sized heap.

Thad placed his lips near Hector's ear, whispering, "Do you know who that is?"

He pulled back and let the boy mirror his movements, so the Hector's lips were close to his own ear. If only Thad had Tom's psychic ability.

Hector's lips brushed the shell of Thad's ear. "Not sure, but I think it's Allison Wildgoose. She wears a *Doctor Who* scarf."

Keeping well back of the railing, Thad studied the pair on the floor below. As his eyes adjusted to the dimness, the dark mound coalesced into a light blue jacket and a multi-colored scarf that resembled one worn by an early Doctor.

A girl this time. Well, why not? No doubt this shadow-stealing son of a bitch had female customers, too. Evil wasn't restricted to one gender. Or did it even matter?

"It's different this time," Hector whispered.

"Because it's a girl?" Thad whispered back.

"No. He's using notes. He's reading the chant like a script. The guy just talked before. Like he had it memorized."

"You sure?" Thad asked. "Jaden said you guys were unconscious." He clung to the notion that they hadn't experienced the pain he had.

Hector screwed up his face, whispering so softly Thad had to concentrate to make out the words. "It was more like dreaming, you know? Like when you wake up and remember what you dreamed in bits and pieces." He gestured toward the other two boys sitting further along the bench, their gazes glued to the scene below. "We told each other what we'd been through. With us, the shadow thief had the chant memorized. This one's a newbie. I'm sure of it."

Thad squinted through the Plexi. As far as he could see in the dim light, the man wasn't wearing loafers of any color leather. Instead, he had on scuffed boots with heavy, non-slip treads. A lot like the ones Thad wore.

Hector was right; this was a different guy.

The bench jerked slightly as Peter joined them, settling in on Thad's left. He pressed up close, his denim-covered thigh warm against Thad's.

"It's not the same guy," Thad whispered, jerking his head in direction of the gym floor.

Peter's eyes widened a fraction, then he studied the scene, nodding. "The antiquarian texts are still in your boss's office, so perhaps I was wrong about him."

"Doesn't matter. Whoever this is, we got him now." Thad squeezed Peter's thigh. "We need to stop him before he completes his ritual." Thad began to rise, but Peter grasped his wrist and pulled him back onto the bench.

Now it was Peter's lips brushing his ear. He shivered but otherwise kept his attention where it should be.

"No, we must let him finish," Peter said.

"*What?*" Thad barely remembered to keep his voice low. "We have to stop him before he takes the girl's shadow!"

Peter held up a hand, then leaned in again. "Sorry, but no. We need to see how it's done in case he's already sold their shadows and we need to detach them from their new owners."

Thad had been about to protest further when Peter's logic

sank in. He snapped his mouth shut, nodding. It made sense, but sitting there watching that evil fucker slice open the back of the little girl's T-shirt and rip her shadow from her spine was the hardest thing he'd ever had to do in his life.

CHAPTER 17

HEXCAPADES

EVENTUALLY, THE SON OF A BITCH put down the knife and the horror show concluded.

The robed man added more chemicals or herbs or whatever to the cauldron. It began to sputter and smoke. A spark must have found its way under his hood, causing him to stumble backward and trip on his robe. He landed on his ass with a thump.

Good. Thad had personal experience with hitting the gym floor on his tailbone and it hurt. The man flailed on the polished floor, catching his boots in the too-long robe as he tried to stand. He flailed about, finally catching his balance. But not before the hood of his robe slipped off.

Thad's mouth dropped open in shock. Standing on the hard gym floor was the last person on earth he'd expected to find clasping the little girl's shadow to his chest as if it were fragile and precious.

Detective Reasoner stepped around the unconscious Allison. Using his free hand, he bound the cauldron up in something that might have been a fire blanket and shoved it in a satchel.

Reasoner looped the satchel across his shoulders and added the boomerang-shaped sacrificial knife to the pouch. He then adjusted the fallen shadow, draping it across his arms where it hung limply in a sad echo of the insensible child on the floor.

The little girl hadn't screamed. She hadn't even moved when

he'd taken her shadow. Thad knew it to be the most horribly painful experience he'd ever had, and that included beatings from his grandfather and a fractured arm when he had once fallen out of a tree.

In fact, she looked dead. Could you steal a shadow from a dead person? If so, then why didn't this asshole confine himself to the shadows of the dead?

But then her chest moved as if she sighed or took a deep breath. So the Detective had probably drugged her. Hopefully she'd slept through the whole thing, pain free.

Reasoner mumbled something at the child. It sounded like an apology. Then he turned and walked away, leaving the little girl prone on the floor. He must have figured she'd be out for a while. He didn't even need to dispose of the body. She'd just wake up and try to go home, but no one would remember her. Inside, Thad shook with rage. Before he could do something rash, like charge down the stairs and confront the bastard, Peter laid a restraining hand on Thad's arm.

"Follow him," Peter whispered. "See where he takes the shadow. Maybe the boys' shadows will be stored there, as well."

Footsteps echoed across the gym as Reasoner headed for the exit. Hands full of stolen shadow, the detective bumped the gym door open with one hip, letting it slam behind him.

As soon as they were alone, Peter ordered, "Go! Go! I'll get the girl. Take the boys. I'll be right behind you." He leapt over the railing, flying across the gym to land silently beside Allison.

"Boys. With me," Thad ordered, charging down the stairs, but still trying to keep his footsteps light. He'd had a lifetime of trying not to attract attention to himself. *Hush and wait. Hush and wait.* He'd hushed this time, but no way was he waiting. He'd done enough of that.

There could be a secret chamber in the building they needed to find, or else Reasoner was leaving. Either way, he refused to let the bastard escape.

The boys followed, their sneakers and boots nearly silent on the stairs from the visitors' gallery. They too had learned not to draw attention to themselves.

Quietly, they entered the hallway, running smack into Reasoner.

"You!" he cried.

"Back!" Thad yelled. The boys rushed back into the stairwell. Thad pulled the door closed behind him. After a moment, he could hear the sound of Reasoner's work boots stomping on the tiles as he walked away, already forgetting their awkward pursuit.

A nasty smile curled Thad's lips. He'd used Reasoner's own villainy against him.

He counted to twenty, then shushed the boys and returned to the hallway. They followed the sound of Reasoner's footsteps as he descended the west stairwell to the basement.

Reaching the basement a few moments later, Thad peered around the steps to determine what hidden chamber Reasoner accessed, what combination of bricks pressed would release the secret door.

But he might as well not have bothered. Reasoner certainly hadn't. No secret chamber or hidden compartments. Just a locked door marked *Electrical,* the word *Hazard* painted beneath it. Reasoner used an ordinary key to let himself in, not bothering to lock or even close the door behind him.

Arrogance would be this man's downfall.

Peter appeared from the opposite side of the basement, the drugged girl in his arms. He must have come down the east stairs at the far end of the building.

Along one wall was a broken pew matching those installed in the Church upstairs. One wooden end had splintered. It was fairly level, though, being supported by a pile of something—a stack of bibles, Thad realized. Peter placed the unconscious girl gently on the pew. Thad noticed he'd dressed her in her coat and *Doctor Who* scarf. He shuddered, thinking how they'd explain her sliced-up T-shirt when she awoke. To her, to her parents and to the authorities.

He'd worry about that later. Right now, they had a rogue cop to thwart.

Thad nodded at Peter across the space, then as one, the two men strode toward the open door. Peter drew his badge from his back pocket.

"Stop where you are, Reasoner! We know what you're up to. By the powers vested in me by Borderless Observers Organization, I'm placing you under arrest. Put down the shadow and step away..." He glanced around the small room. "Step away from those cages."

Thad stood beside Peter, his broad shoulders blocking the entrance. The three boys fanned out behind them. Although Peter had nothing in his hands more threatening than a wallet, Thad noticed an impressive knife dangling from a hilt attached to his belt. In fact, it looked like an antique child-sized sword. Was that how he'd survived on Neverland?

Thad surveyed the room. Against one wall was a stack of cages, like the kind used to transport large dogs on an airplane. Plus one that resembled a mesh locker big enough to hold a full-grown man.

Inside the cages were shadows. Tattered, fading shadows. Thad counted: three youth-sized and one adult. Plus the limp one Reasoner held in his arms.

"You! It's you who's under arrest. How the hell did you break out of jail?" Which was, apparently, Reasoner's cue to drop the shadow and pull a gun.

A gun. Oh, shit! Thad began to shake. Bile rose in the back of his throat, choking him as he flashed back to that day. The bright, sunny day when the hit man shot his mom and walked away, leaving four-year-old Thad to sit in the pooling, cooling blood for hours.

"Thaddeus. Come back. I need you!" Peter hissed, fingers digging into Thad's wrist.

Thad shook himself, leaning into Peter's warm so their shoulders bumped. *Stay focused, damn it!*

"I hate guns," Thad hissed at Peter from the side of his mouth. "I don't suppose you have a special talent for dealing with firearms."

"Not one of my special talents, I'm afraid," Peter said, raising his hands. "I'm afraid he's going to get away. But at least we'll get the boys' shadows back." Peter pressed up against Thad, leaving room so Reasoner could pass them and make his getaway.

Reasoner bent to retrieve the girl's shadow. He'd treated it gently before, but now he couldn't juggle both shadow and gun. He shifted a troubled glance between the men standing with hands in the air and the shadow lying on the ground. After a second, he scooped up the shadow, balled it awkwardly with his free hand and shoved it into the satchel still dangling from his left shoulder.

Thad considered tackling Reasoner, but he couldn't take the risk that the gun might go off and hit one of the boys.

"Go, then. Get out. Ruin these kids' lives, why don't you?" He might be forced to wait, but there was no way in hell he was going to hush.

"You don't understand. It's not..." The detective's hardened expression melted into a look of self-loathing. To Thad's shock, the man's eyes filled with tears. He opened his mouth to speak, but must have changed his mind.

Gun in one hand, the other arm through the satchel strap, Reasoner slithered toward the door. As he stepped past them, still trying to keep the gun pointed in their direction, Thad snatched the wicked knife from Peter's belt.

Although he'd never handled a blade bigger than a carving knife before, it wasn't much different than a hockey stick—and he was pretty good at sports. He deftly slid it between Reasoner's shoulder and the satchel strap, the soft leather parting like ribbon. The satchel and its supernatural contents thunked on the floor.

Reasoner halted, his work boots' excellent traction nearly sending him into a concrete faceplant. He flailed wildly, shouting, "But I need this shadow! A little girl's life is at stake!"

"We know!" Thad yelled back. Beside him, Peter bent down and grabbed the satchel, its contents miraculously staying inside—probably some magical equivalent of Velcro.

Thad brandished the knife at Reasoner, too mad to even think that you don't bring a knife to a gunfight. "If you're going to steal more shadows, you'll have to replace your Goddamn tools." With any luck, shadow-stealing blades and caldrons couldn't be ordered off eBay.

The detective cursed, raised his gun and pointed it at Thad's heart. "I'm sorry, but I'm going to have to take that shadow."

Thad had only ever heard a gunshot at close range once in his life. According to his sad childhood recollection, it hadn't made a thunderous crash like in the movies, just an understated little pop. But this time, in a small, cement room with a low ceiling and concrete floor, the gunfire was deafening. Hit hard, he rocketed backwards, landing on his spine with a breath-stealing *oomph.*

He gasped for air, heart hammering, wondering when the pain would set in. His back and head hurt where he'd hit the cement, but what about the entry wound?

His skull throbbed in time to the sound of boots thudding on the stairs.

"Well done!" Peter said, appearing above Thad. To Thad's relief, the agent clutched the satchel full of magical items.

Jaden's face appeared next to Peter's. "Jeeze, Coach. The way you fell back, I thought you were a goner."

Hector and Stanley leaned into view, worry painting furrows

on their young foreheads.

"I'm glad you're not dead," Stanley added.

"But I'm shot."

Peter looked fondly exasperated as he held out a hand to help Thad up. "You're not shot. I shoved you out of the way and the bullet went wide. In fact, I'm not convinced our misguided detective ever intended to hit you."

"Didn't intend to...? Misguided? What are you saying?" Thad accepted Peter's hand and allowed himself to be hauled up. "Sorry I scared you," he told the boys. "But Reasoner's getting away. And even if we don't think he's the original shadow thief, he could lead us to the other guy. The black loafer guy!"

"Never mind that now. We have work to do." He clapped Thad on the shoulder, grinning.

"Work? What do you mean?" Thad asked.

"How are your seamstress skills?"

CHAPTER 18

SEALED WITH A CURSE

THAD PLUNKED THE SATCHEL he'd nabbed onto the long workbench that lined one wall of the maintenance room. Pawing through the contents, he extracted a wad of rumpled papers. "Reasoner had how-to notes." He scanned the printout. "It's got a recipe for the mixture that goes in the little pot." He flipped the page. "Plus it's got the words to the chant all written out phonetically."

"Sung to the tune of *For He's a Jolly Good Fellow*?" Peter came to stand behind him, close enough for Thad to feel Peter's body heat. Thad relaxed into the heat a tiny fraction. Somehow, this capricious man made Thad feel safe, maybe for the first time in his life. He was sure that, no matter what, Peter had his back.

But for how long? What would happen when they got their shadows re-attached?

Which was, Thad mentally slapped himself, their ultimate priority. He dove back into the satchel, drawing out the knife which was now housed in a dull metal sheath. Thad gripped the hilt so hard his hand shook. A grating, metal-on-metal rasp cut across his eardrums as he withdrew it from its case. He tested the blade with his thumb. "Huh. Not very sharp."

"Probably doesn't need to be since it's only slicing through ethereal matter." Peter picked up the notes and scanned them. His own long blade, which he'd retrieved from Thad and returned to its scabbard, had been exponentially sharper.

Thad laid the magical blade on the table. The last thing in the satchel was the little cauldron, wrapped in a hunk of shiny silver fire blanket. "It's still warm."

Peter examined the papers Thad had laid on the workbench. "It appears that the formula requires the kind of herbs one can easily buy in a grocery store to fill this little, uh, cauldron."

"It's called a censer," Hector said, stepping up to the workbench where the men were examining the satchel's contents. "We used them in Church."

"I suppose you're going to tell us now that you were an altar boy," Peter teased.

"I wasn't always an orphan, dude." Hector sniffed. "When can we get our shadows stuck back on?"

"First, we're doing Thad's."

"Like a practice round?" Hector asked.

"Wait, what? Now we know how to detach them." Thad waved a hand over the contents of the worktable. "How do you know how to re-attach them?"

"I know Wendy sewed mine on once. Then she was able to take it back another time, but as I've said before, for some reason, my shadow used to detach easily."

"So we're going to sew them back on. With what?"

"I thought ahead." Peter tapped his temple, his usual smirk turning positively smug. "On the way over, I descended and popped into one of your dollar stores and purchased a sewing kit." With a flourish, he pulled a plastic box about the size of a thick paperback from under his jacket. "*Voila!*"

Thad held out his hand and Peter passed it to him. "The Bachelor's Sewing Kit," he read the label aloud. "Oh, yeah. Cause that's not at all sexist."

"Well, I suppose if you consider bachelor to be a non-gender specific term such as actor or waiter, which have been redefined to include women, then it's completely not sexist."

Ignoring Peter's logical reasoning, Thad opened the box. He parked it on the workbench next to the knife and censer. "Needle, thread. Right. Okay. But we should definitely do Allison first. Then she won't have to be awake for it. Do you remember if it hurt to re-attach it?" He glanced guiltily at Hector, wishing he hadn't said that within the boy's earshot. "How's she doing? We should check."

Hector led them back into the hallway outside the electrical room. Jaden and Stanley sat on the floor watching little Allison. "No change," Jaden said. "I hope she's not gonna stay like this."

Peter met Thad's gaze, eyes troubled. "Not a chance," he said with more confidence than he had any right to.

Thad didn't need Tom's psychic abilities to know that Peter was worried, too.

"She'll be fine just as soon as we get her shadow back on." He had no way of knowing that, but the boys were looking more and more scared.

"No, we do Thad first." Peter insisted.

"No way. I'd never put myself before the well-being of these children. And that's final."

Peter raised an eyebrow, but his usual smirk was missing. "This time you're going to put yourself first. It's like on an airplane."

"Oh, I get it." The proverbial light bulb flickered on over Thad's head. "The adult puts on their oxygen mask first."

"Right. We're going to see if this works, and then if it does, we'll re-attach Allison's and then the boys' shadows."

"Okay. But..." Thad poked through the contents of the little plastic box. "We're using this." He held up a black rectangle about three inches long by one inch high.

"Velcro?" Peter asked. "Uh, I guess we can try it." He stepped up beside Thad, hip pressing warmly against him. Peter had no sense of personal space and Thad was grateful for the contact.

Which lasted only a second as Peter spun back and stuck his head out into the hallway. "Do any of you happen to know how to thread a needle?"

Now it was Thad's turn to smirk. Too bad Peter wasn't watching. "That's the beauty of it." He said over his shoulder. "It's peel-and-stick. No sewing required."

"Brilliant!" Peter said. "It's time to release the shadows. Now, one at a... Hector, no!"

The smart young man had just done something stupid. While Peter and Thad had been examining their sewing supplies and triaging shadow re-attachment, Hector had opened every cage.

Out drifted the shadows. They floated around the room, bouncing off walls, acting like insubstantial basset hounds in slo-mo. Like something underwater or in zero gravity. They drifted and dodged each other until each found its proper owner. At least Thad hoped that's what was happening. It's not like he had any experience in the area of shadow re-bonding. The grey-brown boy-shaped mists twined around the young people's legs, looking stronger already.

"Sorry, Coach," Hector said, watching his shadow circle him. "I thought you'd want them all out."

"It's okay. Just be careful. And don't make any sudden moves."

"They're trying to re-attach themselves, but they can't!" Stanley looked like he might cry again. "Look! Allison's is trying to stick to her feet!"

"We'd better get on it, then." Thad said. "Do I need to strip?"

"Much as I'd enjoy that, as I recall, you can keep your clothing on. I believe the only reason to cut away your clothing to remove your shadow is in order to get a grip on it. It's probably housed in your appendix or your spleen or some such spot. At any rate, take off your boots and socks."

Thad was way ahead of Peter. He'd hopped up on the workbench and had already begun unlacing his hiking boots and peeling off his once-white gym socks. "Skip the part where you tell me my feet stink and just get on with it."

"Right-o." Peter separated the Velcro strips, then peeled the white paper backing away. He kneeled on the cement floor, bringing Thad's feet up to rest on his thighs.

"That tickles," Thad giggled as Peter applied the male half of each Velcro pair to Thad's heels without comment or innuendo. Thad giggled again, glancing guiltily at the boys. "Sorry," he said, managing to smother another laugh. "I can't help it."

The boys just watched the procedure, eyes wide, faces serious.

"Now where's your shadow?" Peter asked. The adult-sized shadow had remained in its cage, seemingly reluctant to leave. "C'mere, boy. You can do it." Peter patted the side of his leg as further encouragement.

"Oh, wait. The Velcro's not sticking." Thad pointed at his heels. The corners were already curling away from his skin. "I guess you just don't get quality in a dollar store."

"Well," Peter sighed. "They do say magic always exacts its price and I guess a dollar isn't quite enough." He dumped Thad's feet off his thighs and stood. "Perhaps there's something around here we can use as adhesive." He opened a metal storage cupboard. "Ah. Here's some glue." He pulled out a little pot with a handwritten label reading *Glue* and unscrewed the lid. "Gah! This smells foul. It's not unlike the concoction Captain Hook and the pirates used to patch their ship. It'll do."

Thad said nothing. After all that he'd seen and experienced in the last couple of days, he'd pretty much drunk the paranormal Kool-Aid. He was willing to suspend disbelief until it snapped. "Are you sure we want to use something from a sorcerer's cupboard?" Thad asked, drawing his feet in close when Peter reached for them again.

"Please refrain from being a big baby. It's simply glue. Here."

Reluctantly, Thad let Peter swipe the glue onto the backs of his heels, then press the Velcro strips in place.

They then coaxed the shadow out of its cage. Peter managed to sneak up on it and attach the other half of the Velcro sticky tape. It stuck to the shadow without the need for the foraged glue.

"Peter, should it be struggling like that?"

"I'm sure it'll be fine. Let's see how it goes. We can always remove it again if there's a problem, of course. Isn't that why you had the brilliant idea to use Velcro in the first place?"

"Uh, yeah?" Thad said, giggling again as Peter pressed the feet of the shadow against Thad's heels before stepping back. Thad shook one foot and then the other. The shadow stayed firmly attached.

"How's it feel, Coach?"

Thad didn't answer, an uneasy feeling creeping from his heels to his cut. It felt... strange. Odd. You never felt your shadow when you had it, nor when it was gone. But he certainly felt this. After a moment's hesitation, he pulled his slightly damp socks back on and laced up his boots.

Hopping down from the table, he swayed. Peter shot out a hand to steady him. "You all right, Thaddeus?"

The boys edged forward expectantly.

"I feel different. I feel..." Thad put a hand on his forehead and closed his eyes. "I think... I don't know... Is it possible for them to have done something to my shadow so that it's now evil? I'm having all these thoughts. Or maybe they're memories. Oh, God. I want to hurt people. I want— Get your fucking hands off me, fag!" he shouted, shoving Peter away.

Peter banged into the workbench. The items on top of it

clattered.

"Ow. That's going to bruise."

"Good. You deserve it for trying to touch me!"

Peter braced himself and stood. The boys jumped back.

"I don't think they could have... Oh, no! I don't think that's your shadow, Thaddeus. Oh, my God. They've done it. They've swapped your innocent shadow with a bad one, so the recipient can get a fresh start and not end up being punished for his bad deeds. I was just so glad to find the shadows that I never thought..."

"That's a crock. I'm outta here. I can't believe I've been working in this shithole for that asshole for hardly any pay. I've been putting in long hours and now I'm gonna get me some payback. I'm gonna beat that idiot. *Brother* Guy, my brown ass. He's no freakin' brother of mine!"

"No, Thaddeus. Wait. Let me take the shadow back from you. We can— *Oof!*"

Thad followed his right hook with a left upper cut to the jaw, knocking Peter sideways. He held up his stinging fists, inspecting them, delighted in his newfound ability to hurt someone—anyone!

Peter flailed, trying to find his balance. Now all three boys stared at Thad as he rounded on them. They scattered. "You little shits! I'm taking your shadows and selling them to the highest bidder. I'm going to corner the shadow black market. You don't deserve to—"

Something smashed Thad over the head. He spun. Hector brandished a slim board—hardly more than a shim.

"Good thing that wasn't a two-by-four or I'd have to kill you." He laughed. "I might anyway. I should find out if I can take shadows from dead people. Maybe I'll just experiment. On you!"

Hector turned to run, his shadow drifting loose again. Thad shoved him hard. The boy smacked into a wall, blood fountaining instantly from his nose.

The other two boys came at Thad. He straight-armed them both. They fell to the dirty floor, dazed and terrified. Stanley's eye began to blacken and Jaden gained a nasty cut on his forehead from smashing against the workbench on his way down.

The youngest boy's soft cries filled the room

Peter edged between Thad and the boys, fists raised.

"I suddenly know how to box," Thad boasted. "But you. You just fly at people, right? You're no match for me in a tight space like this." He jerked his head to the right. Something had entered his vision. "What? You've called another one of your fairies? A lot of good she'll do."

Peter kept up his defensive stance and circled Thad, but his posture telegraphed a level of confidence Thad found annoying. Almost as annoying as the little lights that were getting all up in his face. He brushed them away.

"I'm getting rid of you once and for all." Thad clasped his hands together, preparing to deliver a two-fisted punch. These stupid fairies or fireflies or whatever they were kept getting in his way, blocking his vision. Their fight must have disturbed a nest of something. He needed to see what he was doing. They sparkled like diamond dust, getting up his nose and in his eyes and mouth.

And on his wrists. He stopped and stared at the cluster of sparkling gnats that surrounded his wrists, thickening quickly. Once settled, the light dimmed and they formed a black band against his light brown skin. "Get off!" he roared, waving his double-clenched fists about. "Get them off!" he howled.

Peter now leaned back against the bench, watching the show. The boys managed to get to his side. He tossed a lazy arm around Jaden on one side and Stanley on the other. Stanley held Hector's hand.

"I've had enough of this shit!" Thad tried to separate his

hands so he could brush away these stupid gnats. But his fists were stuck together. The gnats had congealed or solidified or whatever into diamond-hard cuffs around his wrists. "What the fuck!" he screamed.

"That is enough of that unacceptable language, young man. You yourself said you needed to set a fine example for these youngsters."

A tall, black woman entered, somehow making the small dingy room feel as if it were graced by her presence.

"Who the fuck are you, bitch?" Thad shouted.

"That'll be enough of that, too." She raised her hands and more of the little sparkly gnats flew from her fingertips. This time they formed a mask over Thad's mouth. He could only make the same kind of underwater noises he'd made when his shadow had been ripped from him.

"Peter, would you please remove the offending shadow?"

"Yes, Mother." Peter smiled and moved to crouch at Thad's feet. "I'm very glad to see you."

"And I you, my son."

Thad wanted to spit with disgust at all this family lovey-dovey shit. He settled for trying to kick Peter.

Which the Englishman seemed to have been expecting.

Deftly, Peter used the motion to knock Thad off balance. He landed heavily on the floor where Jaden and Stanley had lain a moment before, unable to break his fall with his hands bound by the strange black band.

Moving speedily, Peter tore off Thad's boots and socks, then tried to peel off the Velcro. "It's stuck to his skin. It's not coming off."

"No matter, dear. Just remove the shadow then."

Thad heard the familiar ripping sound of Velcro being disconnected. It hurt only as much as having his feet lopped off at the ankle, but his screams were muffled by the magical gag.

He tried to yell and curse, and then his world shifted and he slumped to the floor. His eyes filled with tears. His nose clogged. Since he couldn't breathe through his mouth, he knew he was going to die.

Although it terrified him, he knew he deserved it. His last thoughts were of how his grandparents had always told him he was a bad person and now he knew they'd been right. He'd beaten three young boys plus his friend and almost-lover. There was nothing he could ever do to make it up to them.

And then he passed out.

CHAPTER 19

THE MOTHER OF INTERVENTION

EXCEPT THAD DIDN'T PASS OUT. He wished he could, but he didn't. Not at all.

He just lay there in agony, not because his rightful shadow was still gone, or because his heels burned as if they rested on hot coals, but because he had harmed other people, good people, innocent people. He'd never taken up boxing or joined the school wrestling team because he'd hated to hurt people. And now he had.

He'd hurt children. And the man he'd come to care for. The man who would never care for him after what he'd done.

"That is quite enough wallowing, young man." A woman's voice echoed around him. "My son believes you are worthy of his attentions and so you will now rise and make yourself useful."

Wanting nothing more than to pass out or die, Thad found himself slowly climbing to his knees, not daring to look up. The mystic gnats had dispersed while he was preoccupied with blaming himself. No more rock-hard handcuffs. No more solid gag.

Thad was just himself again. He twisted round and slumped onto his ass on the cold, cement floor, drawing his socks and boots to him as if they were of some comfort. At least he didn't have to meet anyone's gaze if he kept his focus on his footwear.

The socks caught on the Velcro as he tried to pull them on.

He picked at the corners that had come loose so easily before, but they were well and truly stuck now. Good thing they'd only glued one half of the Velcro to him. The two female pieces that had been stuck to the shadow lay curling on the ground. They must not have been able to stay adhered to the shadow once it was removed again. He finished putting on his shoes and socks, then stuffed the orphaned pieces in his jeans' pockets and climbed to his feet.

The maintenance room was empty except for him, but voices drifted in from the hall. Reluctant to face the music, Thad stalled.

"We are out here, Mr. Wright." The woman's voice was warm and melodious, but there was no mistaking the steel order under the velvet.

Thad put one foot before the other and forced himself to walk the few paces out into the hallway.

The woman Peter had called Mother sat on the pew at the still-unconscious Allison's feet, humming as she sewed the little girl's shadow back in place. Her hand flickered up and down with a steady confidence as she inserted the needle, then drew up the thread.

The boys hovered nearby, waiting their turn to have their shadows re-attached. "Will it hurt, ma'am?" Hector asked.

"Not at all. I shall make sure it does not," she answered, stopping her rhythmic sewing long enough to grace the boys with a warm and reassuring smile.

Still unwilling to make eye contact, Thad restricted himself to furtive glimpses that revealed bloody noses, scrapes, bruises, torn clothes and a range of other injuries.

"Is everyone—? Did I—? How—?" He couldn't finish. His throat closed and he managed to choke out "I'm so, so sorry," barely distinguishable from the anguished sob that accompanied it. He looked up, steeling himself to face his punishment. Once again he'd ruined everything by failing to *hush and wait. Hush and wait.*

The boys appeared wary. They'd probably been hit before. He'd wanted them to consider him safe, to show them not all adults were cruel. But now he'd disappointed them, had become the same as every other abusive bastard who'd ever betrayed their trust.

"Boys?" Shaking inside, Thad told himself to man up. His grandparents hadn't favored open dialogue, but he did. "I want to make sure everything's all right between us. I'm not trying to excuse my actions, but I am saying it won't happen again. I know what to expect now. If I get an evil shadow again, I'll... I'll rip it back off. Or Peter will."

The boys shuffled around, eyes downcast. "S'all right, Coach. We know you weren't yourself," Hector finally said. He still wouldn't meet Thad's eyes.

"No, Hector. While I appreciate your words, it's not all right. I wish I were a stronger person. That I'd been able to resist the evil impulses. But I wasn't. And I hurt you. I know I can never make that up to you, but I don't want you to say it's okay just to keep from being hit again." All eyes jumped up to meet Thad's gaze now. "Yes, I know. I know what it's like to live with an abuser—someone who hits you and then tells you it's for your own good. And then you have to live with them like nothing happened. Well, I'm not like that. I'll never hit you again, under *any* circumstances. And you can take as long as you like to forgive me. I hope you will someday, but I totally get that it won't be right away." A tear traced its way along his cheekbone. He brushed it away. "I'm so, so sorry," he said again, this time making sure it was clear and audible.

He started to turn away when he felt a warm little hand slip into his. He looked down with disbelief at Stanley's upturned face. The boy was small for his age, but even at twelve, he'd been through more than any child should have. "It's okay, Coach. Ms. Battyeek said you were en— en— en-something."

He screwed up his face, managing to look so cute that Thad couldn't help but lean down and give him a gentle hug.

"Ensorcelled," the woman supplied. "I have explained to the boys that you were not yourself, that you were not responsible for your actions." She fixed her gaze on the point where Stanley gripped Thad's hand. "Thank you for your assistance, young Mr. Greenberg."

"It's 'Batique," Peter leaned close to Stanley's ear, stage-whispering. "Not Battyeek."

"Batique," Stanley repeated, seeming anxious to get it right.

And speaking of getting things right... "Jaden, Hector? You guys okay?" Thad rasped past the choking lump in his throat. "You should go to the hospital and get checked out. See if you need stitches or X-rays."

Peter moved to stand in front of Thad now, lips pressed tightly together so his mouth was just a thin line. Except toward the left side where his upper lip was swollen and oozing a few drops of blood. Where Thad had punched him.

Thad drew in a shaky breath. He'd wanted so much to kiss those lips again, but he'd blown that opportunity. He let his gaze rove over Peter's features. The promise of a serious shiner painted Peter's face from cheekbone to eyebrow. Blood also welled from a nasty cut on his temple.

Peter raised one hand. Thad braced himself for the blow he knew was coming. The blow he knew he deserved.

But when Peter gently laid a hand on his cheek, Thad shuddered, too surprised to react.

"We're going to be all right, Thaddeus. We've all had worse beatings, haven't we boys?"

The boys nodded. Thad's stomach lurched, his throat and heart aching. Those words, although they let him off the hook, were hardly comforting.

Shocking the hell out of Thad, Peter leaned forward and brushed his lips against Thad's. Thad closed his eyes and leaned in, knowing he didn't deserve this. Knowing he didn't deserve forgiveness.

"We're going to be okay. All of us. Even you, although you don't feel like it now."

Something moved behind him and he leapt to the side, terrified the evil shadow would try to re-attach itself to his feet. He huffed out a relieved breath when he realized it was just Hector, collecting the shadow-stealing paraphernalia and stowing it back in Reasoner's leather satchel.

"Where's the... the adult shadow?" Hector asked.

"Trapped in a special containment chamber. Not unlike your Ghostbusters," Peter answered, grinning as if Thad hadn't just clocked him. Twice. "You see, if you—"

"Peter, manners," the stately woman cut in. Her skin shone a rich mahogany, much as Thad's father's must have. Three scar-lines were etched on her cheeks not unlike a cat's whiskers. She wore a navy pinstripe pantsuit and low heels. A creamy silk blouse peeked out from under the collarless jacket.

Unlike Thad, whose light brown complexion reflected his mixed ancestry, there was no way Peter could be anything but adopted by this woman. And that meshed with the story he'd told about living on an island and being rescued. He'd have to ask Peter later—assuming they had a later—for the story of how he'd ended up a son to this striking woman.

Not for the first time, Thad thought about the fact that all five of them—the three teens, Peter and himself—were orphans. No wonder Peter understood him so quickly. He could relate to Thad's upbringing in many ways, even if his own had been incredibly different.

But did Peter know this? Thad had never mentioned his own family in any context. He hoped there wasn't a file on him somewhere at BOO. He never told anyone about his family, but he felt he needed to share it with Peter. About his life, his grandparents, even about his mother. But not right now.

Instead, he turned his attention respectfully to Peter's adoptive mother. He moved to stand before her, clasping his hands behind his back, he waited for Peter to do the honors.

"Sorry, Mother. May I present Mr. Thaddeus Wright. Thaddeus, my mother, Ms. Batique." He actually bowed, which elicited giggles from the boys. A good sign, since they'd just had yet another trauma added to their difficult young lives.

"Pleased to meet you, Ms. Batique." He tried on a bow—his first ever. It seemed to be not too difficult and somewhat appropriate.

"A pleasure." She smiled. "Please call me Jacqueline."

Oh, so this was the Jacqueline that Peter, Tom and Adrian had mentioned. He could see why they held such deep respect for her. She was obviously their superior at BOO. Plus, she could somehow control magical fireflies that turned into handcuffs and a gag. That he was more impressed than terrified said a lot about how he was adjusting to the supernatural in his life. Too bad that would end once the boys had their shadows sewn back on. In just a few minutes.

And Peter would leave, too.

"I'm so sorry for what I just did. Is there any way I can make up for it?"

"That wasn't you, my friend. Don't beat yourself up about it. Now that my mother has this part well in hand, you and I can—"

"But what if it *was* me? What if the shadow just released what's really in my heart? I sometimes have these impulses..." Thad resisted the urge to turn and run away. "My mother..."

He cast about for the words. How could he explain? He chewed the inside of his cheek until he tasted blood.

Peter eyed him, his usual smirk noticeable by its absence. "What do you think, Mother. Is our Thaddeus here a villain?"

"Please do not be foolish, Peter. Thaddeus, you are not a violent man by nature. You must not judge yourself so harshly.

You did not kill your mother. Now, gentlemen, it is high time you learned to sew."

"But how did you...?" Thad let the rest of the question go unsaid. He'd never told anyone about how he felt responsible for mother's death.

"We will discuss it at the right time and place, but now, you must put your needs aside and help these young boys."

Thad's mind sizzled with emotion, thoughts, memories, accusations and responsibilities. Jacqueline rose and reached out one hand, resting it on his bare wrist and he calmed. He didn't forget any of it—he was just able to compartmentalize it for later.

"Thanks," he said, figuring she'd know why he was grateful.

"Now Thaddeus, take this needle and thread. You will sew on young Hector's shadow straight away. And Peter, you will begin with Stanley."

Thad cringed at Jacqueline's tone. Not because he didn't know how to sew, and not because she'd given him an order, but because she'd given Peter an order. He truly expected Peter to protest, to make a scene at having his mother show up and take over his first assignment.

He arched an eyebrow at Peter, who seemed to understand.

"Whatever helps the children," Peter shrugged. "It's not about me." He turned away and began to poke thread at the eye of the needle.

Thad was impressed with Peter's sudden display of maturity and wondered just how much of the youthful boisterousness was an act to put Thad and the boys at ease.

"But wait. You, Jacqueline, you looked away and yet you remember me. The boys and me. How? Why?"

Her gaze tracked to his. "I remember many things, Thaddeus. Some of them may even come to pass." She handed him a needle and a spool of grey-brown thread.

He opened his mouth to ask if she'd lost her shadow in the

past, but Peter caught his eye and grinned, shaking his head. "Give it up, my friend. Jacqueline tells you only what she wants you to know."

"I just wish she'd—" Thad began, sick to death of all this mumbo-jumbo. Then he noticed anew the damage he'd done to Peter's face and closed himself down, hushing and waiting yet again. "I just wish she'd Show me how to do this." He held up the needle.

Jacqueline threaded their needles for them, but once they got going, the sewing part wasn't too bad. The quality of the stitches was questionable, but it seemed to be a sort of metaphysical activity because the thread quickly disappeared and the shadows re-attached as if they'd never been taken.

By the time the adults had re-attached the boys' shadows, Allison Wildgoose had begun to stir.

"Now, gentlemen, I want the three young men plus my son to go and lock yourself into those cages while I escort young Ms. Wildgoose to her father's car."

"Lock ourselves—?" Hector began, but Peter cut him off.

"You'll see," Peter said. "It'll all work out for the best." He smiled reassuringly at the boys and gestured for them to precede him back into the maintenance room. A little unsure, they moved in slowly. "Not you," Peter stopped Thad from following. "Sorry, but you have no shadow, so you can't be part of the rescue scenario."

"How do you—"

Jacqueline moved to Thad's side, taking his hand and patting the back of it. "You must now return to your apartment. You are no longer required here." After one more reassuring squeeze, she released Thad's hand and returned to the propped-up pew where Allison was struggling to sit up, looking sleepy and confused but none the worse for being drugged and briefly relieved of her shadow.

Peter winked at Thad and punched his shoulder. "Welcome

to my world. Imagine trying to live a mis-spent youth when you're saddled with an omniscient mother. Anytime I got into trouble, I knew it was only because she'd allowed it. Took the rebellious wind right out of my sails." He rolled his eyes and followed the boys into the maintenance room.

Speechless, Thad stood in the dank basement hallway staring after Peter until the door slammed shut.

"If you would be so kind as to lock them in, please," Jacqueline said, using the *sounds like a request but is really an order* manner Thad was already becoming familiar with.

Allison had finally surfaced. "Wha—? What happened? Where am I? Who are you? Oh, hi, Coach Wright."

Thad smiled at her. Now that he could see her clearly, he realized she was on his Wednesday after-school volleyball team. The rest of the kids called her Allie, so he hadn't made the connection. "It's okay, Allison. This lady is going to take care of you."

Had Allison been shadowless long enough to remember him or would she forget him as soon as she looked away?

She turned her face toward Jacqueline, a little afraid, but inclined to obey Thad's authority. She probably had a loving family and didn't live in uncertainty and fear like the orphans caged in the next room.

"You fell asleep here at the community center, young lady. I have summoned your parents to come and retrieve you. Your father should be arriving..." Jacqueline paused a moment, a far-away look in her eyes. Then, looking satisfied, she continued. "He is pulling into the parking lot even as we speak. Shall we?"

Jacqueline rose gracefully and Thad wondered if she, too, could fly. She held out her hand. Allison eyed her for a moment before grabbing it. "Bye, Coach Wright."

It seemed even the briefest time in a shadowless state allowed the young girl to remember Thad even after she'd looked away.

Jacqueline stopped before Thad. "Remember, please, Thaddeus Wright. You are to return to your apartment posthaste."

They started away again. Allison waved to Thad and led Peter's mother up the stairs on shaky, young legs, unaware that she'd almost been trapped in limbo.

While Thad still was.

CHAPTER 20

COP 'TIL YOU DROP

THAD WONDERED IF ANYONE had ever disobeyed Jacqueline Batique before or if he was the first.

If she was truly omniscient—and he was about ready to believe anything at this point—had she already known he wouldn't head back to his apartment right away, or did his shadowless state render him immune to her psychic abilities? But he'd been reachable by Tom and Adrian's two-step mind-reading act, so probably not.

Still, whether Jacqueline knew or not, whether she approved or not, didn't matter. There was no way on earth he was leaving the boys he considered his charges locked in cages in the dingy basement of the Church of the Gnomon.

Nor was he leaving Peter.

He crawled behind the nearby giant beast of a furnace and hid in the shadows. The irony was not lost on him.

He wasn't worried about capture. He knew the cops would forget him as soon as they looked away. Once again, his shadowless state could prove useful. Besides, he just wanted to observe.

Plus, if things didn't go well, someone had to be there to unlock the door and the cages. At least that's what he told himself.

He didn't have to wait long. Not five minutes after Jacqueline and Allison's departure, he heard sirens, followed by car doors slamming and police radios crackling. The sounds were familiar to him from cop shows, and somewhere back in the dusty corners of his memory, from the day his mother had been killed. *Hush and wait. Hush and wait.* Old pain spiked anew. If only he had. If he'd only hushed and waited, she might still be alive today. It was an old refrain and one that he wished would stop echoing through his mind in times of trouble.

The cops didn't search the building. From the footsteps and voices calling back and forth, he could tell they headed right for the basement. Someone had tipped them off. Jacqueline maybe?

A plainclothes cop, probably a detective, hustled by Thad's hiding place. He barely held in a gasp of shock and surprise when the man turned around to dispense orders to the uniformed officers tramping down the stairs in his wake.

The posse was led by none other than Detective Reasoner! The balls on this guy. Thad almost stepped out and accused him, but knowing it would prove pointless, he stayed in his claustrophobic hidey-hole.

Reasoner led the way to the maintenance room. Did nobody wonder how he knew exactly where to look? Even a tip wouldn't have been that detailed.

"Cut it off, Charlie." Reasoner stepped out of the way as a tall female officer strode forward, wielding a pair of giant bolt cutters. She wedged them in place and leaned into them. The shank snapped, the severed padlock clunking as it hit the cement.

Officer Charlie stepped back, leaving room for Reasoner to take her place before the door.

"Ready?" he asked. Nightsticks and stun guns fanned out behind him. Officer Charlie kept her bolt cutters poised.

Reasoner flung the door wide. The detective stepped inside and gasped. "Oh, my God. They're here. They're here! Charlie, get those cutters in here now!" He dashed into the room with the female officer, then dashed out again. "Get some emergency blankets. And have some bottled water ready if the medics say it's okay for them to drink. Who knows what's been done to them?"

You do. You were here less than an hour ago. Reasoner was playing the big hero. He'd get tons of media attention and maybe a promotion for locating and rescuing the missing boys. Thad's guts roiled with the need for justice. How could this man steal a little girl's shadow, taking her ability to live on this earth with it, and an hour later, claim credit for the heroic rescue of the very people he'd put in harm's way?

But how much did Reasoner remember? Once he'd taken her shadow, he'd forget her. Would he also forget what he'd done? Jack Stabler seemed to remember, although he was only the procurer. Surely Reasoner remembered figuring out how to steal shadows, relieving Allison of hers. But the boys? Maybe this really was all new to him. Thad's brain hurt trying to figure out how all this mystical stuff worked. He stopped trying and focused back on the big *rescue* scene.

Thad wished he could see inside the room. He could only assume Peter had staged a tragic crime scene, which indicated the boys had been stashed down here for days. Despite the seriousness of the situation, Thad found himself smirking. Peter's favorite expression must be contagious. Then he recalled how beat up they all were and just how they'd gotten that way. The smile slid off his face, along with a tear or two.

He watched as the boys, followed by Peter, were led out of the maintenance room by paramedics and uniformed cops. Those shiny emergency blankets lent Thad's friends a ghostly glow and he had to reassure himself they were fine. At least they'd get medical attention for the damage he'd inflicted.

"Isn't that the guy we arrested?" one of the cops asked, pointing at Peter as he filed by.

"Yes, it is. He's obviously a victim, though. And not the perp," Reasoner declared. It had a fake ring to it. Was he hoping that if he drew suspicion off Peter, the agent would keep quiet about Reasoner's own involvement? He'd see what Peter thought about it later.

Then it occurred to him that there might not be a later. The boys had their shadows back now. What if Peter felt the case was solved and just went home? Thad had, after all, beat on him and the boys. Thad's insecurity kicked him in the gut. If he hadn't felt awful before, he did now.

Once the boys had been taken away, Reasoner ordered the maintenance room sealed off. The same female officer he'd addressed as Charlie produced a roll of *Crime Scene* tape and used it to seal off the room.

Next, Reasoner ordered the other cops to fan out and search the premises. His final orders sent an icy trail down Thad's spine: "Proceed with caution. This perp is dangerous in ways you can't even imagine."

Yeah. A cop gone rogue always is.

Then he remembered that Reasoner was not the original shadow thief.

Who had done such terrible things? How could they find out? And just how dangerous was this perp?

CHAPTER 21

HEXPOSITION

THE COPS VACATED THE BASEMENT without checking behind the old furnace and the forensics techs began their careful analysis. Thad slipped out of the Church using his usual "Look over there!" technique, his heart breaking each time someone forgot him, forgot they'd ever seen him and forgot his very existence on this earth.

He'd always tried to fly under the radar, to not draw attention to himself, to never make a scene. But this fell into the *be careful what you wish for* category. What if he never got his shadow back? What if Jacqueline and Peter had forgotten him?

Telling him to go home wasn't much of a plan. And not very reassuring.

At least they'd rescued the boys and Allison and restored their shadows. He'd been so focused on saving them, he hadn't had an opportunity to confront his own feelings about his shadow-loss. About his future. About Peter.

He had the time now.

What kind of justice could BOO exert on Reasoner? Thad had no idea. Should he step in and exact punishment? He could kill the man in front of a thousand witnesses and get away with it in his shadowless state, but Jacqueline was right. That level of violence wasn't in his nature. Still, it would be a long time before he'd forgive himself for hurting the boys and Peter. If he'd had more self-control, he reasoned, he'd have been able to fight the violent impulses as he always had before.

Except that one time.

He pushed thoughts of his mother away. Jacqueline somehow knew about that. He hoped to one day have that conversation with her. Was that likely now?

Peter and his mother were busy agents. They had criminals to catch and justice to carry out. Thad's needs were probably low on their priority list.

How would they find the real shadow thief? He hoped Peter and Jacqueline would continue to pursue the case and bring the thief to justice.

He couldn't help but feel his own involvement had come to an end. What did he have to offer? He'd been a lead, a walking, talking clue. What was he to them now? What was he to Peter?

Thad trudged home, feeling alone and friendless. Before the whole shadow thing, he'd been alone and friendless, and that had been fine.

Mostly.

Acceptable, anyway.

Now it wasn't. He'd grown attached to the boys and to Peter. He hadn't realized how isolated he'd become since Clint had dumped him. To keep from being alone in his apartment, he'd thrown himself into his work as much as possible. He loved his job, but knew he could never go back. Without his shadow, he'd soon he'd have no cash and no home. If technology wouldn't work for him, he couldn't work an ATM, couldn't pay his rent or buy groceries. He'd be stuck shoplifting or doing dine-and-dash as the boys had suggested.

Or living out of dumpsters.

Reaching his apartment building, he grabbed the outside door as a neighbor exited. Usually he was friendly with the neighbors, even if they didn't reciprocate. This time he didn't bother saying hi. What was the point?

Of any of it?

He pressed the elevator call button and stood there, lost in thought. After maybe five minutes, it hadn't come. Had even basic mechanical technology forgotten him? Or was the elevator just out of service again?

Was his presence in the world stable at this level or would it continue to deteriorate? It wasn't like he could google "shadowlessness: symptoms."

He climbed the stairs to his apartment.

In all the excitement, he'd never asked Peter how he'd found him in the first place. He'd implied it had to do with Thad's initial google search that had triggered some sort of investigation. But Peter had arrived mere hours later.

Where, exactly, was this island they lived on? Had Peter already been in town on the missing boys' assignment? No, Adrian had said they had only just found out it had a supernatural component. How had Peter known to come to him? How had Jacqueline known to send Adrian and Tom? If she truly was omniscient, then why hadn't she known it was a supernatural problem? Why hadn't she known about Reasoner's involvement?

Thad guessed he'd never know the answers to his questions. Or the limits of Jacqueline's powers. He'd been useful for a while, but now he'd been dismissed. Would they even bother trying to get his shadow back now that the boys had been rescued?

Depressed as hell, he sprawled on his sofa bed. The boys hadn't bothered closing it up when they left that morning. After a few minutes, he sighed and began setting the apartment to rights. He didn't need the reminders that, for a brief time, he'd had company. A family.

He unlaced his heavy outdoor boots and shoved them in the hall closet. His heels itched like the bad case of athlete's foot he'd contracted in junior high. Once he pulled off his less-than-fresh gym socks, he scratched at his skin, only to be reminded of the half-Velcro pieces glued to his heels. Probably homemade superglue, he figured. He'd need acetone to remove it. Hadn't he read somewhere that nail polish remover was made with acetone? Maybe Mrs. Petrone next door had some nail polish remover.

She'd be happy to lend it to him, except as soon as she turned away to fetch it, she'd forget what she'd been going to get. Or that she'd left him standing at her open door. He would probably have better luck just buying a travel size bottle.

Or shoplifting it.

His brain churned as he examined his options. No wonder Peter had ended up on Neverland and stayed there for a hundred shadowless years. Maybe Thad could... but no. He couldn't fly, and he had no idea how to "pass the third star on the right and fly straight on 'til morning" or however the old story went.

Thad moved into the bedroom for a fresh pair of socks. Then he allowed himself to be distracted by his unmade bed. He lifted the pillow Peter had slept on and buried his face in it, inhaling deeply. It smelled of Peter, although what that was comprised of, he had no idea— probably fresh air and fairy dust.

That damn lump in his throat was back. If this continued, he should find an ear, nose and throat specialist and get himself checked out. Of course, he wouldn't be able to make an appointment or get a prescription filled.

He tossed the pillow back on the bed and pulled up the covers. He nearly tripped as he rounded the far side to draw the comforter up evenly. What the—?

Peter's knapsack. Thad's heart soared. At least he'd get to see Peter one more time when he came to pick it up.

And with that bit of hope filling his heart, he crushed the knapsack to his chest and returned to the living room to await his... acquaintance? Colleague? Paranormal Service Provider?

His friend, he finally concluded.

Although he briefly considered just leaving the knapsack out on the balcony, where Peter could fly up and retrieve it without having to see or speak with Thad, he couldn't bring himself to do that. Along with realizing that he wasn't a violent person and that magic was real, he also realized he was falling for Peter. He needed to put some closure on the love that might have been.

After sitting on the couch for a while, real life kicked in. He grew bored, hungry and nature called. He made sure the apartment door was unlocked. Three times. And the balcony door, as well, of course. He never locked that, what with living on the third floor. But he checked that, too. Five times.

He grabbed a fresh apple out of his full-to-bursting fridge and sat at the little table for two, wondering where he'd get the energy to ever do anything again.

By the time he heard the door creak open, he'd resigned himself to his fate. If Peter was done with him, he'd survive. He'd survived so much already.

But it wasn't Peter who walked into the room.

Stanley appeared first, holding the door open as the others poured in. He listed to the left, weighed down by the leather satchel presumably refilled with supernatural tools. There was no sign of the slice in the strap where Thad had cut it in two.

"Hey, Coach. We got pizza with all that organic stuff you like!" Jaden called, his arms piled high with flat whitish boxes. Hector followed him in, a bulging plastic bag in each hand.

Jacqueline Batique came next. "Thank you, Stanley. That was very gentlemanly of you."

Stanley beamed. After closing the door, he stepping over to the couch and plopped the satchel onto the coffee table with a metal-on-metal clunk.

Thad took another head count, but no, Peter wasn't among the ensemble. Thad's heart dropped low in his chest.

He gave himself permission to grieve for a moment for lost possibilities as the boys bopped around the apartment gathering plates and glasses and setting the tiny table for two before dropping on the couch with their own juice and pizza.

Juice, a tiny part of Thad's brain noticed. Not pop. At least he'd had a good influence on their beverage choices.

"Thanks, boys. I'm so glad we can all have another meal together." He turned to Jacqueline. "And thank you, Ms. Batique." He assumed she, or BOO, had covered the cost.

Stanley placed a fragrant pizza box on the table while Jacqueline seated herself in the chair opposite Thad, a knowing smile on her face. Of course, if she really was omniscient as Peter had claimed, or just wanted people to think she was, then that was probably her go-to expression. He tried to smile at her but it felt too fake to maintain. What did it matter anyway? She could probably read his emotions as easily as his mind.

Or was she a seer and not a psychic? What the hell did he know? Was it only two days ago that he'd been safe in his belief that the supernatural didn't exist?

Then a pair of gentle hands dropped over his eyes. Before he could figure out which of the three youngsters was pranking him, an English accent sing-songed, "Guess who?"

Thad sat frozen, afraid if he moved it would all go away. Instead, he felt warm breath on his neck and the hands moved down to massage his stiff shoulders. "You're so tense. You should learn to relax, my friend."

The hands withdrew as Peter crossed the apartment toward Thad's desk. Grabbing Thad's wheeled office chair, he rolled it back to the table. His usual grace deserted him and he plunked down in it hard enough that he had to grab the edge of the table to keep from wheeling away again.

"Dig in, love. I'm famished."

Love. Thad's heart filled again. It was getting quite a workout. He opened his mouth to say something—anything—

but his brain refused to engage and nothing emerged.

"You are no doubt wondering what transpired at the hospital," Jacqueline prompted.

Thad nodded. That he could manage.

Peter gifted him with a lopsided grin and flipped up the pizza box lid. He placed a piece on a plate for Jacqueline, then grabbed a slice and shoved it in his own mouth, his teeth gleamed as he bit through the chewy topping.

Thad realized he was starving. The apple hadn't done anything to fill his empty stomach. He lifted a slice to his mouth and bit down. Nothing in the world had ever tasted so good. "I hope you don't mind dining on the same thing two evenings in a row," Peter said after swallowing a mouthful of pizza.

Thad smiled for the first time in hours. "'Course not." He'd gladly eat pizza every night if it kept Peter near him.

"The boys were examined by a physician, who pronounced them healthy," Jacqueline said. "As you can see, the small cut on Peter's temple is the only injury that required so much as a bandage."

Since Peter obviously did not speak with his mouth full when his adoptive mother was at the table, he merely made exaggerated pointing motions to the butterfly bandage affixed near his hairline.

His lip didn't appear swollen at all, and his black eye seemed to have skipped the purple stage altogether, going straight for yellow and green. If Thad hadn't known better, he'd say the injuries looked several days old and almost healed.

Question after question formed in his mind. He ended up asking the least supernatural one. "Why are the boys here? I mean, I'm very glad to see them, but why aren't they at home with their foster families?"

Peter waved the air as if he'd been subjected to an unpleasant smell. "Media circus. And their *devoted* foster families are wallowing in it. The papers snapped a few shots of the boys returning home, then the police officers who'd escorted them ordered the paparazzi to leave the kids alone. The two families were so busy giving interviews about how they'd worried and grieved for the missing boys that they didn't even notice when Mother and I collected said boys and left to purchase another round of pizza." He held up his current slice by way of demonstration.

"The cuts and bruises. They look almost—" but before he could ask his next question, someone pounded on the door.

"Don't answer it without checking first," Peter warned the boys, but Stanley raced across the room and yanked the door open. He probably couldn't quite reach the peephole yet anyway.

Thad's pizza splatted back on his plate as, for the second time in a so many hours, he was shocked at the gall of Detective Reasoner.

"What the hell are you doing here? Sorry." The latter was said to Jacqueline in response to her disapproving look at his use of the mild curse word.

Reasoner stepped into the room. Stanley slammed the door behind him.

"I..." Reasoner began, but nothing more followed.

Awkward, uncomfortable silence reigned until Stanley whispered loudly, "Isn't he a bad man?"

Thad was about to leap up and do... something when Jacqueline placed a restraining hand on his wrist. He relaxed a fraction. He hadn't known what he planned to do anyway. Punching people wasn't high on his list of favorite activities right now.

"Yes, Detective. Please explain your presence here," she commanded.

"I..." Reasoner said again, then his spine straightened and his jaw firmed. "Why did you allow me to play the hero back there at the Church? I'm just what this young man said." He pointed to Stanley who ducked behind Hector. "I'm a bad man."

A different kind of person might have followed that statement with guilt, hung his head maybe. Instead, Reasoner glared stubbornly around the room, and his gaze jumped from person to person. Only Jaden kept on chewing his pizza, as if he had total faith in the adults in the room to handle the situation. Hector placed an arm around Stanley's shoulders.

Jacqueline rose and crossed the room to stand before Reasoner. If the detective was six feet tall, in low heels Jacqueline was of equal height. The bare bulb above her head cast her features in sharp relief, her all-seeing dark eyes shining beneath shadowing arches.

"I am afraid I must disagree with you, Detective Reasoner." She crossed her arms, returning his defiant gaze. "You are not a bad man."

"But I tried to take that little girl's life essence. I don't even know. I just—" Once again, Reasoner managed to surprise Thad, this time by breaking into a harsh, guttural sob.

What happened next shocked Thad even more. Jacqueline took a single step to Reasoner's side. Placing a hand on his shoulder, she began to stroke his back in a soothing manner. She whispered low into his ear. What the hell was she saying to him?

Peter seemed shocked too, if his gaping mouth displaying half-chewed pizza was anything to go on. He stared at his mother and the latest visitor to Thad's apartment in disbelief.

The detective cried great wrenching sobs, disturbing and distressing as only a grown man's crying can be. Thad's own eyes filled with sympathetic tears and the lump in his throat put in a return appearance.

After only a few moments, Reasoner seemed to come back to himself, realize where he was and who he was with. He accepted a small lace handkerchief from Jacqueline. While the tiny square shouldn't have been up to the task, it handled the detective's tears just fine.

Finally, eyes still shining, Reasoner whispered something in return. Jacqueline appeared satisfied and gestured for him to turn and face the room.

"I'm not... I'm not trying to justify my actions. What I did was wrong. I can't thank you enough for saving that little girl."

Jacqueline must have told him that Allison's shadow had been restored and that she'd been returned home safely.

"I'm always the one who saves folks, but this time it was me she was being saved from." He gasped as if he'd been struck. "I went a little crazy. My Emily. My daughter. She's sick. She's... The doctors say she's not going to make it." He took a moment to collect himself. "She hurts all the time, and slips away from her mother and me a little more each day. I guess I got obsessed with saving these boys since I couldn't save my own daughter." He looked at his hands.

Even from across the room, Thad could see where he'd picked at his cuticles until they'd bled, scabbed over and bled again.

"I thought that Coach, Thaddeus Wright, had kidnapped these three." He jerked his chin toward the couch where the three orphans stared at him wide-eyed, pizza forgotten.

"But I'm a victim, myself," Thad said, rising from his chair.

"Oh, when did you get here?" Reasoner looked puzzled. "Yeah, I got that. Just not in a way that's admissible in court. Hell, none of this is admissible in court." He stared out the big balcony window.

"Go on, Detective," Jacqueline prompted, still standing at his side.

He shook himself. "Back at the beginning, before I knew about all this hocus-pocus stuff, I thought Coach Wright was the perp. I wanted to catch him— Oh, when did you get here?" His puzzled expression deepened. "Anyway, I wanted to catch you in the act of something incriminating, something I could use, so I set up surveillance. I couldn't get a search warrant, not enough evidence, but I was beyond obsessed. I picked your crappy door lock with a credit card and hid a camera on your shelf." He pointed without taking his focus off Thad. "Right there. I had just gotten home and tuned in when you and that guy, Jack Stabler, arrived. I almost turned it off, figuring all you were up to was a little hanky-panky." He glanced guiltily at the boys, then back at Jacqueline. "If you know what I mean."

Hector rolled his eyes. "We're not children."

"Yeah, dude. We're not children," Stanley repeated.

"Please continue with your explanation, Detective. The boys deserve to understand."

Thad figured he and Peter were included in "the boys."

"Okay. Then weird stuff started happening. Stabler drugged Wright..." He glanced around the room. "Oh, when did you get here?"

"That's what being shadowless does, Reasoner. Keep your eyes on me or you'll forget I'm here again and again."

The detective seemed to buy this without question, staring at Thad as if afraid to blink. Maybe he, like Thad, has seen enough supernatural hoodoo in the last few days to have entered a state of complete credulity. Man-eating unicorn on the balcony. Sure. Why not?

Thad glanced at the balcony. He rolled his eyes at himself.

Reasoner cleared his throat. "So I'm watching on the screen, ready to rush over here at any second. Then the robed guy arrived and Stabler let him in. They began to strip you. I thought they were going to... you know... *rape you.*" He whispered the last two words loud enough for everyone to hear. "I was stuck. Do I stay and observe or rush over? Then they'd pulled out that stuff.

"I told myself it was some sort of kinky sex..." He glanced at the boys. When his gaze swept over the room again, he noticed Thad. "Oh, when did you get here?"

Jacqueline shook her head. "Thaddeus, would you come here, please?"

Thad crossed the living room to stand before Jacqueline and Reasoner.

"Thank you. Now if you could please place a hand on the detective. No, it must be on bare skin."

Thad wasn't comfortable laying a hand on the man who'd tried to frame him and then committed the same horrible crimes he'd accused Thad of doing. But if Jacqueline said so, then he would. He was beginning to understand why Tom and Adrian were fine with obeying her orders, and that Peter didn't mind her arriving and taking over.

There was a certain comfort in leaving things up to her, a feeling of worthiness when contributing to what she was attempting to achieve. She was the sort of person people signed on to follow. She made you strive to be the best person you could be.

He stepped to Reasoner's side, then touched the man's wrist with and the tip of his index finger for minimal of contact. The three then stood in a little line facing the room, Jacqueline on Reasoner's left, Thad holding his right wrist.

"Now he will remember you are here. Please continue, Detective. You were watching Thaddeus be ensorcelled upon your closed circuit television system."

He glanced at her sharply at the word *ensorcelled*, but sighed and continued. "I began to get really nervous. I thought they were going to do some sort of Satanic sacrifice. Then Wright, you, started screaming. I left the camera recording and drove over here as fast as I could and broke into your apartment again."

"But you didn't call for backup," Thad accused.

"I couldn't. I would have had to explain how I'd been observing you. Look, I know what you're thinking, but I couldn't risk getting locked up or anything. I needed to be available for my daughter. They say she has only a few more days."

"So you busted into my apartment. Twice. You found me lying on the floor. You didn't call 9-1-1 or anything?"

Reasoner's brow crinkled. "No, that's not what happened. I came in here and found nothing. You weren't here. I retrieved my camera and left again. When I went back home and replayed the video, it got fuzzy and you just disappeared. I couldn't figure out what was going on, but after fifteen years as a cop, I know hinky when I smell it. That's when I arrested Stabler. You were there?" He asked. "I know he was." Reasoner jerked his head in Peter's direction.

Peter nodded. "Yeah, we both were."

"Sorry I arrested you, son. By then I was in such a state, I would have arrested the Easter Bunny himself if he'd showed up."

"She usually vacations during the first few weeks following Easter," Jacqueline murmured. Thad shot a glance in her direction. She seemed dead serious.

Let it go. He had quite enough supernatural craziness to deal with at the moment.

"Stabler, as you probably know, was useless. Just a henchman for hire. He'll be charged as an accomplice in a different crime since we can hardly pin this one on him. But the tape showed me enough. I tracked down the real perp. I confronted him. We'd met before in the course of the investigation, and he was aware of my daughter's illness. He said if I let him go, he knew a way to save my daughter."

Reasoner spread his hands in a helpless gesture. "I'd seen him do this ritual on you on the camera. I figured it was bullshi— Sorry. I figured what did I have to lose? Worst-case scenario, it doesn't do squat and I tell the kid I'd drugged that she fell and hit her head. But what if it worked? I was desperate. Not myself. He promised Emily would be saved if I did this ritual with another girl about her age, took her life essence, her soul, and gave it to my daughter. He said in time, the other girl would grow a new one."

The detective looked at his feet, drawing in a shuddery breath. His confession was killing him. Thad was beginning to feel that maybe he understood, just a bit, what had motivated this guy to do something so horrible. He circled Reasoner's wrist and squeezed, encouraging him to go on.

Reasoner came back to himself with a start. "I agonized over the decision, believe me. But in the end, I gave in to temptation and got him to give me the instructions for how to extract a soul. I was going to give it to my daughter and save her life."

Jacqueline turned slightly toward the miserable detective. "But that is not what would have happened, Detective. He lied to you. It was not a soul you were taking from young Allison Wildgoose, but her shadow. Even with a new shadow, your daughter would not have survived. And Allison would have been lost to this world, possibly forever."

"A shadow? Is that what I was taking? But I don't want that. It's a new soul we need. Can I get my daughter a new soul?"

Was he still willing to do anything to save his daughter? Would anyone?

"I am afraid not. Souls are very special, and there is no way to separate one as it is the very essence of one's being."

"But what if he just took Emily's shadow off her?" Hector leaped into the conversation. "She'd live in limbo, right? Isn't that what happened to Peter? He lived a hundred years without aging."

The smart young man must have read *Peter Pan* or else eavesdropped.

"Like Thaddeus here?" Reasoner jerked his wrist where Thad clung to him. "So I wouldn't be able to interact with her, but she'd live and that's all that matters!"

"That is correct. She would live in limbo, in the extreme pain that she now suffers. Unable to get better or to die. She would starve and suffer and be alone in the world. Is that living? Is that what you want for her?"

Reasoner clapped his free hand over his face. After a moment, his head snapped up and he grabbed Jacqueline's arm. "But you can heal her. Save her. That Wildgoose kid. You fixed her T-shirt with your mind or a spell or whatever. It was like I hadn't sawed through it with the stupid knife." A muscle in his cheek jumped.

She had? Thad hadn't been aware of this. And the satchel strap had healed as if he'd never sliced through it. He looked at Jacqueline with new awe. And not a small amount of fear. If she could fix things, could she also break them? Instead of the mystic handcuffs, she could have just broken both his legs. He glanced at Peter. And he called this powerful being Mother?

Jacqueline calmly met Reasoner's gaze and held it for a long minute.

He released her, leaving a damp imprint on her sleeve. "Sorry. I guess repairing a T-shirt and repairing a child aren't exactly the same thing."

In a gentle voice, she said. "It is I who am sorry. You are going to lose your daughter this very night."

Reasoner collapsed in on himself, seemingly aging decades and shrinking inches right there in Thad's apartment.

"You must go now to your child's bedside. Your wife awaits you. Take this and place it around your child's wrist." Jacqueline slid a small beaded bracelet off her own wrist, holding it out to Reasoner. "It will ease the passing. She will be without pain for her final hours and you will enjoy for one last time the happy child you loved and raised."

He accepted the bracelet, tears streaming down his face. "I— Thank you. I can never make up for the things I've done."

"Ah, but you will. You are a good man driven to do evil by grief and desperation. But you have spent the past fifteen years 'paying it forward,' as the young people say. And you will spend the rest of your life atoning for your one evil deed."

"Yes, of course." Hope blossomed on his face. He clutched the bracelet to his chest. Thad felt the pulse below his fingertips throb and race. "But how? What can I do to ever earn redemption?"

A sad little smile formed on Jacqueline's lips. "First, you will grieve. Your daughter is the center of your world, and shortly she will be gone from you. You will never cease to grieve for her, but time does, indeed, heal all wounds. In a few weeks, you will return to your worthy role as police detective. And then you and your wife will contact the appropriate agencies. You will tell them you wish to adopt these two youngsters, Hector Gonzales and Stanley Greenberg. Both of them, even if the foster system has separated them by then. You will be an excellent father and in return they will be kept together and raised in a good home as brothers and beloved sons."

She didn't say this as any sort of request, but rather as if she were rattling off exactly what the future held. Peter beamed and did a little bounce.

Reasoner nodded. He shook his hand free of Thad's and held it out to her. "Thank you. Thank you." When she clasped his hand, he shook it hard, focusing on her entirely. "I don't know how to thank you." He turned to leave, bumping into Thad. "Hey, when did you get here?"

Thad ground his teeth as he opened the door for the confused and grieving detective and ushered him out into the hallway. He resisted the urge to slam it behind him.

"But..." A small voice, thick with tears, came from the sofa. "What about me, Ms. Batique?"

Outside, a crack of thunder sounded, although there wasn't a cloud in the sky. Inside, Jaden's voice broke into a sob, and once again Thad's own eyes filled with sympathetic tears.

And the damn lump in his throat was back.

CHAPTER 22

BRAWL IN THE FAMILY

THAD HELD HIS BREATH while Jacqueline gazed at the young orphan. She nodded once, as if arriving at a decision. "We will speak of this more at a later time, young Jaden. Please do not worry. I believe we can find a place where you will be happy."

Jaden looked unconvinced, a little defiant and a lot disappointed. Thad bet he'd heard that before—from counselors, caseworkers and families who'd let him down easy as they shoved him out the door. His heart ached for the boy, and for the first time in his life, Thad was grateful to his grandparents for taking him in. They might have been overly strict and appallingly behind the times, but at least he'd always had a place to call home.

Jacqueline interrupted Thad's thoughts, saying, "Thaddeus, Peter. Please get ready now. We have another visit to make yet this evening. Jaden, you will stay here and supervise the younger boys."

"Yes, ma'am." Jaden clearly wasn't happy with either her earlier vague response about his future or his baby-sitting assignment, but it would be a rare individual who argued with Jacqueline Batique.

Thad felt a thrilling little echo of teenage rebellion at his own disobedience when he'd stayed behind in the Church basement after she'd ordered him home.

She chuckled low in her throat. Had she known all along that he wasn't going to desert his friends? He wished he knew the extent of her abilities.

"Where are you going, Ms. Batique?" Hector asked, helping Stanley lug the pizza debris into the kitchen.

"We are going to have a word with the man who stole your shadows."

Thad smacked himself in the forehead. "But we still don't know who that is. We should have asked Reasoner."

Once again, the all-knowing smile settled on Jacqueline's dark features. "You may not have obtained the perpetrator's name, Thaddeus Wright. But I did."

Peter brushed past him, stopping long enough to waggle his eyebrows in Thad's direction. "See. Omniscient. Just as I said."

Or maybe that was what Reasoner had whispered to her before he began his explanation.

Thad pulled his hiking boots on over his clean socks, thinking again of acquiring some acetone to unstick the Velcro from his heels. But he had better things to do than worry about that at the moment. Besides, unless that had been some kind of magical superglue, the Velcro would peel off in a day or two.

A taxi awaited them when they reached the ground floor. Peter swapped the satchel of supernatural tools to his other hand. A carved wooden box Thad hadn't seen before stuck out of the leather pouch. Peter opened and held the door for his mother.

Jacqueline slid gracefully into the taxi. Peter walked around the cab and climbed in, leaving Thad to decide if he should squeeze in next to Peter as he so wanted to, or if he should behave himself and ride in the front passenger seat. Something about Jacqueline brought out the responsible adult in him. Mostly. He yanked open the passenger door and got in.

The cab was surprisingly clean and smelled fresh. Not cardboard-pine-tree fresh, but actually clean and new. Now he was really impressed with Jacqueline's supernatural portfolio—because being psychic, controlling magical fireflies and the ability to repair things with her mind was one thing, but the ability to conjure a clean cab tested even his current state of credibility.

She gave the driver an address in the ritzy part of town. Thad hadn't been to the area very often, even though he'd lived in Barriesville all his life. The driver pulled out into traffic without engaging the meter. Thad glanced at him, but the man remained focused on the road.

The driver was immaculate and well-dressed, wearing a suit and tie. If Jacqueline wasn't actually magical, she was certainly lucky. Maybe he could get her to stop and buy a lottery ticket.

Peter chatted with his mom—no, make that *mother.* Jacqueline would never be anyone's *mom.* They spoke in hushed tones about people and things he had no clue about. He thought he heard Tom and Adrian's names mentioned at one point but couldn't figure out the context. What was a Quechua anyway?

About twenty-five minutes later, they pulled into the circular, faux-cobblestone drive of a mansion—not just a big house, but an honest-to-God mansion. Like something Lex Luther would own. It had a certain broody gothic charm and radiated wealth. Thad climbed out of the cab and rubbernecked right to left to observe the house in all its grandeur.

"Who lives here?" he whispered, wondering why he'd lowered his voice.

"This is the home of Mr. Franklin Boniface. He is not expecting us, nor do I believe he will be happy to see us," Jacqueline answered, stepping from the cab.

"Then why are we here?" Thad asked, feeling very much outside his comfort zone. His grandparents had been poor immigrants who'd come over after a local revolution had cost them their tiny patch of farmland. He'd spent his life in blue-collar neighborhoods and equated wealth with snobbery. It intimidated him. Some of the wealthy parishioners at the Church had been warm and friendly, true to the tenants of love and acceptance that the Church of the Gnomon preached, while some, like that silver-haired man who'd called Thad a fag, were the farthest thing from Gnomonistic ideals.

"Although he may not wish to see us, he very much needs to." She climbed the cut-stone steps and stood to one side. Peter seemed to know what she wanted and flew up the steps to land next to her. He grasped the heavy bronze knocker shaped like a fist and rapped loudly.

"*Si?*" A small, round maid answered. Thad had never seen a real maid in uniform before.

"We wish to be presented to Mr. Boniface, if you please."

"Do you have an appointment?" the maid asked in heavily accented yet perfect English. It sounded like: *Do chew haff an appoint-i-ment?*

"You may give him my card and tell him he wishes to see us." Like a magician, Jacqueline produced a card seemingly from thin air and presented it to the maid. The woman rubbed her hands on her frilly apron before accepting the little cream-colored rectangle. "You may also say it is regarding his son."

"Wait een here, please." She led them to a large parlor off the grand entryway.

The décor matched the house—opulent and intimidating. Planned and purchased by some high-priced designer who'd never have to live with the stuff they'd picked out. Thad's gaze roamed from a gracefully curving sofa stuffed to within an inch of its life to the brass-studded wingback chairs constructed of artfully distressed leather.

He decided he'd rather stand.

Jacqueline and Peter had no such issues and immediately seated themselves on whatever was handy. Peter selected a cantilevered brass-and-stone end table that probably would have overbalanced if someone who had a more formal relationship with gravity sat on it. Jacqueline selected a straight-backed chair with pure white upholstery that Thad would never have dared touch.

To keep his nerves at bay, he wondered what kind of place Jacqueline and Peter lived in back on their island home. Peter may have lived in a thatch hut or an underground burrow on Neverland, but he couldn't imagine Jacqueline Batique living in anything but the height of luxury.

No, wait. That wasn't right. She would live in quiet comfort and efficiency. Not for her were the gilded dust-collectors and multi-layered ruffled curtains. A picture grew in his mind of a bright and spacious home, wooden shutters open to allow the sea breeze to sweep across the terra cotta tiles. Simple, comfortable furniture in conversational groupings, a color palette of rich earth tones, a few treasured pieces and rare books held places of pride about the room, an open staircase leading to the bedrooms.

He didn't know how he knew this, but he did. Maybe some psychic abilities were rubbing off on him. Despite squinting hard, he failed to determine the winning lottery numbers.

They had waited only a minute or two when they heard a shriek. Peter caught his gaze only long enough for Thad to know that Peter was going to hurl himself toward the sound of distress.

Before meeting Peter, Thad's usual *modus operendi* would have been to grab a weapon but proceed with caution. Even now, his mother's voice crooned in his brain: *Hush and wait. Hush and wait.* He closed his eyes and gritted his teeth, the muscle along his cheekbone pulsing.

"Shut up, Mom!" he said aloud, eliciting a surprised look from Jacqueline and dashed after his flying friend.

Their heroic save-the-day charge ground to a halt almost immediately. They stood in the main foyer, slowly executing a 360 degree arc. So many doors spoked off the central entrance.

Which one had the scream—?

There! A second shriek had them racing through another couch-filled room and sliding down a long marbled hallway just like young Tom Cruise in *Risky Business*, only with less Bob Seger and more screaming.

They paused again. Once more they heard a raised voice, this time a man's angry bass tones. They ran toward it. Thad managed to catch up with Peter, who'd stopped mere inches from the open door. Thad grabbed Peter's jacket, hauling him back a step. Trying to quell his panting, he put his finger to his lips, then pointed to his ear.

Peter nodded, apparently reading Thad's charades correctly as "we should listen at the door first." The brash agent had gotten as close to the door as he could without being seen by the people arguing within.

On the opposite side of the hall, facing the room, Thad noticed a huge gilt mirror. Challenging himself to be as silent as his flying friend, he pressed up behind Peter. Keeping his thoughts on the situation and not on the sexy agent, he tapped Peter's shoulder and pointed toward the mirror. They couldn't see very much, just that it appeared to be a study or office.

Before they could begin to make a plan of attack, the maid raced from the room, her eyes wide and wild. *"Madre de dios, que tiene un arma!"*

Arma? Thad's already pounding heart lurched in his chest. Surely even Peter would be cautious now that they knew a gun was in play.

But did Peter speak enough Spanish to know that's what she'd warned? He tapped Peter on the shoulder, drawing his attention. This time, he cocked his index finger and mimed firing. Peter's eyes widened like the maid's and he nodded. Feeling mostly relieved that Peter wasn't going to race in and get shot, Thad tuned in to the loud conversation within.

"I may never have done a single worthwhile thing in my

entire life, but I'm gonna this time. You gotta get back the fancy woo-woo stuff and help me do this." The voice sounded older, thick, nearly pleading, yet it sounded to Thad like the voice of someone used to being obeyed.

"Not a chance. They know it was me. Reasoner may not be able to prosecute me through normal channels, but who knows what he'll do when he finds out I duped him and his kid's going to die anyway. He might even shoot me."

Thad knew that voice—Brother Guy. So Peter had been right to be suspicious. Thad felt like a fool. How could the man be a church and community leader, so nice to work for, and then go around stealing shadows and ruining people's lives? He cringed inwardly at the betrayal, grinding his teeth hard enough and loud enough to drown out his mother's crooning voice.

Then the other, older voice spoke again. "I gotta give it back. Whoever's it is, I can tell he's a good kid and deserves his life. I've never been a good man. I see that now. I was a bad man and a bad father. I'm so, so sorry, son."

A slow light dawned in Thad's brain. He knew the other voice, too. Not well. He'd only heard it once, and it had been a lot angrier, a lot more entitled. The house belonged to a man named Boniface, Jacqueline had said. Of course. Thad had been so focused on magic and rescue and Peter that he just hadn't made the connection. He always thought of his boss as Brother Guy, but the man had a last name—Boniface.

He knew what he had to do next. It was up to him. Jacqueline laid a hand on his shoulder. Somehow, he knew that she hadn't just arrived, but had been there as long as he had.

Stepping around Peter, Thad gestured for him to stay put. He hoped that Peter had come to trust him and to work with him as a partner so that he'd actually do as Thad asked. Thad entered the study, his hiking boots sinking noiselessly into the thick carpet pile.

His boss, Guy Boniface, stood with his back to Thad. Farther into the room was Guy's father, Franklin Boniface—the silver-haired man he'd seen at the Church only a day or two ago.

Had it really been that recently? It seemed like a lifetime.

"You!" Franklin Boniface shouted, pointing at Thad. "I remember you. You work at the Church."

"You think I'm falling for that old trick, Dad?" Guy laughed. "You're not going anywhere."

Thad moved a step to the left, giving him a slightly different perspective. Now he could see that Guy wore his usual designer suit, sundial pendant and, he glanced down, expensive black loafers like the ones that had peeked out from under the homespun robe in Adrian's pictures.

This time, however, Guy had an added accessory—a big, grey handgun he pointed at his father.

A vague plan to disarm Guy began to form. Thad was just about to jump the fake religious leader when movement by Boniface Senior's feet caught his eye.

Although the room's lighting hadn't changed, Franklin's shadow was moving. It fluttered a little, then floated in Thad's direction, just as the boys' shadows had back in the Church basement. It reminded Thad of the way spineless sea creatures moved about underwater—slow, graceful, deliberate. It traveled as far forward as it could, tugging and straining at the connection to Franklin's heels.

A new plan now struck Thad. He took another step into the room, moving into Guy's view.

"You! What are you doing here?" Guy swung the gun to aim it at Thad and backed up so he could keep an eye on both men.

"I've come for my shadow, *Brother* Guy." He spat the word *Brother*. There was nothing sacred or even good about this bearded charlatan.

"Your shadow? What's he talking about, Guy? You said you get 'em from kids so they're pure."

Thad pointed to the floor. Both men watched the shadow affixed to Franklin's feet strain like a tethered octopus, attempting to float toward Thad. He sidled to the right a few steps. The shadow adjusted its trajectory, trying to get to its rightful place.

"What the hell is going on?" Franklin demanded, his entitled tone returning. "You promised me the shadow of a young innocent!"

Guy glared at his father, hatred darkening his eyes. "That was what *you* wanted, Dad! What you ordered me to get you." Thad's boss's tone was bitter, spiteful.

Ex-boss, Thad realized. He was never going back to the community center and that was another crime done to him by Guy. He'd loved that job.

"Just because you asked for it," Guy continued, "doesn't mean I have to do it. I'm not your little kid anymore. You're so used to being obeyed by your servants and lackeys that it never occurred to you I might disobey you. But I did. The joke's on you. I decided to give you what you deserved. You were the worst, neglectful father in history. More interested in your mobster deals and sleazy affairs than in your only son. I used to cry myself to sleep when you promised to spend time with me and then didn't come home for days. It's why I started the Church. So I could demand respect and admiration in the community. To try and fill the hole your neglect left in my heart!" He clutched his pendant with the hand not holding the gun.

"That's a bunch of clap-trap. I never shoulda let your mother drag you to that psychologist."

"And then I came to you for financial assistance," Guy carried on with his rant as if his father hadn't spoken. "A little donation to help the Church keep going. You laughed at me and sent me away."

"Your stupid Church is bleeding money. It's a shitty

investment," Franklin said. "I don't make shitty investments."

"I needed cash. Do you think I would have come crawling to you if I hadn't been desperate? I'd worked every bit as hard to build my Church as you did to build your empire of crooks and crime. But no. I got nothing from you."

"You shoulda come into the business like I wanted." Franklin sounded bored. Like they'd had this conversation many times before, the loaded gun notwithstanding.

"When you turned me away, I thought maybe I could find something of value in the old train station's cellar to sell. An antique maybe. There's guys out there obsessed with trains. They'll pay big bucks for train memorabilia."

Guy's rant was taking on steam, just like a train. "And I did. Not train stuff. No, I dug up an old book of spells in the basement. It was written in some foreign language. I posted a scan of some text online and somebody identified it as ancient Kharamaic, a long-dead language. Once I knew what it was, I found an internet site that translated Kharamaic to English. The accuracy wasn't great, but I managed to translate a couple of spells. One was for drawing off shadows.

"I thought I might be able to sell the spell, but when I put the details into Google, I discovered there's a black market for shadows. There's a website—hard to find, but I managed. I got the boys' shadows, and posted the details. The offers poured in. I planned on holding out for a few more days to see if I could up the ante some more. Then I'd package 'em up and ship 'em off to the highest bidder." He laughed—a harsh, rasping sound that grated on Thad's eardrums. "You can find anything on the internet. Isn't that how you found out about shadows, Dad?"

"No way. I built my fortune without the damn internet and I don't need it now. I got the info off one of my business associates. He and a few other guys my age are startin' to think about the afterlife and how our just rewards might not be something we really want. When you're a fifteen-year-old orphan starving in the gutter, you don't think about how you might end up payin' for your actions down the line. But what we didn't know, is that the shadow you get affects you. You gave me the shadow of this guy..." He pointed at Thad accusingly. "And it's making me all warm and fuzzy inside. That's why I want him to take it back."

"That was never my intent. I wanted you to have a shadow every bit as bad as the one you were shedding. I want you to rot in hell or whatever punishment comes after you die as payback for my rotten childhood. Thaddeus here is not a good guy. He's a bastard and a half-breed and a queer. How can his shadow be pure?"

Thad gaped at his ex-boss. Guy, this supposedly saintly man, founder and pastor of a church based on ideals of kindness and righteousness had schemed to let him rot in limbo so he could get revenge on his neglectful, mobster dad? Anger and insecurity battled within Thad.

He knew he had issues to deal with, but he'd had it better than Peter or the lost boys waiting back in his apartment ever did. Or either Boniface, it seemed.

Those two men, like his mother, had chosen to sink into illegal and immoral activities as a way to deal with their issues. He only hoped Jaden and Hector and Stanley continued to be the good, clean-living kids they had managed to stay up 'til now. At least Hector and Stanley would have a chance once Detective Reasoner adopted them. His heart ached for Jaden— so like the teen Thad had been.

He shook off his introspection and stepped toward Guy. The gun swung back his way.

"Bastard, half-breed, fag," he repeated Guy's accusations calmly. Words that had wounded him all his life suddenly were just words, letters strung together with no power to hurt. "There is nothing inherently evil about a child born to an unmarried woman, a person of mixed race or a gay man. And if you actually believed any of the loving and caring doctrine you've written into your so-called religion, you'd know that."

"Well said." Jacqueline entered the room, Peter at her side. "Those are not flaws, nor are they sins. They are part of what makes Thaddeus Wright the good man that he is. The question you might ask yourself, Mr. Boniface the Younger, is not how could his shadow be pure, but rather how could it *not* be pure?"

"Get this goddamn thing off me!" Franklin demanded, kicking at the straining shadow. "Quick, before I give my entire fortune to charity." Sweat appeared on his forehead, although whether from frustration or from fighting the urge to reach for his checkbook, Thad couldn't tell. "But maybe I should. I'm gonna change my will so you don't inherit a penny, you ungrateful brat. You're a big, fat disappointment and no son of mine!"

So my shadow is pure, Thad thought, the idea sinking in for the first time. He had real, irrefutable, albeit magical, proof that he was a good man. If only his grandparents could see it, but they wouldn't get it anyway. He needed to let their ignorant beliefs go.

Thad stood up taller, feeling lighter and more self-assured than he had in years. He'd been living a half life, a shadow of what he deserved. *I need to step out of the shadows—of my mother, of my grandparents, of people like these evil Boniface men—and start casting one of my own.*

Just as soon as he managed to get his back.

Peter stepped to his side and clapped his hand on Thad's shoulder, fingers brushing the bare skin where it emerged from his T-shirt collar. Thad leaned into the reassuring touch, beginning to feel that he just might be worthy of this fascinating man's attentions.

Guy walked over to the large mahogany desk that faced into the room. He must have been aware of the memorability issue because he kept his gaze on Thad. Without looking, he dropped the gun on the blotter behind him. It landed with a thud. "Guess I don't need this anymore. It seems while I was preventing you, Dad, from making a new and difficult problem by trying to return Thaddeus's shadow, the problem has now come to me."

"We brought the censer and the special knife, so you can go ahead and do your thing, Boniface." Thad gestured toward the satchel that once again dangled from Peter's free hand.

"You know what?" Guy said almost conversationally, leaning back on the big desk. "Swapping back your shadows would actually accomplish exactly what I want. I don't care what happens to you, Wright, but I'd be really happy to see my father stuck with the shadow that's filled with the evil he's done—a guarantee he'll burn for all eternity." He stroked his beard and gave one of those demonic laughs Thad had thought only happened in old movies. "Then I'll be avenged for the way he treated me all my life."

"So, what's stoppin' you, son?"

"I couldn't remove his shadow from you if I wanted to. The adhesive I used to attach it? I got the formula for mystic glue out of the spell book, too. As far as I was able to translate the Kharamaic, it, like a diamond, lasts forever."

Another bad-guy style laugh rang out, cut short when Thad stepped up and punched his former boss in the teeth.

CHAPTER 23

BLOOD IS SLICKER THAN WATER

GUY BOUNCED OFF THE DESK and hit the floor ass-first.

"You're lying!" Thad stared down at the evil son of a bitch.

The study was carpeted with a thick Persian rug, so the landing couldn't have been too hard, but the punch sure had been. Thad's hand ached. Guy clutched at his jaw. A bit of pink drool decorated one corner of his mustache.

Good.

Jacqueline appeared at Thad's side, also peering down at the man on the floor. She stepped back to avoid him as he grabbed the edge of the desk and levered himself to his feet. Thad expected Guy to take a swing at him or, God forbid, at Jacqueline. Or at the very least, yell and insult them.

But he didn't. His shrewd eyes narrowed at them over his rapidly swelling nose. He gritted his teeth and glared.

"Do you happen to have with you, Mr. Boniface, the book of spells you have mentioned?" Jacqueline asked, matching his earlier conversational tone.

"Yeah, sonny-boy. You got the damn book? This gal here looks to be an expert, so maybe she can figure a way to unstick this goody-goody shadow."

"Sure. I got the spell book, although a lot of good it'll do you if you don't happen to read Kharamaic." He pushed off the desk. "I left it with my coat. I'll just go and get it." He began to walk away, but as he reached the door, Thad blocked his exit.

"Hey," Guy said. "When did you get here?"

Moving slowly to avoid further physical confrontation, Thad reached out and slid his hand down the side of his ex-boss's suit jacket which hung in a lopsided manner. Feeling a book-shaped lump, he reached into the inside pocket and slowly, holding Guy's angry gaze, drew out a fragile and worn old volume.

"This it?" he asked, more smug than questioning.

As if producing the volume wasn't enough to put a Peter-like smirk on Thad's face, Guy's cartoonish pose of bad-guy-thwarted—shoulders high, fists clenched at his sides—would have been. Thad almost expected to see steam shooting from Guy's ears. Heck, with the goings-on he'd experienced in the last few days, maybe ear-steam wasn't an unreasonable expectation.

Thad stepped around Guy to close the study door in case the bastard decided to make a break for it.

Peter took the slim volume from Thad, ignoring both Guy and Franklin and handed the worn black book to Jacqueline. "How's your Kharamaic, Mother?" he asked.

"Somewhat rusty, I suspect. I have not had much call to practice it this millennium."

Thad started. His mind flooded with images of long-ago lands gleaned from the *National Geographic* channel—Mesopotamia, Egypt, Byzantium—until he recalled the last millennium was less than two decades ago.

"Gentlemen, please be seated. Perhaps Mr. Boniface Senior would be good enough to ring for tea?" She seated herself at his impressive desk and opened the spell book.

"I don't suppose we could get something to eat, as well? I'm famished," Peter said to Franklin.

The elder Boniface harrumphed but used the desk phone to call for tea and snacks. Thad's shadow was certainly working to make Franklin a nicer person despite his best efforts to remain a mean old man.

Peter turned his back on the group, sprawling on the fancy long sofa situated in the bay window. It was one of those with a curved back, so only one person could sit comfortably in it. Thad assigned himself guard duty and hefted a ladder-back chair—probably a priceless antique—and set it down near the door.

To Thad's satisfaction, the two Boniface men looked at a loss. This was Franklin's home and probably the house Guy grew up in, yet they seemed like the outsiders while their unwelcome guests made themselves at home.

Eventually, Franklin and his son took chairs set along the far wall, arranging them so they sat side-by-side facing the newcomers. *United against a common enemy.* Maybe this was the first time in their lives that they were united in anything. Of all the men and boys involved in these weird shadow dealings, only Guy had had a living, present father. And Franklin had chosen to squander the opportunity and hadn't been a proper father at all. Thad slowly shook his head. What a waste.

The room remained silent, except for the rustle of a page being turned every few minutes.

And Peter's snoring, although Thad, trying hard to stifle a grin, was pretty sure it was faked.

A single *tsk* from Jacqueline put an end to Peter's self-entertainment. Thad doubted it was the first time, nor probably the last.

Before long, a thump on the door had Thad leaping to attention. He opened it a crack, then widened it enough to admit the same maid bearing a tray of nicely arranged little crustless sandwiches and a silver tea service. She deposited it on a side table without looking up. She'd probably done this a thousand times.

She fussed with the tea things, arranging them on the table just so. "Will that be all, sir?" she addressed her question to the person seated at the big desk. "Oh, uh. *Perdón.*"

"That will be fine, thank you, Juanita."

How had Jacqueline known the maid's name? Oh, wait. It was embroidered on her uniform. Never mind.

Peter crossed the room and picked up a sandwich. Thad closed the study door behind Juanita and strode quickly to Peter's side, stopping the agent's hand just as he was about to bite down.

"What?" Peter demanded.

"I already have some experience with being drugged by these guys. Let's not make it both of us, okay?"

"Yes, of course. Good thinking." Peter dropped the sandwich back on the tray. He punched Thad lightly in the bicep. "Messrs. Boniface? Would you be so good as to break with convention and help yourselves first? We guests will dine after you."

Peter picked up the tray and lugged it over to the two men.

They selected sandwiches and poured themselves tea like somebody from *Downton Abbey*. Peter returned the tray to the side table. Thad waited for each man to take a sip and a bite. Then he waited a bit longer.

"Okay, then. Guess I worried for nothing," Thad said, reaching for a triangle of bread with a beige filling peeking out between the slices that could have been tuna, hummus or who knew what. He bit into it and still wasn't sure.

Peter took a cup of milky tea to his mother. She thanked her son and sipped it silently, never looking up from her reading.

The clock ticked on.

Thad had always thought the life of a secret agent would be filled with gun battles and car chases. James Bond never sat in a room and watched someone read. The Velcro on his heels itched. To take his mind off it, he glanced at the shadow—his shadow—straining away from Franklin's feet.

Huh. Merely wearing his shadow had turned a lifelong

criminal and all-around creep into a nice-ish man who felt compelled to do the right thing for probably the first time in his life. Or at least made him uncomfortable enough to want his old shadow back, no matter what the risk.

Thad had blamed himself for falling under the influence of Franklin's shadow and hurting the boys, but watching the silver-haired man struggle to stay evil, he realized all the self-control in the world couldn't counter the good or evil influence of the shadow you wore.

Franklin Boniface had been such a bastard that wearing his shadow for five seconds had turned Thad into a brute. Realizing that put to rest Thad's worry that the beating he'd enacted in the Church basement had been the result of something bad within his own character. Nope, it had been beyond his control. He added that particular guilt to the list of things he needed to let go of.

He turned his attention to the weird and supernatural beings and events that had become his life over the past few days. On that topic he'd ping-ponged around, first believing in nothing, then believing in everything. Now, he felt a little more at home with the notion. Going forward, he'd make it a point to listen with an open mind and take each mystic encounter on a case-by-case basis. He'd reserve final judgment until he had enough evidence.

And then there was Peter. From nowhere, this mercurial character out of classic fiction had swept into his life. He'd been instantly attracted to the handsome agent. And apparently, despite Thad's insecurities, the attraction was mutual. He couldn't wait until everything was settled and they could finally spend some time together. Preferably naked. At least initially. There's nothing like afterglow to get someone to really open up about themselves. And he'd respond in kind. He briefly imagined what it would be like to have a partner like Peter. He shifted on the hard chair, wishing he were alone with Peter right now.

Then his spine stiffened while other parts of him deflated. Once the shadows were all set right and Guy Boniface was taken to task for his evil doings, there'd be no reason for Peter to stick around. The boys had been the original impetus for BOO to send in an agent and they were settled now.

Except for Jaden.

Thad wondered if he could adopt the young lad, but even though he'd tried to keep a low profile, thanks to his involvement in several GBLT organizations, his orientation was a matter of public record. Although more and more gay couples were successfully adopting infants and young children, Thad doubted any agency was going to let a single twenty-five-year-old homosexual male adopt a fifteen-year-old boy, regardless of his good intentions. That would raise a few too many well-meaning eyebrows.

No, Jaden would eventually go to a new foster home and Thad would never see him again. Hector and Stanley would go to live with the Reasoners in a nicer part of town. Peter and his mother would return to Azunya. Thad would go back to his boring, lonely life, only this time with no job.

And that was all dependant on whether or not he could get his shadow back. His gaze traveled to the grey cloud that still strained toward him.

There was a time when he'd thought he'd had someone. That he wasn't alone. But Clint had never been much of a partner. He'd liked having a younger man on his arm and in his bed, but he'd made all the decisions—and kept most of their stuff. Thad realized he'd barely thought about Clint in days.

Not since Peter flew into his life.

And was about to fly back out again.

Abruptly, Thad needed to move, to not sit and wait to find out if he'd get his life back and watch Peter depart. Given the chance, he could love Peter more than he'd ever loved anyone.

Because Peter wasn't like anyone he'd ever met. Nor would again.

Sick of his own navel gazing and too angsty to sit, Thad stood, shaking out his muscles. "Hey, Peter. Would you take a turn watching door while I go use the little billionaire's room?" Turning toward Franklin Boniface, Thad asked, "Which is where?"

"Down the hall to the left," Franklin answered. Having had his own shadow swapped out had left him able to remember Thad when he'd looked away. Unlike his son, who now leaned toward his dad and whispered, "When did Thaddeus get here?"

Thad rolled his eyes as he exited the room and headed left.

The bathroom was huge, complete with a sitting area in addition to the basic necessities. After washing up, he sat on a gilt chair to remove his boots and socks. His heels were itching like crazy and he needed to give them a good scratch. Good thing he was already leaning forward with his head nearly between his knees, because what he saw made black spots jiggle before his eyes. His breathing grew rapid and shallow.

The Velcro was no longer just stuck to his heels—it had sunk into his flesh and become a part of him. Or the flesh had grown around it like a tree that had imbedded a fence within its bark.

It was as if it was normal to have tiny Velcro fronds growing from one's flesh like short, wiry hair. No wonder it itched like crazy.

There'd be no unsticking it now. Not without painful surgery.

Or possibly amputation.

And the same must be true for his shadow since Guy had used the same glue. It would never, ever be extricated from Franklin Boniface.

Thad would be stuck outside the world forever.

CHAPTER 24

FROM BAD TO VERSE

THAD STAYED IN THE POWDER ROOM with his head between his knees, trying to calm his breathing, trying not to pass out or puke.

Before too long, he pulled on his socks and boots, rose and splashed water on his face, using a little linen towel to wipe drops of water and cold sweat from his brow. He couldn't stay away too long or Peter would come searching for him. Then Jacqueline would be left alone with two evil men. And Thad didn't want to think about how they might overpower her.

Or her, them. Which would be much better.

Leaning one hand on the wall for support, he made his way back to the study.

He arrived to find Jacqueline no longer bent over the book. It lay closed on the desk. The gilt-edged pages were now on the left-hand side, meaning she'd turned the last page. Had she found nothing?

"It is a very interesting book. It will make a respectable addition to my library." She rose to pour herself more tea. "I am afraid that Mr. Boniface is correct, though. The potion he has formulated is permanent. There is no counter-spell that I am aware of."

Thad's knees gave out and he sat heavily, nearly missing the ladder-back chair. Peter rushed over and crouched beside him, gripping Thad's forearm. "Wait. Don't despair. My mother has more to say."

"Indeed, I do. As my son has said, do not despair. There is a solution."

"Great," Thad said, swaying a bit. He might have toppled off the chair if Peter hadn't been holding him upright. "Let's do it."

Jacqueline returned to the desk. "I merely have yet to find it."

So much for omniscience. Once again, the spots began to gather and dance before Thad's eyes. And not the kind Jacqueline shot from her fingers.

"We'll think of something, love. We'll take you back to Azunya with us. At least Mother and I will always be able to remember you."

"You'll have to take me, too," Franklin Boniface supplied helpfully. "I've got the shadow. Oh, shit. I've done it again. I've been helpful." He spat. "Get this stupid shadow offa me!"

Thad grimaced. Just what he wanted. To go live in some foreign paradise where he couldn't contribute to society and only three people would remember him, one of whom was the vicious old mobster stuck to his shadow.

And what if something happened to Franklin? He had to be well past sixty, and one eye drooped as if he'd suffered a stroke already. If he died before they figured out a way to swap the shadows, Thad's would die with Franklin. Isn't that what Jacqueline had told Reasoner about his daughter?

How were they going to fix this? His eyes burned. His throat got lumpy and more than anything he wanted to hit something. Preferably Guy Boniface again. Thad wasn't worried that this violence would overtake him and cause him to attack Peter again, or Jacqueline. He'd finally got some perspective on his impulses. And discovered they were pretty much normal.

Allowing his hands to fist, he was about to trade light-headedness for satisfaction by jumping up and punching Guy again when music began to play.

What the—? A jangling version of AC/DC's *Highway to Hell* rang out. It brought back memories of Thad's teenage rebellion and calmed his nerves a little.

"Who's playin' that devil's music?" Franklin demanded.

Thad rolled his eyes. That was exactly what his grandparents had called most rock 'n' roll. That it pissed them off had been part of its appeal. That it wasn't what the other black kids in his high school were listening to had also been part of his I-don't-fit-in rebellion against, well, everything.

The song stopped playing, then began again. It finally dawned on Thad that it was a cellphone ringtone.

And it appeared to be his own, although he'd never set it to that particular tune. He'd downloaded Queen's *We Are the Champions* just like every other coach in the world.

He pulled his phone from his pocket, thrusting it at Peter since he knew it wouldn't work for him. One of the boys must have installed it on his phone as a prank. Or possibly it was Peter's idea of a joke.

"Hello?" Pause. "Oh, hey there." Peter had managed to catch the call before it forwarded to voicemail. Thad could hear a tinny voice speaking but couldn't make out the words. "Yes. Alright. Thanks for checking in."

Peter clicked off the call and returned the phone to Thad. "That was Jaden, checking in to tell us he and the boys were okay. He wanted to know if they could—"

"Shhh!" Thad cut him off.

"Well, that's not very—"

"Don't speak. Don't say anything. I'm... Almost..." An idea danced just out of Thad's grasp. If only he could... Everyone in the room stared at him. He closed his eyes to avoid the distraction. "Almost. Almost... Devil's music. AC/DC. *Highway to...* " he said aloud, trying to work out the puzzle.

"Backwards!" he shouted, rising to his feet. "If we want to

reverse the spell, we do it backwards!"

A grin spread across Peter's face like an especially happy sunrise.

Jacqueline stood up, arms crossed over her chest, brow furrowing. "It is not beyond the realm of possibility."

"Oh, right. Very clever. Like back-masking music, only reversing the spell," Guy said. Everyone looked at him. "What? You're surprised I know what back-masking is? It's playing rock songs backwards to find hidden alleged Satanic meanings. I had a rebellious youth, too, you know. Neglectful father—" He jerked his head in Franklin's direction. Franklin looked at his knees. "Rock and roll music, yada yada." He rolled his eyes, whether at them or at his own lack of youthful creativity, Thad had no idea. "But there's one thing you idiots haven't thought of. How do you reverse glue?"

CHAPTER 25

ALL SPELL BREAKS LOOSE

THE INGREDIENTS FOR THE GLUE, just like those needed for the censer in the shadow spell were mainly common household herbs and spices. Thad kept watch on the Bonifaces while Peter ransacked the kitchen—kitchens plural. It turned out the maid and her husband, the resident groundskeeper and handyman, had their own private apartment over the garage. Most of what the cook didn't have in the main kitchen, Juanita had in hers.

Then Peter flew to the corner store, easily purchasing the final few items.

They decided the study wasn't a good place for spell-casting, so with Franklin's new shadow-induced helpfulness, they descended to the basement. They set up in a large workroom-cum-laundry room. It was essentially an open area with a sink. Everything they needed.

Predictably, Guy tried to make a break for it during their little parade down the stairs. Thad felt slightly ashamed of himself for tackling Guy so hard. His ex-boss's suit wasn't quite as pristine when he climbed back to his feet. Done with guilt and insecurity, Thad blamed his excess violence on residual evil from having briefly worn Franklin's shadow. He dared anyone to prove otherwise.

Of course, Guy's reaction had been to wonder when Thad had arrived. Which was getting very old very fast. To prevent the constant memory lapse, he clasped a hand over Guy's bare wrist.

Once in the basement, Jacqueline had Peter clear off the long workbench of tools and projects that no doubt comprised the handyman's to-do list. She then had Peter fetch a few more things and began to mix up potions. Thad kept his hand on Guy and an eye on Franklin. Due to his personal experience with Franklin's shadow, he didn't trust the older Boniface for a second.

Things progressed quickly. The ingredients were mixed in reverse order, and the words of the spell were spoken backwards. The super-*undo*-glue was ready about ten minutes later.

Thad released a held breath. This had to work.

"The accoutrements, please, Peter."

Peter carried the leather satchel to the clear end of the workbench. He lifted out the carved wooden box. Thad glanced at Guy, but he looked puzzled, too. The box was about the size of a thick old bible. It hadn't been part of the items used to amputate shadows, nor had it been in the workroom back in the Church. Jacqueline must have added it later. Peter placed the other items on the workbench—the knife, the censer and the typed instructions.

"Check the box, please," Jacqueline asked.

Peter fiddled with a complicated latch and opened the box a little. Thad hadn't even realized he'd let go of Guy and moved to peer over Peter's shoulder until he saw a foggy grey-brown shape floating near the bottom of the box.

Instinctively, he knew it was Franklin's shadow. They'd said they'd contained it.

He stepped back quickly, hoping that during his brief possession of it—or by it—it hadn't bonded or imprinted on him or something.

In the five seconds he'd let go of Guy's hand, Guy had once again tried to escape. This time Jacqueline worked her mystic gnats magic and created rock-hard manacles around his ankles. The bearded man toppled to the linoleum floor when he tried to run. He landed with a grunt, his hands flying above his head with the momentum.

In a few seconds, his wrists were wrapped in her supernatural handcuffs. The proud and evil man lay prone on the cold, hard floor—exactly as Thad had when they'd taken his shadow. Thad couldn't help the warm feeling spreading through his chest. *Not nice,* he chided himself. *Although the son of a bitch totally deserves it.*

"I am afraid, Mr. Boniface, that I am going to have to ask you to lie next to your son on the floor."

"I'm an old man. Can't I remain standing?"

"What?" Peter asked. "You were willing to travel to Azunya with us in order to restore Thaddeus's shadow, but you won't lie on your own floor?"

Thad joined Peter in rolling his eyes. It was then he noticed the lawn furniture shoved up into the rafters for out-of-season storage. Thad couldn't reach it, but Peter could. *Handy.* Peter landed gently on the floor clutching an overpriced canvas and mahogany poolside lounger that Franklin had probably never used.

He set it up next to Guy, who was swearing under his breath, making threats aloud and wasting his time straining at the cuffs. Thad knew from experience that only Jacqueline could undo that awesome bit of magic.

With an air of satisfaction, Franklin lay face-down on the lounger. It raised him about eight inches above his son. It seemed so petty to Thad, who was seeing his own upbringing in a new light. Apparently money didn't make a difference when it came to shitty parenting.

Resisting the urge to pace, Thad flexed his fingers and ignored his itching feet. He feared this was taking too long, that the counter-spell would lose its strength. Jacqueline caught his gaze and shook her head once.

"Gentlemen. If you are quite ready?" Without waiting for any kind of response, she took the little dish of anti-glue she'd whipped up and a clean paintbrush Peter had located among the workshop tools over to Franklin.

Peter removed Franklin's shoes and she began brushing on the rather stinky mixture over his socks.

"Don't you need to take his clothes off?" Thad asked. "They cut mine off me."

"Do you not have a shadow, even when clad?" Jacqueline asked, not looking up from her work.

Thad started. "You mean they didn't have to do that? They stripped us and wrecked our clothes for no damn reason? Sorry." He was really going to have to watch his language around Peter's mother.

"I compared the typed instructions to the original Kharamaic. I'm afraid it included a number of mistranslations."

"So sue Google Translate," Guy said.

Everyone ignored him.

"Now, Peter, if you would set the contents of the censer alight and hand me the book." She passed the brush and the little bowl of non-glue to Thad.

Was he supposed to apply it to the Velcro on his own heels?

"Thaddeus, if you could put that down safely and then come over here and hold the knife, please." He did as she asked and she passed him the curved blade. "Now Peter, if you would manage the censer."

Peter accepted the censer, swinging it gently back and forth. For once, he took his duties seriously, his regular smirk wiped from his face. The censer hung on three chains, each one about eighteen inches long. Thad had no idea what the smoke was for. Did it purify the room? Lend ambiance? Appease some god? He recalled what Guy had said and made a mental note to google "magic spells, censer" *when*—not *if*—he got his shadow back.

In her confident, soothing tone, Jacqueline read the spell backwards. Or at least that's what Thad assumed she was doing since he'd never even heard of Kharamaic before today, let alone recognized a single word.

She held out her hand for the knife. Thad passed it to her. Continuing to chant, she moved around Franklin's lounger until she stood in the narrow space between the two Boniface men. "The box, please, Thaddeus?"

Thad grabbed the box from the workbench and carried it over, just in time to see Jacqueline swipe the knife across Franklin's heels. Franklin didn't seem to be experiencing any pain or discomfort. Obviously, Guy had been doing something very wrong when he'd ripped away Thad's shadow.

Once detached from the old man, Thad's shadow floated there as if stunned. Then it extended a tentative feeler or two—his earlier analogy about the octopus appearing more accurate than he'd originally thought. The smoky cloud seemed to find him, floating slowly toward him until it reached his ankles where it curled around him but couldn't quite seem to attach.

This had to work. It just had to.

He held out the box, but instead of opening it and restoring Franklin's shadow, Jacqueline spun around and—in one perfect swoop of the knife—sliced Guy's shadow from his heels. His ex-boss screamed. If Thad's hands had been free, he would have clapped them over his ears.

"What's going on? Where's my shadow?" Franklin shrieked.

Guy continued to scream.

"What do you need, Mother?" Peter yelled.

Everyone was screaming and yelling. The laundry workroom had turned into bedlam. Was that all part of Jacqueline's plan?

Guy's shadow wasn't sluggish like Thad's had been. It struggled, trying to attack Jacqueline.

"Stay where you are!" she shouted when both Peter and

Thad moved to help her. "You must not touch this evil thing."

Sickeningly elongated grey fingers reached for her throat. The knife slipped from her grasp to thud on the floor. She had the thing by the faux-wrists now, her teeth clenched in concentration, her exotic face contorted with effort.

"Now, Thaddeus, the box!"

He extended the box to her and opened it a crack.

Franklin's shadow tried to make a break for it.

Like father's shadow, like son's.

CHAPTER 26

THE BITCHING HOUR

JACQUELINE WRESTLED WITH GUY'S SHADOW. It seemed to become aware of Franklin's shadow, which escaped from the box like a wisp of smoke.

Guy's shadow turned from Jacqueline and attacked his father's shadow. Franklin's shadow fled, funneling itself back into the box with Guy's shadow in hot pursuit.

As soon as all grey, smoky limbs had piled inside, Thad slammed the wooden box closed. The lock clicked into place. He stood there panting, as if he'd been the one struggling against the evil shadow.

Franklin labored to sit up, the canvas lounger providing little support. Guy lay struggling and crying on the cold floor.

"Are you all right, Mother?" Peter tossed the censer into the nearby sink, where it landed with a crash. He rushed to her side.

Of all the strange things Thaddeus had seen over the last few days, perhaps the strangest was Jacqueline with her hair out of place.

He wanted to rush to her side, too, but he needed to stay poised to prevent either Boniface from escaping. He placed the shadow-filled box gently on the floor.

Jacqueline lips moved, but Thad couldn't make out her reply since both Boniface men began to yell and curse, giving orders and demanding answers.

"Shut it!" Peter yelled louder than anyone. "If you don't shut up this very moment my mother will make gags for you out of the same material that is currently holding your hands and ankles together."

Remembering how that had felt, Thad shuddered. Guy continued to threaten, but Franklin studied the situation. "You're not gonna return my shadow, are you?" He jerked his chin toward his struggling son. "Or his, neither."

"Very astute, Mr. Boniface. As Director of the internationally sanctioned Borderless Observers Organization, it is within my purview to decide your punishment for your crimes against humanity. I hereby sentence you both to twenty-five shadowless years."

Guy had managed to maneuver around until he was lying on his side, staring at Jacqueline with disbelief. "No, you can't do—"

She raised her hands. He shut up.

"I can and I have. You now exist in a state outside this world and as such can neither age nor die. I am sending the two of you to an island that does not appear on any map. Peter once lived there so it will sustain you, but not easily. The two of you will need to depend on each in order to survive. At the end of the twenty-five years, I will observe you and see if you have earned back a place in this world."

As she'd been speaking, she'd also been creating the threatened magical gags over the two complaining and cursing men. They were restricted to making the same underwater noises that Thad had experienced in the past. Of course, they were both doing their best to shout, but at least the decibel level was no longer eardrum shattering.

The particular shade of red that Franklin Boniface had turned would have been worrisome at his age if Thad hadn't known that he couldn't die without his shadow. Guy, on the other hand, turned a frightening shade of white and shook. Thad figured the prospect of spending twenty-five years with the man he'd just tried to trick into eternal damnation wasn't as appealing as it might sound.

Guy's gaze met Thad's, and he knew his ex-boss wouldn't forget him when he looked away.

He heard water running behind him and saw Peter snuffing out the censer. "We almost ready, Mother?"

Thad's heart shifted in his chest and the cold rush of panic clenched it tight. What about him? What about his shadow? The smoky cloud curled around his ankles like a lonely cat, trying to re-attach itself.

"Uh. Did you bring needle and thread, Ms. Batique?"

"Yes, of course, Thaddeus. In all the excitement, I have neglected you. If you would be so good as to remove your footwear and seat yourself on the workbench, I shall sew your shadow back on permanently."

"Uh, no. I don't think so."

"What?" Peter's head snapped up from his washing duties.

"I beg your pardon?" Jacqueline looked shocked.

Thad felt a twinge of satisfaction that he'd managed to surprise the mostly omniscient head of BOO. Even the two Boniface men stopped making unintelligible yet angry noises. Seemed he'd managed to surprise everyone.

The idea had come to him so suddenly that he was almost afraid to say it out loud. Almost.

"Uh, can we use these, instead?" he asked. He dug into his front jeans' pocket, drawing out the female halves of the Velcro that had fallen off Franklin's shadow back at the Church. He kept his focus on the black loopy fabric, afraid to meet Jacqueline's gaze. "If you use the magic glue, this'll embed in the shadow, right?"

Slowly he raised his eyes, feeling like a kid about to be told yet again that he couldn't have something he wanted with all his heart.

Jacqueline ran her hand over mouth. Her fight with the

shadow had broken a nail. It caught on her lip and she stared at her own hand.

Thad gave a nervous chuckle. He'd always heard that in books and movies, magic had a price. Apparently, in real life, that price was a chipped manicure.

Peter flew past him.

"We'll have none of that now." He retrieved the knife from the floor just as Guy had wormed his way around to grab it with his bound hands. More frustrated noises came from behind his gag.

"So, Mother, I believe I see where our Thaddeus is going with this. Can it be done?"

Jacqueline sighed. "It is without precedent, but that only means no one has thought of it before. It could be dangerous, Thaddeus. You may find that your bond with your shadow becomes weakened, and you may slip from this world again."

"Exactly. If I can detach my shadow at will, then I can do things without being remembered. Sneak into hostage situations and rescue people. Retrieve stolen items. Remove children from abusive homes."

"These are very noble ambitions, but you could not work within the policing systems of the everyday world."

"No, ma'am. I, uh..." Thad shuffled his feet, sending his shadow scuffling about before it drifted back toward him again. "Sorry," he told it. It pressed up against his ankles again. He was pretty sure the purring was only in his head.

"Look," he said, stiffening his spine. "Two days ago I'd never heard of magic. Well, of course I'd heard of it, but not like this. Not like it was real." He waved toward the men lying on the floor, bound with magical cuffs and gags. "Two days ago, I was somebody I didn't much like. I'd been treated badly and then dumped by my ex and believed I deserved his bad treatment. I was living in a crappy apartment, working almost every waking hour for a paltry salary for a false pastor who ripped off the parishioners for cash and ruined the lives of children. I let people manipulate me and felt I had it coming. In short, I've allowed myself to be overshadowed."

Thad paused, shaky and cold inside, but unwilling to *hush and wait* on this, the single most important thing he'd ever done. He stood up straighter still, holding out the Velcro tabs again. "But if I'm able to detach my shadow at will, then it's like magic, right? Hell—sorry—Heck, it's like a superpower. I can go where others can't. I can do things like we did at the precinct—sneaking into a high-security building and gaining Peter access. I'll be able to do rescue and reconnaissance. I can work with Tom and Adrian to get you pictures of places I've accessed." He realized he'd given away his entire plan. "So hire me. Take me with you to Azunya. Make me a BOO agent. I'm dedicated, hardworking, resourceful—*Oof!*"

When Peter finally released Thad from his bear hug, Jacqueline tried very hard not to smile. With hands on hips, she attempted to appear stern and failed. "Peter, I believe you have with you the original glue that Mr. Boniface created? Yes, dear. Thank you."

She took the Velcro from Thad and coaxed his shadow up onto the workbench. He had to climb up and put his feet on the surface before it would go along.

His heels no longer itched. *Was that a good or bad sign?*

Filled with trepidation that he'd just risked his real-time existence on a crazy idea to marry technology and magic, he took a deep breath. Was he insane committing to an organization he scarcely believed in, following a man who claimed to be Peter Pan and a woman who defied definition?

He untied his laces, worrying that his feet smelled. His hiking boots thunked onto the floor, followed silently by his socks.

"There," Jacqueline said, putting down the paintbrush and straightening up. Peter took the glue and the brush, wrapping them in wet paper towel and sticking them in a plastic bag he'd dug up from somewhere. He added them to the leather satchel along with all the other magical items: carved box containing two warring shadows, cooling censer, curved blade, magic spell book and both the glue and the unglue. The satchel didn't appear strained at all. Perhaps it was bigger on the inside like the TARDIS on *Doctor Who.*

While Thad had been taking mental inventory, his shadow had once again drifted over to his ankles. This time, when the female Velcro glued to the shadow rubbed against the male Velcro embedded in the flesh of his heels, it stuck. He could feel it.

It tickled and left him feeling the good kind of shivery, like a cool breeze on a hot day. He walked over to the staircase and called to the maid.

"Jes?" she answered.

Thad hoped Juanita could see only him and not her bound employer or his equally bound son from her position at the top of the stairs.

"Sorry to bother you, Juanita, but I have something very important to tell you about Mr. Boniface. It's that—" Thad cut himself off and stepped to the side, lost in shadows, out of her field of vision.

"Jes, what is eet?" she called down, taking a tentative step to the first stair.

Thad counted to ten, then popped back to stand between the newel posts. "Ili, Juanita. Do you remember me?"

The maid looked at him like he was crazy. "Jes, of course. Now what was eet you wanted to tell me?"

"That we really enjoyed those sandwiches. Mr. Boniface said to tell you that he just doesn't thank you enough."

"Gracias. " She gave a little curtsy and left.

With that, Thad skipped away from the base of the stairs, light of heart, foot and shadow.

He had returned to the land of the living. He whooped and leapt about, pouncing on Peter with a bear hug of his own.

He released Peter and spun around, barely stopping himself from hugging Jacqueline. Now that would have been crazy.

Her hairstyle and her manicure had repaired themselves. Once again, she was perfect. She headed for the staircase. "Gentlemen, it is time for us to take our leave. And Thaddeus. Your dedication, courage and resourcefulness have made a very good impression. I am willing to grant your request. You will, indeed, make a fine agent and a welcome addition to our ranks. I believe I can speak for my son as well when I say I will be glad to have you join us on Azunya."

Peter whooped, following his celebratory cry with, "A hand with the bad-guy wrangling, please, Thaddeus?" He stooped down and grabbed one of Guy's arms.

Thaddeus, however, was totally overwhelmed with emotions ranging from terror to joy. He stared into space, rocking slowly back and forth on his heels, his shadow contentedly rocking with him.

"Thaddeus. Thaddeus!" Peter snapped his fingers in Thad's face before returning to wrap his fingers around Guy's upper arm again.

"Oh, hey. What? Right." Cheeks burning, Thad reached down and seized Guy's other arm. Together, Peter and Thad hauled him to his feet. The tiny black gnats that had been binding them together dissipated and the man was able to stand on his own, although he needed some support. "I've got this one," Peter said. "Get the father, will you?"

If I'm going to be some sort of agent, I guess I'll have to get used to escorting unsavory characters to their just deserts. He hauled Franklin to his feet a little more gently in deference to his age and herded him up the stairs.

"Hey! What are you doing with Mr. Boniface?" A male voice rang out, sounding like, *Hey, what are chew doing wit Meester*

Bon-ee-fac-ee? This must be Juanita's husband. Thad eyed the burly man, mentally adding bodyguard to his other duties.

"Look behind you," Thad yelled, pointing behind him. Of course when the man turned back, he wouldn't remember seeing his de-shadowed employer and dad being taken away in magical irons. He'd just remember three visitors exiting the house alone.

This was going to be great.

CHAPTER 27

PAST DITCH EFFORT

THEY EMERGED INTO DARKNESS, the sun having set hours ago. Headlights winked as a vehicle pulled up to the curb near the front walk. The spotless cab, of course.

Thad congratulated himself on becoming blasé about the whole magic/psychic thing, only to drop his jaw as a background hum quickly morphed into the noisy roar of a helicopter. Spotlights and swirling debris blinded them, nearby trees bent in its passing maelstrom.

The chopper thudded down halfway between the sidewalk and the mansion on the perfectly manicured lawn. Juanita's husband was going to be pissed. Of course, with his boss missing, he might not care so much about the state of the grass.

A woman pilot hopped out before the blades ceased spinning. Initially, Thad thought it was the lighting that painted a rainbow of colors in her chin-length hair before realizing she wore it streaked pink and gold. Blue too, he observed, squinting against the glare. A number of tattoos and piercings adorned her face and hands. She waved at Peter.

"Cheers, Wendy!" Peter yelled, waving back.

Wendy marched over and clapped real handcuffs on the Boniface men. Jacqueline did whatever she did to dissolve the magic ones. As soon as their gags dissolved, both men began protesting loudly. Jacqueline raised her hands and they shut up again.

"Thanks," Wendy said. Without further conversation, she herded the two prisoners to the chopper.

Peter stepped up to Thad. "I've got to go with them or they'll get away. Wendy can't remember them, right?" He leaned in and pecked Thad on the cheek. "But we'll see each other in a few days. Pack up your apartment and my mother will look after the travel arrangements for the three of you."

"You— I'll—" But Peter was gone. He hovered about fifty feet in the air, waiting for the helicopter to catch up.

"The three of us?" Thad turned to ask Jacqueline, but she was already gliding toward the taxi, the satchel over one shoulder. He rushed after her to open the door and she slid in with her usual grace. Thad hiked around the car and climbed in the back next to her, feeling very much like he'd usurped Peter's rightful spot. He bit the inside of his cheek, then stopped immediately. He was done with that. He stared out the window, awkwardness joining him. The darkness offered a little shielding, but he felt fragile and vulnerable after all he'd been through. Then they'd pass beneath a streetlight and he'd rejoice anew to see his shadow stretch long and merge with the others until they again passed into the light again.

They'd travelled a few blocks when Jacqueline spoke, starling Thad. "Thank you for your assistance in this little contretemps. It is not usually the victim who solves the crime."

"You're welcome," Thad mumbled, a little surprised by her words of appreciation and wondering what contretemps meant.

"I commend you on the clever strategy for shadow flexibility. It is not often a Natural is able to gain a gift whereby he becomes a Super."

"A what...? Oh, I get it. Supers and Naturals."

"Yes, that is the modern nomenclature."

A swell of pride tickled Thad's chest. Not only had he done something that Jacqueline found commendable, but he'd managed to do something special in order to join an elite force.

But a moment later, his confidence wavered.

"I hope you don't feel, ma'am, Jacqueline, that I forced myself on you, uh, I mean on your organization."

She let that hang in the air as the cab sped along a block or two. If she were truly omniscient, would she need a moment to compose her thoughts? Or was she about to let him down easy? He cleared his throat, wondering what to say next.

"I am not omniscient, no matter what Peter may have told you. People, Peter included, can be predictable at times." Whatever expression she wore was difficult for Thad to determine in the dark cab interior, but the tone of her voice suggested it might be a smile. "In fact, you surprised me with your clever plan. I have not experienced a similar surprise since Adrian discovered his abilities. I do enjoy surprises of this nature. And like Adrian, you will be a useful member of our little band of brothers, sisters and others."

He got a bit stuck on that last part but decided new and different genders were not the main issue here. In fact, they might prove interesting. "It's just that... I don't always put myself forward like that. I usually..."

"Hush and wait?" Jacqueline asked.

Thad spun around to stare at her fully, ignoring the seatbelt cutting painfully into his abdomen. "How do you know that? What do you know about my mother?"

Passing streetlights lit her face in short bursts, the light gleaming off her dark skin. "I know that you feel responsible. That you believe if only you had remained still as your mother asked of you, that your entire life would have been different. I know that her final words to you have guided your entire life. And I know that you need to let them go."

A soft whimper escaped Thad. His shoulders slumped. At least the darkness hid his burning face. "It's my fault," he whispered. "She would have lived. Things would have been different."

Jacqueline placed her hand gently on his bare wrist. He could feel warmth and something else. Some kind of energy maybe, flowing not just from her to him, but back again. Different than Tom and Adrian. She wasn't trying to read him, just help him to read himself.

"Do you know why that man killed your mother?"

Thad hung his head. "She was an addict. She owed her dealer money."

"Not just owed money, Thaddeus. She had stolen from them. She had earned their trust and was using you to smuggle drugs for them. Using you. She hid drugs in your pram, your stroller, even in your clothing, against your skin. If you had ingested any, you would have died. She put drugs ahead of your safety."

Thad's eyes burned. He felt four years old again. He turned away from Jacqueline, the truth resonating with him, even if his memories were vague.

She tightened her grip on his wrist, firmly, but not painfully. And his memories cleared, solidified, the fog of youth and passing years lifted.

For the first time in his life, he could remember exactly what happened. Not like earlier, when he'd allowed Tom to read the early part of the day, the good part where he drew pictures in the sunshine. He never thought beyond it, blocked it out and refused to see. But now, it was as if he was there again, in that dumpy apartment, experiencing the entire tragic day again. Only this time, it was with an adult's frame of reference.

"She ripped them off," he murmured, watching the scene play out across his mind's eye. "She told them she'd been robbed when she'd actually sold the drugs to another dealer."

Jacqueline squeezed his wrist. Scalding tears splashed down on his skin, dampening the back of her hand. "I remember now. I remember it all."

The day continued to play back in all its horror. His mother dragging him under the bed, clutching him close and crooning softly in his ear, *"Hush and wait. Hush and wait."*

But the air had been stifling and the floor hard. He'd wanted to play with his toys. He wriggled in his mother's arms until she shoved her hand over his mouth. *"Hush and wait. Hush and wait."*

Unable to breathe, he panicked. He struggled, kicking, scratching. She would have smothered him to save herself. *"Hush and wait. Hush and wait."*

He bit her hand as hard as he could, his little baby teeth proving more than up to the job. She hissed, bringing her bleeding hand to her mouth.

He'd sucked in a big gulp of air and begun to wail. So much for hushing and waiting.

The man with the gun sang, "Come out, come out, wherever you are" as he crossed the apartment toward them.

Thad's angry wails turned to screams of terror as the booted feet clomped into sight. The single bed suddenly flipped up and off them, bouncing against the bedroom wall. An angry crack and his mother's arms loosened. A dark spot blossomed on her forehead, dribbling scarlet just like the red in his paint box.

The man had pointed his big black gun with the long, finger-like nose at Thad, then mumbled, "No freebies, kid," and left.

Thad hadn't known what that meant at the time, but now he knew. It meant she'd taken drugs from them without paying. That he wasn't going to kill the Thad because he hadn't been paid to.

Hours later, a neighbor stuck her head in. His mother's assassin had left the apartment door ajar. The neighbor, a recovering junkie who lived down the hall, probably thought there might be something to steal in their apartment. Thad knew they'd had nothing—nothing but drugs and a few second-hand toys his mother had stolen from the local kiddie park. Eventually, the neighbor had called the police, no doubt hoping her one good deed would count in her favor the next time she was arrested.

His recollections of the time between his mother's death and when the police arrived were hazy. He remembered trying over and over to get his mother to wake up, but that wasn't so unusual. The red paint all over the floor was. For some reason, it made him queasy and he felt no urge to fingerpaint with it. Instead, he looked after himself, as he'd had to do as far back as he could remember.

He recalled being proud that he'd gone to the bathroom all by himself. He'd even managed to get himself a snack—leftover pizza in the fridge. It was a miracle he hadn't tried to eat any of the white icing-sugar-like powder hidden in the crisper.

When the police had arrived, there'd been a nice policewoman and a doctor who'd checked him everywhere. She'd had a biologically correct doll but he'd shaken his head when she'd asked about *bad touches* and *down there*.

Social workers cared deeply during their shifts, and handed him off to someone else so they could go home to their own lives, their own beloved children. Eventually, a pair of wrinkly white strangers had come for him, puzzled at his very existence.

"Dis is our grandson?" they'd asked. "But he's is *czartzan!*" It was the first time he'd ever heard the derogatory term for black in their mother tongue, but certainly not the last. He'd come to know their word for bastard, too.

They'd never known he was gay.

He'd left them as soon as he was old enough, calling once a year at Christmas.

It was time for him to let that go—all of it. Time to stop blaming himself.

He wasn't responsible for his mother's addiction, her debts or her self-destructive lifestyle. In fact, she hadn't been a good mother to him, putting him at risk. *Hush and wait, my ass!*

He suddenly realized his grandparents had actually been the

better parents. Oh sure, his stoned-out mom had been lots of fun—when she was around, when she was conscious and when she wasn't wrapped around the toilet bowl. But his grandparents had been well-meaning, uneducated immigrants doing their best to raise a grandchild they'd never asked for. That their best wasn't great was just the way things were. They'd done the same oppressive job of raising his mother and that had led to her escape into illegal drugs.

Thad could just as easily have followed her down that path. Instead, he'd chosen a life of helping others. She could have, too, but she hadn't. She'd squandered everything.

"My father?" he asked Jacqueline, but he already knew the answer. "The man who killed her was my father."

"I am afraid so, yes. He was the dealer's henchman. They sent him after her. He did not even know you were his son." She paused, giving Thad time to adjust to the information—both old and new. "He died shortly thereafter. A work-related incident."

Thad barked out a laugh. Hired killer gets killed. Of course he did.

"Your mother did stop taking drugs while she was pregnant, which was, for her, a sacrifice and gesture of love," Jacqueline explained. "However, she just did not do well with temptation. Once you were born, the drugs, the money, it overshadowed her desire to be a good mother."

The lump in Thad's throat prevented him from saying anything.

"In their own manner, your grandparents did care for you, Thaddeus. Indeed, how could they not?" She released his wrist to run her hand down his cheek, gently thumbing away his tears. "I am proud to have you as a member of my team. And as a member of my family."

Thad pressed back into the vinyl seat, staring out the

window but seeing nothing. *Hush and wait. Hush and wait.* His mother's voice crooned in his mind, growing softer and softer until she ceased to croon altogether.

CHAPTER 28

ONE GOOD TURN DESERVES A MOTHER

JACQUELINE AND THAD ARRIVED back at his apartment to find the boys still up despite the late hour.

"Why aren't you at your homes?" Thad asked.

"We were, but our foster families were too busy trying to record all the different news shows where they're interviewed about our *miraculous return* to even notice we were there. "He formed air quotes while simultaneously rolling his eyes. "We might as well not have our shadows back for all they noticed us."

"But, hey," Jaden said. "Don't you worry. We don't feel *marginalized.*"

Thad cringed, recalling how he'd spewed a bunch of psycho-babble at the boy about being ignored when Jaden had really been trapped outside the world.

"Hey, sorry about that, but the shadow thing? Came as a bit of a surprise, you know."

"Yeah," Hector chimed in. "Besides, me 'n Stan are going to go live with that detective soon. We're gonna be real brothers! I think I wanna be a detective when I grow up."

"Me, too!" Stanley chimed in. "Only I like friend-sicks."

Thad barked out a surprised laugh. "I think you mean forensics."

"S'what he said." Hector came quickly to his step-brother's defense.

Thad tried to hide his smile. These boys were going to be okay. They might need a ton of counseling, but they'd always have each other.

Jaden said nothing, but a tiny sniffle escaped him. Thad's heart went out to him, but he wasn't sure what to say. An unexpected gust of wind whipped the cheap lawn chairs around on the balcony.

Jacqueline looked up from the open spell book she'd pulled from the satchel. "I have not forgotten you, young Jaden, and I believe I have arrived at an arrangement that will please us both. How would you like to accompany us to our little island nation? Peter has grown and moved on." Her gaze cut to Thad. A tiny smile played around her mouth. "I find that I am in need of a new son to raise. Would you like that, Jaden? To be my son?"

Stanley whooped and Hector punched Jaden in the arm. "Awesome, dude!"

But Jaden's eyes continued to look glassy. Thunder boomed in the distance. Thad worried about BOO's helicopter if there was a storm, but a glance out the big window showed a clear evening.

"Peter told us about Azunya." Jaden's voice cracked. "Everyone there's got magic powers. And I'm just, you know, *ordinary.*" He whispered the final word and dug his teeth into his trembling lower lip.

"That is not entirely correct." She said this to Jaden and turned her gaze to take in the rest of the people in the room from her position at the table. "Thaddeus, I will return to my hotel now, but I will be back in the morning to begin the paperwork. Boys, I will see you safely to your current foster homes. Jaden, be ready early. We must be in touch with the appropriate authorities."

"Yes..." the young man hesitated, then raised his chin and added, "Mother."

She chuckled low in her throat as she placed the spell book back into the satchel on the table.

"Hey, Jaden," Stanley said, following Hector toward the door where they'd left their shoes. "You'll get to have a brother too!"

Jaden's light brown complexion paled. Maybe gaining a new home in a new country, a new mother and the mercurial Peter as a brother all in five minutes was a bit overwhelming.

Thad moved over to stand by Jaden. The poor kid had been through so much.

"Haven't you always wanted a brother?" Thad asked, "I know I did." He was happy for the boys. What he wouldn't have given to have someone to share his unhappy childhood.

"Uh, yeah. I guess. It's just... I never had anyone before and now I've got, like, a family." A big, fat tear rolled down his cheek.

To hell with possible lawsuits. Thad tossed caution out the window and wrapped the young man up in a gentle hug, holding him until he stopped shaking.

"Don't forget I'll be there. And it's an adjustment for me, too," Thad told the boy. "I've lived in Barriesville all my life, and suddenly I'm going to go to some strange place with some pretty strange people. No offense, Jacqueline."

She harrumphed, watching the two intently. "I suspect that *strange* may be something of an understatement. And if Peter were here, he would say that for *people*, as well."

Thad laughed, although not without some anxiety. Just what had he and Jaden gotten themselves into?

"Jaden, may I give you a hug?" Jacqueline held out her arms.

After an exchange of looks between Thad and Jaden, the young man marched resolutely across to the little table where Jacqueline sat. He stood stiffly as she wrapped her arms loosely around his shoulders. A moment passed, and he relaxed, slowly leaning into the hug until it looked as natural as if they'd done it all their lives. Jaden's café au lait coloring looked warm and healthy, practically glowing against Jacqueline's much darker skin.

Something about the hug made Thad relax, too. Supernatural or just plain old natural, this would all work out.

A tiny bit of envy snuck into Thad's heart. Jaden would have a fun brother in Peter and a stern but caring mother in Jacqueline. These were things he would have killed for when he was younger. A loving family was everything. He hadn't really had it. Neither had Guy or Franklin Boniface.

Well, he might not have had the best family growing up, but it had been better than some. And he'd have a great family going forward—an entire island of them. He shoved the envy away, looking toward the future.

Maybe, Thad considered, he could understand Reasoner's behavior a little better in what he'd tried to do for his dying daughter. Family was everything.

Suddenly, a snippet of earlier conversation drifted back into his brain. Jaden had said that everyone on Azunya had magic powers while he didn't. Jacqueline had responded with "That's not quite true."

She hadn't said which part. And even in their brief acquaintance, Thad had learned that she phrased things very carefully. In this case, had she meant not everyone on the island had magic? Or that Jaden was not entirely ordinary?

He looked at the young lad appraisingly, wondering if there was something about him they had yet to discover.

CHAPTER 29

PACKING THE DECK

AFTER PACKING UP the non-perishable food items for the food bank, Thad and Jaden sorted through the hall closet's contents. The paperwork and passports should have taken weeks, months even, but apparently bureaucracy-busting was one of Jacqueline's superpowers. Within hours, they had adoption papers and gleaming travel documents.

Thad had never owned a passport before, never been further than spring break in Key West. Jaden confided that he'd never been out of the state.

"Never seen the ocean?"

"Never even seen the Great Lakes." He wrapped his thin arms around himself as if he were cold, whispering. "Like I said, water makes me nervous."

"Jaden, I know we're not at the community center or anything anymore and I'm no longer your counselor, but I gotta ask. Did someone... Did you have...?" He hesitated, careful of his words. "Like, a bad experience with water at some point?"

"What? No, man. Nobody tried to drown me. I just, like, don't like it. It scares me. Well, not the water really. I'm more scared of the way it makes me feel. I freaked out over a documentary about the ocean in school one time. Fell into some sort of *fugue state,* the principal called it. Sometimes I stare at a glass of water like I could get lost in it. I have dreams, Coach."

Outside, a breeze sprang up, making the old windows rattle.

Replacing the crumbling grout would be the next tenant's problem.

"Oh, you better call me Thad now. We're going to be, well, friends, I guess." Or if things worked out with Peter the way Thad hoped they would, he and Jaden would end up the next best thing to brothers-in-law.

"Hey, Coach, Thad. You're blushing."

Thad had wanted to ask more about Jaden's water phobia, but that moment seemed to have passed. There'd be plenty of time to talk about it after they landed on Azunya. There were probably qualified counselors there that could help more than he could. And someone would need to help the young lad deal with the fact that he would be living on an island. Surrounded by water.

So instead of asking all the questions that bubbled around his brain, Thad piled the last of the stuff he wasn't taking into the box marked Goodwill. The light glinted off a silvery item on the top of the pile. He ran a finger over the shiny surface of the staple gun he'd used to put up the posters of Jaden. He'd never returned it to the Church of the Gnomon. Why bother? With its charismatic leader gone, the sect would probably dissipate as quickly as it had arisen. And it did owe him one last meager paycheck that probably he'd never collect.

The City announced they'd received a large donation from an anonymous source. It was specifically directed toward the purchase of the building, and to keeping the gym and community center open while converting the former Church space into a day-care center. Thad figured anonymous meant BOO.

And speaking of BOO. "Let's get back to packing. Jacqueline—your mother—has us booked on an early flight tomorrow."

"My mother. Hmmm" Jaden taped another full box shut. "I like the sound of that."

In the end, the Goodwill pile outgrew the keeper pile.

He wouldn't need his text books or winter clothing anymore—except a few items for when he went on assignment—and his furniture had been secondhand when he'd gotten it. So summer clothes, laptop and a few photos fit into two well-stuffed gym bags.

At the last moment, he tossed in a photo of his mother standing next to his grandparents. Although they were smiling, no one looked happy. But they had been his family and he knew that counted for something. He'd finally reached the point where he could appreciate them for who they were and that they'd done their best for him.

It's just that their best had really sucked.

CHAPTER 30

SEXUAL PEEK

Barriesville, USA / Azunya, somewhere in the Caribbean

JACQUELINE MET THEM DOWNSTAIRS with the clean cab once again. They hurtled through traffic, arriving at the airport in exceptional time. Thad had feared that Jaden would be nervous about his first-ever plane ride. Instead, the young man seemed excited, taking to flying as if he'd been doing it all his life.

The first leg of their journey dropped them in the closest country to Azunya with an international airport. That was followed by a short puddle-jumper flight to a neighboring island. Although the first flights, which had been over land, had gone smoothly for Jaden, this time he dug his fingers into Thad's arm as the plane bounced and jostled.

Jacqueline asked Thad to switch seats with her. "It's the water," she explained, seating herself next to the anxious young man and placing her hand on his bare wrist, just as she had with Thad the other night. After that, Jaden seemed to settle down. Oddly, so did the plane.

Upon landing, they found Wendy waiting for them next to BOO's helicopter. Thad wondered at the range of the chopper, but decided not to ask. He had a lot to learn about a tropical island of supernatural beings and decided that a helicopter appearing just when and where they needed it wasn't high on his list of concerns.

His top question was, of course, where was Peter? He waited until Jacqueline had disappeared to deal with some administrative matter before asking Wendy.

"He's busy getting the place ready for you," Wendy grinned, punching Thad on the bicep. Equatorial sunlight glinted off her mirrored sunglasses as well as her nose and eyebrow jewelry.

Jaden snickered.

Thad glared at him to cover his blush.

Wendy snickered right along with the teen before elaborating. "He wants you to like it. He only moved out of Jacqueline's home recently and he's still nesting." Thad guessed Wendy was in her late thirties, and she seemed to have an easy relationship with Jacqueline and Peter.

"You'll love it here. We're a strange bunch but a lot of fun, when we're not off saving the world," she added.

Feeling daring, Thad ventured to ask, "So, Wendy, what are your powers?"

That elicited a laugh from the rainbow-haired woman. "Me? I'm a *pi-lot.*" She enunciated her job title slowly, as if Thad were a little slow. "I fly."

"Like Peter?" Thad asked, fascinated.

"I wish. My grandmother did. Unfortunately, there's not enough fairy dust left in the world." She shrugged. "Another species going extinct thanks to pollution and global warming," she added bitterly. "I'm on the committee to save the fairies. Oh, and just so you know, that's actually not a socially acceptable question on the island. You don't ask people what they are or what they can do. If someone wants you to know, they'll tell you."

Thad started to blush again and apologize, but Wendy waved it off. "You couldn't have known, but now you do. Let's get aboard, 'kay?"

Of course, Jacqueline reappeared at exactly that moment.

The short flight to Azunya seemed to take forever. Thad's eyes burned from scanning the skies, expecting Peter to show up and execute death-defying aerial maneuvers at any moment. But to Thad's great disappointment, the sky remained Peter-free.

A sparkling silver Bentley awaited them on the tarmac, next to a dusty, open-top Jeep. Jacqueline guided Jaden toward the gleaming car. Thad began to follow, but Wendy grabbed his arm and tugged him toward the other vehicle.

"Nah, I'll take you. I'm a better driver anyway."

Thad waved at the departing Bentley, hoping they were waving back from behind the tinted windows. He hadn't expected them to go their separate ways so soon.

Once in the Jeep, he found himself hoping the Bentley's driver drove a lot better than Wendy. She whooped and spun in the open-topped vehicle, leaving Thad's fingers aching from clutching the roll bars and his stomach roiling from her reckless road antics. How could she be such a cautious chopper pilot and then go wild on the ground?

Not wanting to distract her from her daredevil driving, he watched the scenery, trying not to hurl.

It was time he learned something about the island. He'd googled it, but the internet was strangely limited on the subject. A Google search turned up only two entries: a Wikipedia listing and a dedicated website. The Wikipedia entry had described the island as a tax-free paradise just off the Caymans and not a lot more. The Azunya Tourist Board website played tinkly Caribbean music and encouraged visitors. A flashing banner warned that it was *carnero* season, so swimmers and boaters should be careful of this deadly fish that swarmed the surrounding waters. It seemed this fish would enter the body via the penis...

He'd shuddered when he thought of that, thinking Jaden was right to be afraid of water. But when he'd googled *carnero* fish, he'd discovered that they didn't live in the area and couldn't survive in salt water.

"It is merely to discourage tourists," Jacqueline had explained, even though Thad hadn't asked.

Google maps just kept giving him the *404 server temporarily unavailable* message. He'd given up.

With a spray of sand and gravel, Wendy skidded to a stop a few yards from a rustic little house. It fit in with its surroundings, looking as if it had grown where it stood on a dune above the beach. It was no hut, regardless of the bamboo walls and thatch roof. It probably held a couple of bedrooms. A small satellite dish peeked out from the thatch.

"We're here," Wendy said, leering at Thad. Then she lowered her voice so it could barely be heard over the Jeep's growling engine, "He's just as nervous as you are. He's never lived with anyone other than Jacqueline before. Well, my grandmother and the lost boys aside. He was just a kid then."

Thad hadn't had the courage to ask where he'd be staying and was both relieved and thrilled that Peter expected him to move in—at least short term. His heart thumped faster at the idea of being with Peter.

He'd barely had time to grab his luggage and tell Wendy he hoped he'd see her soon when she floored the Jeep and spun away, sending a spray of sand and grit over his shoes.

Fine. He shook himself off. Beach shoes topped his must-buy list. He wondered if there was shopping on the island or if he'd have to order them online. Hadn't Peter said something about the internet when they'd first met?

Gathering his courage, Thad climbed the wooden steps to the thatch-roofed, wrap-around porch. He nearly tripped on the final stair, nervousness rendering him clumsy. He tightened his grip on his two gym bags, afraid they'd slip from his sweaty hands. Not that his belongings were particularly breakable. Even his laptop was swaddled in five T-shirts and a hoodie.

He halted before a plain screen door, its lines and edges worn smooth by years of wear and coats of paint. Obviously, Peter was not its first occupant. Its latest color was a soft, light green that blended well with the island's bountiful plant life. Thad panted as if he'd climbed 300 steps instead of just three, staring at the door, incapable of figuring out how to open it with a bag in each hand.

The door shot outward, barely missing Thad's face.

"Oh, sorry. Well, um. Glad you're here." Peter straight-armed the door open while Thad tried to enter, turning sideways to avoid knocking into his host with his bags. "Missed you."

I missed you, too. Had Thad said that aloud or not? His lips tingled and he realized he'd been pressing them together in a thin, straight line. He snapped his mouth open, air escaping with a *pfft* sound.

"Not sure what to make of that." Peter reached for the gym bags, which, for no reason Thad could imagine, he refused to release. Whereas before he'd been afraid he'd drop them, now he couldn't seem to let go.

"Relax, love. Relax."

Peter gave up on the bags. Since his arms were already out and he stood just six inches from Thad, he stepped closer. Gently, inexorably, he pushed Thad up against the wall next to the door. Despite the slow moves, Thad managed to lose his balance, flail about and hit the wall with a thunk. He finally dropped the bags, thinking that if ever he'd deserved Peter's signature smirk, it was now.

"I'm, uh. I..."

"Yes, love. Me, too." Peter didn't smirk. Instead, he wore a slightly stunned look Thad could only call starry-eyed. He imagined he wore a similar expression.

Peter slid his right hand down Thad's T-shirted chest. *Oh, God. Do I smell?* It had been a long day of travel, after all. Peter leaned in and nibbled on Thad's ear, teeth clicking against the little gold hoop.

Thad sighed long and loud, relaxing into this mercurial man's touch while his breathing and heartbeat sped up. How could he be relaxed and aroused at the same moment? He'd never felt like this before. But even in their short acquaintance, Thad had learned that Peter was a big, handsome bundle of contradictions. Apparently, it was contagious.

He sucked in a surprised breath as Peter slid his warm hand under Thad's T-shirt, stroking his abdomen lightly but firmly enough not to tickle.

"Missed you," Thad managed to say the words aloud this time. He felt a little ridiculous. They'd only been apart two days. In fact, a week ago they hadn't even known each other.

Peter released Thad's lobe from between his teeth and drew back. "I'm so glad you're here and going to stay. I hated the idea that I might have to leave you in the States and return to Azunya without you. Have I mentioned the Velcro idea was brilliant?"

"I don't think you can say it often enough," Thad whispered.

"Okay. Let me tell you again, then that—" It was Peter's turn to make underwater noises as Thad gently slapped his palm over his host's mouth.

A low, intimate chuckle escaped Thad. He dropped his hand from Peter's lips and his gaze from Peter's eyes to his sexy, insolent mouth. Caging Peter's face gently between his large palms, Thad slowly moved in for a kiss. It was even better than the one they'd shared while fleeing the police station—at least this time the only pealing bells were in Thad's heart.

And hopefully in Peter's as well.

Peter drew his hand out from under Thad's T-shirt. He brought up the other hand and snagged Thad's hips. Without releasing his mouth, Peter bent his knees slightly and began a slow slide upwards, rubbing his prominent erection along the length of Thad's.

Even through both pairs of pants, the move was incredibly sensual. An electric thrill leapt along Thad's spine. Being pinned to the wall by Peter was the best thing that had happened to him in ages—maybe ever.

Outside, a gull shrieked, angry and plaintive at the same time, a harsh contrast to the gentle panting between Thad and Peter. It struck Thad that this was perhaps the first time he'd ever begun something with only solitude and quiet as orchestration to their lovemaking. No pounding club beat, no carefully planned playlist, no traffic noises nor sound of any city in the world. There was only silence and, in the distance, the ocean slapping at the sandy shoreline.

Thad allowed his hands to drift down to Peter's shoulders. He released Peter's swollen lips and smiled at him. "I don't suppose this place has any amenities?"

"Like what?" Peter looked positively dazed. "Oh. Oh. Yes, a bathroom. And something to drink. Where are my manners? Mother would wring my graceful, swan-like neck." The smirk put in an appearance. Thad couldn't help himself. He cupped Peter's chin and ran his thumb across those kissable lips, Peter's light stubble rasping against his skin.

"Actually, I was thinking more along the lines of a bed." Thad gifted Peter with a smirk of his own.

Peter's expression morphed into a look of surprise and delight. Thad was surprised and delighted by that in itself, although maybe not as surprised as he might have been. He'd been so out of his depth with all of the supernatural stuff that he'd done a lot more following—a lot more *hushing and waiting*—than was actually in his true nature.

At least he hoped so. He had his own superpower now, and he'd joined this amazing crew of badass... people. He fully intended to be a lot more outgoing and maybe work his way up to brazen.

But following along did seem like a great idea when Peter grabbed his hand and tugged him down the hall, through something that might have been a living room—they moved through it too fast and were much too distracted for Thad to notice or care—and into a bedroom.

The bedroom was something right out of Thad's fantasies, complete with a mesh-draped bed so tall it needed a tiny footstool to climb onto. He tried not to think about the bugs that the white mesh was there to keep out, nor how much damage could be done if one of them fell out of bed and landed on his head. Like Humpty Dumpty.

Then he realized that he was exactly the right height... or rather the bed was. *Think of the traction!*

"Think of the what, Thaddeus?"

Thad might have blushed at actually saying that out loud, but he was too far gone. He pulled Peter to him with the same velocity that Peter had used to drag him into the bedroom. When Peter tried to kiss him, Thad pushed him away, taking charge as he never had before. He began to unbutton Peter's shirt—a short-sleeved, linen shirt like those worn by every model in every tropical photo shoot.

As he undid the line of buttons, he kissed and licked each newly revealed inch of skin. Of course he was tall—although only an inch or so taller than Peter—so when he neared the navel area, he got down on his knees, nosing into Peter's belly button, pleased at Peter's sharp intake of breath.

Or maybe it was his own. It was hard to hear over his own panting, so he needed to get Peter to make more noise.

Much more noise.

He nuzzled down the front of Peter's trousers, pleased but not surprised in the least to find a rock-hard erection straining against the light cotton.

He grinned so hard it made it difficult to continue to nuzzle effectively, so instead, he began to work on the button and zipper—with his teeth.

"Oh, Thaddeus! That's so hot. I have never been so turned on in my extra-long life."

Finished with the zipper, Thad climbed back to his feet feeling very accomplished... he hadn't even really started yet. When Peter reached for him, he once again pushed the other man away. Stepping back a pace or two, he slowly drew his own T-shirt up, gradually revealing his trim belly. Even though they'd dined on pizza for two days straight, followed by airline and airport meals, he was pretty sure his six-pack was visible in the bright afternoon sunlight flooding Peter's—no, *their* bedroom. He wasn't vain by any means, but he knew this was one of his best features and with shy joy, wanted to share it with Peter.

A slow, appreciative clapping had him turning around to hide his blush. With his back to Peter, he concluded his little striptease by dropping his jeans and stepping out of the pool of denim. Cool air from the desultory ceiling fan wafted past his bare legs, cooling his skin, drying the fine, dark curly hair. He'd been too nervous and distracted to realize how hot he'd been. A summer-weight wardrobe went on to the must-buy list. He'd never owned linen before. Or an iron.

His wandering thoughts were yanked back to the present when Peter moved up behind him and pressed up against Thad's backside. "Aren't you going to take these off?" he ordered, reaching around and sliding his fingers under the waistband of Thad's boxer-briefs. His blunt nails grazed the tip of Thad's hard-on. Thad had to stop and close his eyes to survive the waves of pleasure.

"You're making it hard," he gasped.

"That's the very idea." Peter ground his own hard cock against Thad's ass.

"No. Well, yes, but I meant, I can't get these off with you glued to my ass."

"I want to be glued to your ass." Peter shoved up against Thad, hard, wrapping his long-fingered hand around Thad's cock and squeezing.

Thad groaned, deep and guttural. He grabbed Peter by the wrist and gently drew his hand out, then skimmed his briefs down his legs and stepped out of them. "Bed. Now."

"Yes, sir!"

Peter's submissive response sent a sizzle through Thad's belly. What had he been missing all these years letting his partner take the lead?

Peter pulled back the mesh curtains and the two men scrambled for the four-poster. Thad leapt on, then had to climb off again at Peter's insistence that they pull back the white duvet. "Sheets are so much easier to wash."

Sexy and practical. What's not to love?

Thad grabbed a corner and helped yank the duvet to the bottom of the bed. "I can just picture you down by some river, pounding these sheets with a rock."

"I'll have you know, young Thaddeus, that Azunya might not be a sprawling metropolis like Barriesville, but it definitely has all the modern conveniences. Besides, this beautiful decorative bed ensemble is brand new. I bought it especially with you in mind."

Thad had to admire Peter's wisdom in decorating: the sheets featured a busy pattern in tropical earth tones. Stains would hardly show at all.

Once the cover was piled out of the way, Thad leapt back upon the bed again. After his double bed back in the city, this one seemed huge—at least a queen. Maybe a king. Peter seemed like the king type, definitely.

Peter made a show of flying up toward the high ceiling. He then dive-bombed Thad. Thad threw himself to the side, ending up dangerously near the edge. Peter drifted back onto the super-thick mattress, landing with a gentle bounce.

"You dickhead!"

"You love it."

Thad nearly blurted out, "I do," but thought less than a week was too soon for declarations. He couldn't hide behind cultural habits like Peter could. Although if Peter hadn't lived in England in a century, how had he picked up the sixties nickname, "love?" He'd call him on it... someday. But today was not that day.

Peter made himself comfortable and lay back, head on the great, fluffy pillows.

Thad thought he looked entirely too comfortable, so naturally he pounced on Peter, finding a ticklish spot right away.

Peter giggled and struggled, quickly begging for mercy. He didn't sound very sincere, but Thad wasn't one for begging, so he stopped. He stared into Peter's hazel eyes, seeing a vision of himself reflected there that made his heart clench with happiness. His eyes misted. His smug grin turned goofy, mirroring Peter's. Then their grins drifted away altogether as things suddenly turned from playful to serious.

Peter reached up and cradled the back of Thad's skull in one hand, drawing him down for a kiss. It began light but quickly deepened until they were kissing as if their lives depended on it.

Kissing turned to groping and thrusting, Peter's uncut cock leaving silver trails along Thad's flat stomach and hip. Suddenly, it wasn't enough. None of it. Thad growled low in his throat. He'd managed to maneuver himself between Peter's legs and he now raised himself up on his knees. He grasped Peter's tan flanks and yanked his legs up until he was able to thrust directly against the root of Peter's cock.

"Oh! Oh!" Peter's voice rose as the thrusting grew harsher and faster. Thad set a bruising pace, wishing he were inside Peter. Wishing they'd taken time to prepare, but knowing that was not going to happen. Not this first time.

"Next time," he whispered, low and husky, grinding and pounding against Peter's body. He hadn't rubbed off like this since high school. "Next time, I'm going to fuck you silly."

"Next time." Peter might have said more, but he was too far gone. "Yes, yes. Oh, God."

Thad hadn't been with anyone in months, but there was no way he wanted this to be over quickly. Maybe this way was better, after all.

And then Peter groaned, his whole body shivering. Peter's cock, trapped between their bodies, pulsed and sent scalding strands of come over both their bellies.

So much for wanting it to last.

Thad pistoned against Peter, sliding in the slippery puddle of come and sweat. He gritted his teeth and forced his eyes to stay open. Rearing up, he watched his dark purple cock spew strings of white-hot come all over Peter's belly and chest.

And maybe a drop or two on his chin.

Thad remained kneeling over his lover, hands still trapped behind Peter's knees. He panted softly while admiring the mess as if they'd created the most beautiful artwork ever.

"Oh, man," Peter said, dropping his head back on the pillow. "That was brilliant."

Out of consideration for Peter's thighs, Thad fell to one side, bracing his head on his hand. "Was it?"

"Fishing for compliments, are we?"

"Yes." Thad felt no compunctions about asking for what he wanted anymore. From now on, he was going to reach out and take life by the balls. But in the meantime, Peter's balls would do just fine. He ran his index finger along Peter's sac, eliciting a shiver and a flinch.

"Sorry," he said. "Didn't know you'd be that sensitive."

Peter just sniffed, as if his balls had somehow been impugned.

Thad drew his finger up Peter's abdomen, stirring their come together like a murky, primordial stew. The whole room smelled of sex and the sea. Thad drew in a great breath, rolled over on his back, sweat cooling on his body, making him shudder.

"We should shower, love. Before we dry like this."

"You go ahead. I'll wait here." Thad was way too comfortable to move. While he'd never been the kind of guy who drifted off right after sex, he figured it was never too late to start.

"Did I mention Mother's expecting us for dinner?"

Thad was up and off the bed faster than you could say *omniscient*. "Uh, what time? What time is it now? How long—?"

"Hours and hours. Can you bring me a towel before you get in the shower, love? Bathroom's on the right." Peter didn't bother to open his eyes, just pointed to the mess on his belly.

He'd been conned. Well, probably not the last time. Thad laughed and retraced his steps to the front door where they'd left his stuff. He found his shaving kit and a fresh pair of boxers and carried them back down the hallway until he found the bathroom.

He'd bring Peter a towel after he'd showered. It wouldn't do to let the guy get too spoiled.

He turned on the water and stepped in, almost sorry to wash the evidence of their first time together down the drain.

EPILOGUE

SEA NO EVIL

Azunya, a few weeks later

PETER AWOKE SLOWLY, groggily, as he often did. As he had never done back on Neverland, where waking up quickly might mean the difference between life and a pirate cutlass to the throat.

And for a moment he struggled, thinking he was back in Neverland, the soft breathing beside him calling him back to the days when the lost boys had slept around him. With Wendy—the first one who'd been their acting mother—safe in the next room.

But the memory faded and he surfaced, coming back to the present. He had a different mother now, and most recently, a brand new brother. And now a partner. He couldn't stop the goofy grin that seemed to have replaced his usual smirk a great deal of the time now.

He stroked Thaddeus's arm where it had escaped the cotton top sheet, eliciting a contented sigh from the man in the bed beside him. His noticed how his partner's mocha skin had tanned a deep, rich brown in the few weeks he'd been on Azunya.

Knowing he wouldn't sleep again, Peter rose quietly, finding yesterday's pair of linen shorts draped over the desk chair. He pulled them on and crept from the room, gliding down the hall to the kitchen. He poured himself a glass of filtered water from the jug by the sink, drinking deeply.

What should he do until Thaddeus awoke? Maybe he should wake him. Thaddeus was so warm and pliant when he was only half-awake. Peter's dick certainly thought that was a good idea.

He took another long draught of water and, as he lowered the glass, he noticed movement out the window. He thought about going out on the verandah, but there would be bugs. Instead, he just closed the distance to the window and gazed out.

A lithe young figure stood in the sand, silhouetted by the pinkish light sneaking over the horizon. Peter recognized the outline of his brand new brother, the spiky hairstyle the dead giveaway. Peter's brow furrowed as he tried to figure out why the young man was out on the beach alone so early.

As Peter watched, Jaden took halting steps toward the ocean.

Peter knew Jaden was afraid of water. Or more specifically, afraid of the way water made him feel. What had that even meant? And why was the boy heading straight for his worst nightmare?

Peter made his way softly out onto the verandah, ready to fly to his new brother's aid should the need arise.

On the shore, Jaden had reached the waves. It looked to Peter like he was going to keep walking. Maybe this was some sort of desensitization process Jaden had dreamed up to deal with his phobia. It would be good if he got over it before he started at Azunya High tomorrow. The other kids—

Peter was in the air before the scream finished sounding.

Continued in MYSTERICAL, Tales of B.O.O., Book #3

NEW! MYSTERICAL

Tales of B.O.O., Book #3

The lies that blind

Imagine being the only un-magical kid at Hogwarts. That's how sixteen-year-old orphan Jaden Raines feels as he enters Azunya High. He struggles to fit in, but he's really a fish out of water.

The magical isle of Azunya, where paranormal policing agency B.O.O. is headquartered, is shocking to Jaden after having lived his entire life in the American Midwest. Back there, his classmates were freaks, geeks and gangstas. Here, his classmates are genies, witches, healers... A whole pantheon of beings and monsters.

And worse yet, he'll have to read The Old Man and the Sea. Again.

Jaden might be the new kid in town, but he's still a teen. It's love at first sight with handsome skater-boy Stiltz. They have three things in common: neither is able to use magic, they're both petrified of water, and, lucky for Jaden, they're both gay. They should bond, but their relationship's stormy from the start.

To try to fit in, Jaden hides his powerless state, accidently creating the myth that he's the most powerful being of them all.

But when the entire school demands a demonstration, what's Jaden to do?

New lies and cruel deceptions leave Jaden and Stiltz stranded at sea in the middle of a deadly tropical storm.

In order to survive, the boys must spill their secrets. It's sink or swim for our heroes.

Only the truth can set them free. And keep them alive.

MYSTERICAL: A young adult, gay, contemporary paranormal adventure romance. Novella approx. 150 pages. Available in both digital and print formats.

MYSTERICAL: EXCERPT

CHAPTER 1

SCALES PITCH

Something inhumanly strong wrapped around his legs, clamping them together, ankle to thigh.

"Nooo!" Jaden yelled, toppling into the cold surf. He struggled, gasping for air. Salt and sand stung his eyes. He flailed in the waves, grasping useless handholds of sand and grit.

He was going down. Oh, God. He was going to drown.

With a yell, he kicked out at his attacker, No good. His legs were tightly bound.

Buffeted by whitecaps, he gasped, inhaling seawater, choking. Panicking. He shoved hard at whatever clamped his legs together, putting all his strength into his trembling arms.

His fingers met a strange, alien surface. Slippery, yet warm and sleek. Scales. Jeeze. Had some giant sea snake swallowed his legs? Panic tore through him. A glimpse through the foam. Glossy black scales and a slick, menacing fin.

A sea monster? In the ocean surrounding Azunya! Why had no one warned him? No one cared enough to warn him.

No one had ever cared.

Then from behind, another attacker. Rough hands grabbed his arm, fingers like claws digging in hard.

Jaden bellowed.

He swallowed more salt water, sputtering. His thudding heart shook his entire body. A second pair of hands grabbed him under his other arm, dragging him roughly up and out of the ocean.

Coarse volcanic granules sandpapered his bare back as he was hauled up the shore, away from the waves and their terrifying inhabitants. Turned out his fear of water wasn't so irrational. He quickly added fear of land to his list.

Once up on the shore, the hands eased their iron grip, but stayed. Warm. Supporting him. Keeping him from collapsing back onto the sand.

Jaden coughed, spewing water, inhaling precious air along with a last few choking droplets.

"Turn him on his side. Recovery position."

The words were clear, but made no sense to Jaden. He kicked at his new captors, his legs now free. He forced his burning eyes open. Slammed them shut again, blinded by the sun. He scrambled up the wet beach like a startled crab, falling back into dry powdery sand when his legs scuttled faster than his arms.

"Jaden! Jaden! It's okay. It's okay. We got you."

The words made more sense this time. The voice familiar. A voice he was used to obeying, although it wasn't telling him to pass the ball now. "Coach? Coach Wright?" Jaden gasped, gagging as the last of the inhaled seawater flooded his throat, tasting foul and poisonous. His eyes streamed as he blinked hard, trying to see through salt, sand and tears. "What... What happened?"

"That, my brand new brother, is what we need you to tell us."

ALSO FROM STORM GRANT

SHIFT HAPPENS

Tales of B.O.O., Book #1

A change is as good as a quest.

Three years out of grad school, anthropologist Adrian Thornapple is still stuck in that "temporary" office job. When his former mentor invites him on a rainforest expedition, he says he can't. He has obligations. He has security. He has... a dead neighbor on his doorstep? It seems she's fallen victim to a new and deadly designer drug shipping up from the rainforest. Accused of involvement in her death, Adrian suddenly gets that life is short, that civilized doesn't mean safe and that he should follow his dreams.

Captain Thomas Ferrell hates the supernatural. When the Army kicked him out for weird behavior, he signed on with paranormal investigators Borderless Observers Org. Three missions in, Tom's learned that BOO does a lot more than observe. And that their paranormal investigators really are paranormal investigators. Sent to stop a drug operation in the Amazon basin, he's unwillingly shape-shifted into a huge black jaguar. He believes he must regain his humanity before he can complete his mission. Is he wrong?

Adrian's expedition morphs into a nightmare of illegal drugs, slave labor and a terrifying quest through the rainforest and the spirit world. Worse yet, his companion and protector is a giant man-eating jaguar with whom he might be falling in love!

Adrian just wants to go home... until he learns that saving the world is a lot more fun than returning to his corporate cubicle.

SHIFT HAPPENS: A male/male paranormal adventure (previously published by Amber Quill Press)

Full-length novel, approx. 300 pages. Available in digital and print formats.

AND MORE FUN, GAY, ACTION ADVENTURES...

THE RELUCTANT REAPER SERIES

Death is what happens while you're making other plans.

A pun-filled romp through the underworld. (m/f)

WHAT PEOPLE ARE SAYING ABOUT
STORM & GINA'S BOOKS

GLOWING PRAISE FROM USA TODAY: "I loved the way Ms. Grant developed the nuances of this story. Lost Boys 2.0 is a character-driven book wrapped in an intricate plot that runs smoothly."

"Storm Grant delivers a story filled with drama, comedy, and romance. The one-liners kept me in bouts of laughter." ~*Fallen Angels Reviews*

"Storm Grant created a very impressive storyline with some surprising twists, heartwarming characters and a little intrigue that I enjoyed immensely. I loved the intrigue and the creative way the story flowed to a happy ending with a few surprises along the way." ~*Literary Nymphs*

"...a fresh and original story. The story had great characterization, not only just filled with some steamy sex scenes and overall just a great piece. This is another author to look out for." ~*Rainbow Reviews*

"I could not put this book down, I even skipped dinner to I finish it! ...fully fleshed-out characters that are quirky... and utterly adorable. The novel seamlessly weaves between the real world and the supernatural, taking the reader on a wild ride filled with funny dialog, action, adventure and true love. But the most important selling point on why I enjoyed this book so much was the author's wit and her ability to twist words into such humorous dialog kept me laughing throughout the entire novel. A truly delightful read. Storm Grant goes on my auto-buy list from this point forward!" ~*Dark Divas Reviewer*

"This is a novel that masterly mixes together adventure, thriller, romance, but above all comedy: it's not often that, while reading about drug dealers and dangerous situations, you find yourself laughing..." ~*Elisa Rolle*

ABOUT THE AUTHOR

Storm Grant writes and publishes engaging male/male fiction, more light than dark. Since 2007, she has published with a variety of e-publishers including Riptide Publishing, Amber Quill Press, Phaze, MLR Press and Torquere.

Writing as Gina X. Grant, she is represented by Rosemary Stimola, the agent who also represents the Hunger Games series. Gina's RELUCTANT REAPER trilogy is available from Simon and Schuster's Pocket Star imprint.

Gina's and Storm's books are available at all your favorite online booksellers.

Gina lives in Toronto, Canada, just blocks from the house she grew up in. She's married to a friendly curmudgeon from a mining town in Northern Ontario, where he played hockey against Shania Twain's brother. Gina and Mr. Grumpy have two rescued dogs that might just be a bit spoiled.

Follow Storm's exploits on her blog at www.stormgrant.com or on Twitter, Facebook, Goodreads or wherever fun people hang out.

Email Storm at storm.grant@gmail.com

I hope you enjoyed LOST BOYS 2.0. If you did, why not post a review on Goodreads or Amazon or your fave review site?

Thank you, again, for taking the time to enjoy my book.

Stormy

Quirky fiction that's pretty, witty and gritty